Imperfect Strangers: A

CU00687239

by

Lea O'Harra

Table of Contents

Introduction by Paul Johnston

Foreign-based crime fiction is enjoying a golden age in the English-speaking world. While Scandinavian novelists currently occupy the limelight, with Italians also making a strong impression, there are many other countries in the frame. It is necessary to make a distinction between novels written by foreign writers translated into English and those written by native English-speaking writers who set their fiction in foreign countries. Each has its own strengths – the best of the locals are critical members of the societies in which they locate their stories, while foreigners can achieve a degree of objectivity that is beyond natives. They may also be able to examine issues that are taboo in their adopted countries.

Lea O'Harra's *Imperfect Strangers* is a good example of the second group. Having lived for several decades in Japan, she is well versed in the complexities of its society, one very different to Western models despite the influence of the West on it. One of the factors that makes crime fiction so popular globally is the genre's conventions. O'Harra shows herself to be an assiduous reader of classic detective fiction. *Imperfect Strangers* has a cast of standard characters – the policeman Inoue, who is oppressed by his superior, Takenaka; Professor Nomura, the unscrupulous man who has many enemies;

Andrew Thomas, the Canadian who is out of his depth in more ways than one; the various minor characters who all have secrets and all could have been the murderer. However, convention only works up to a point. Having drawn the reader in by fulfilling genre expectations, the successful novelist must bring something new to the table, something original enough to pique the interest. This O'Harra does with commendable skill.

The trick, as in all good novels, is in the title. *Imperfect Strangers* has several layers of meaning. The most obvious refers to the group of non-Japanese primarily employed to teach English at the university in Fujikawa. This makes a subtle point about cultural imperialism – in order to get on in the modern world the Japanese must learn a foreign language (unlike many Britons or Americans). But, as the novel progresses, it becomes clear that the Japanese characters are both imperfect and strangers to their own kind – for example, the liberal college professors have no point of contact with the nationalistic army personnel; some of them act arrogantly to their social inferiors; and some males treat their females colleagues according to the old- fashioned patriarchal structures that endure.

Beyond that, O'Harra's most effective stroke is to present couples who are imperfect strangers to each other. Chief Inspector Inoue is deeply in love with his foreign wife, Ellie, but they only partially understand each other. Other mixed marriages show lack of communication and awareness in various ways. Even marriages between foreigners, particularly Andrew Thomas's, are compromised by secrets, lies and indifference. Ultimately, everyone is an imperfect stranger, which seems to me a highly accurate vision of society in both fictional and real worlds.

Lea O'Harra also provides much information about Japanese institutions, such as the higher education system, the police, the legal system, and the military. She uses Christianity cleverly – the university is a Christian foundation – by introducing the question of faith. As she is well aware, the detective novel is nothing without the reader's mutable faith in characters and motivation. Indeed, Christianity is another defamiliarising factor in *Imperfect Strangers* and, as such, plays an important role in the plot.

Crime fiction, especially the more traditional type based on deductive reasoning, is sometimes seen as out of touch with reality. Interestingly, post-WW2 Japanese crime fiction is grounded in such conventions. As Lea O'Harra shows, the traditional form is not necessarily regressive or conservative. *Imperfect Strangers* is a novel that probes the society in which its characters live. As such, I commend it highly and wish it well on its voyage across the choppy seas of international crime fiction.

Paul Johnston, author of the Alex Mavros series, set in Greece.

Prologue

The instruments of murder were assembled on the bed. Most were items of clothing, bought the day before at the local shops.

Objects innocuous enough, inspiring thoughts of working in a garden and making things grow, rather than purchases for plans to make someone die.

It was shortly after dawn. Outside, despite the early hour, Mother Nature was engaged in a stunning display of strength, unleashing her fecundity with every tool at her disposal. If the scene were filmed in slow motion, it would show the frenzy of activity as flowers, bushes, shrubs, trees, grass, and weeds writhed, twisted, and pushed. All were in the grip of an irresistible power that urged the budding and blossoming of life.

One item stood out among the things displayed on the thin white summer blanket. It lay between a hat and a pair of trousers on the bed. It was a little knife, brand-new, its blade shining brightly in the shaft of sunlight slanting down from the open window. It had a black handle. It was the type of utensil to be found in any Japanese kitchen for peeling fruit and vegetables.

This knife had a different purpose. It would be used to slice through the soft, flabby neck muscle of a certain middle-aged individual.

Would the victim squeal? Like a pig feeling the sharp cutting tool at its throat? The would-be murderer picked up the would-be murder weapon and gently stroked the blade.

A sharp exhalation of breath. A drop of blood now adorned the blade, glistening red and ruby-like. A sigh of relief. The weapon was fit for purpose.

Three hours later, the items had been packed in a bag, ready to be transported to the place where they would fulfil their fatal purpose.

It was an unlikely venue for a murder, the campus of a small private university on the island of Kyushu in western Japan. The university was recent, founded less than seventy years before. Its campus was unassuming, an assortment of functional two and three-storey cement buildings linked by tiled pathways, which were lined by dusty bushes and trees.

It was a hot, bright morning. A man in his forties dressed in a business suit, rubbing a large nose, hurried to the administration building – a squat block covered by imitation brick in the centre of campus, with a cement forecourt in front and a dirt courtyard behind it. Just before entering, he encountered a slightly older man with an aureole of white hair in a crumpled grey suit who was exiting the building. The two bowed.

"Kawane-*san*, always so reliably early," the older man said.

"Thank you, Professor Nomura," the other replied. "I do my

best." "Of course, it is a busy time of year," Nomura said.

"Yes, sir," said Kawane, trying not to look at his watch.

After Kawane had rushed in to check the monitor on his desk for any urgent messages, Nomura strolled around the cement forecourt. He looked white and exhausted. He derived consolation from the sight of the camphor trees whose upper branches were waving slightly in the faint breeze, their new leaves still a vivid green. He sighed deeply and then bowed to a short elderly man with work-gnarled hands. Wearing a wide-brimmed straw hat and white work clothes, the man was wheeling a trolley to the rubbish bins in the forecourt.

"Ah, thank you for all your hard work," Nomura said in a kind voice, noticing the worker looked tired and that he grunted lifting a heavy bin to empty its contents into his trolley. "Always keeping our campus so clean and tidy," Nomura continued, and the white-clad man bowed deeply, grateful for such unexpected praise from the president of the university.

Students who had arrived a good hour before the start of the first period were gazing intently at noticeboards lining the east wall of the administration building, checking whether any of their classes for that day had been cancelled or would be held in a different room than usual. With their fashionably frayed jeans, expensive trainers and carefully groomed hair conferring an air of studied casualness, the students formed a curious contrast to the cleaners – stooped old men and women already hard at work, dressed in big straw hats, surgical masks, loose white shirts and trousers.

Like the man Nomura had greeted, some were emptying bins into trolleys that would be wheeled to a collection area at the back of the campus, shielded from sight by large white aluminium walls, where the rubbish would be sorted for recycling or incineration. Others were sweeping paths with big bamboo brushes or raking the dirt

courtyard. A few were trimming bushes or washing windows. Some were inside the classrooms, washing the blackboards clean of yesterday's work.

Two middle-aged female office workers, dressed neatly in dark mid-calf skirts and pastel blouses, emerged from the glass doors of the administration building with small brooms and whisked away a medley of leaves, balled-up paper tissues and discarded snack containers littering the forecourt. They were joined by a frail Japanese man in black trousers and a white shirt who deposited a long pair of tongs and a plastic bag on the verge of the path and then, with his own broom, swept with an energy at odds with his exhausted appearance.

Two clerical workers employed at the university library came out and hung grimy cloths on bushes to dry. They had just wiped down all the desks and chairs in the strikingly modern building behind them, its silver roof constructed as a gentle ripple that mimicked the undulating silhouette of a mountain range in the distance.

Professors appeared at intervals, briskly and purposefully striding between the buildings. Heads down, they avoided the students' curious glances, intent on reaching their destinations. They were aware of their role as the minor celebrities of the institution, the lesser deities to whom the students paid homage. They self- consciously assumed expressions of modest cleverness. Some carried briefcases, others had big satchels or woven bags. Male and female alike, they were conservatively dressed in two-piece suits of black, grey or brown over crisp white shirts, and whether it was because of the heat or the end of the academic term, or a combination of the two, they looked tired and careworn.

There were two exceptions to this. One was a foreigner in his early fifties whose blonde-grey hair shone in the early sunlight and who walked with a slight spring in his step. He was a thin, pale individual of medium height dressed from head to toe in black. He punctiliously bowed and exchanged greetings with everyone he met as if he had risen that morning for that purpose. The other was a gaunt Japanese woman in baggy orange trousers and a tunic of faded yellow. She was carrying a large bag. She had a long purple scarf around her neck. A thin grey tail of hair trailed down her back, twitching slightly, bouncing up and down as she strode along.

The woman entered the administration building shortly before the man, and they exited its rear entrance at the same time, the man holding the door open for the woman. As if aware of the tenuous link between them, that they were both anomalies

among their more conventionally suited colleagues, they stopped and spoke to each other in Japanese.

"Professor Hunter," the woman said, "you're up and about early this morning."

The man composed his features in a benevolent expression. The woman thought his face seemed oddly naked, but she was in a hurry and didn't look carefully.

He bowed. "Professor Yamamoto, now that it's summer, early morning is the only time of day I can enjoy, before it gets so dreadfully hot."

The woman nodded in sympathy as the pair instinctively moved further into the shade cast by the awning over the glass door behind them. Professor Hunter shifted the heavy-looking briefcase he was carrying from his right to his left hand. "And anyway, you know, the end of term, so much to do."

"Of course. Well, good luck to us both," Professor Yamamoto said, pulling at the strap of her bulging bag to settle it more firmly on her shoulder. "We just have to carry on and do our best."

"And, of course, good luck to our students. I'm praying they've actually cracked open a book or two and done some studying for the exams we'll be giving them today."

Yamamoto said, "I'm praying too, but I'm not looking for miracles."

They both smiled in chagrined amusement – they didn't expect their prayers to be answered. They then bowed to each other again before setting off in the bright sunshine in opposite directions.

Chief Inspector Inoue Longs for Excitement

Chief Inspector Inoue of the Fujikawa police force was lying in bed early one Wednesday morning in July, his American wife, Ellie, beside him, as motionless and beautiful as an enchanted princess in a fairy tale. She kicked off her light covering and curled up facing him. Inoue propped himself on one arm and looked at her. They had been married ten years, but the sight of her still filled him with the same tender awe he felt when she was his bride. Her hair lay in a thick yellow plait on the pillow. Her face was rosy and soft.

Inoue was accustomed to waking early, especially in the heat and humidity of summer. It was a habit adopted in childhood. He liked the freshness of the morning. But even at 5.30 the sun was already well above the horizon: the sky a dark blue dominated by a blistering orange ball, its rays beating down on the roof of the inspector's modest home. Inoue sat up, adjusting his pillow behind his back. He looked out the window, squinting from the glare.

The air shimmered. The bedroom felt like a sauna. Inoue coughed, trying to dispel the sensation that he was being suffocated. He hated the heat. He also hated the explosion in the insect population every summer. It was a source of amusement for Ellie that he was squeamish about creepy, crawly things. He shuddered seeing a huge hairy black spider dart up the wall beside their bed to disappear behind a picture.

He hated how summer in Japan was so noisy. Outside, cicadas buzzed with a sound that reminded him of the noise of a stone being rubbed maniacally on sandpaper, amplification on full. From dawn to dusk an army of tiny frogs in the paddy field beside the house kept up a rhythmic croaking that was sometimes punctuated by the mournful bellow of a big bullfrog.

Inoue looked at his alarm clock and gave a grunt of satisfaction. He needn't get up yet. He plumped up the pillow and settled back on the mattress. Even that slight exertion made him perspire. He could feel tiny rivulets of sweat coursing down from his forehead and trickling through the bristles on his scalp, offering a hint of coolness as they dried. He turned towards his wife.

He wondered if Ellie had been put on earth to remind him there was heaven even in hell. As if she had intuited his thought, she moved slightly. Now her yellow plait draped over her pillow and across the twisted thin cotton sheet that lay between them. On an impulse, he lifted her plait and kissed it.

Inoue was a big, burly man. Anyone who saw him striding purposefully around Fujikawa might have thought he looked stout. But there was not an ounce of fat on this veteran policeman's body. It was all muscle in the broad shoulders and sturdy legs. His voice was deep and commanding. The officers and policemen under his control held him in awe. They would have been astonished to see what their curt, terrifying chief did next.

Inoue was still gazing at Ellie. Deep in her slumbers, she was oblivious to the tenderness he longed to express. That was just as well. It would only have embarrassed them both had she woken and seen him as he stroked her plait gently. Ellie never used perfume, but she exuded a soft sweetness. Inoue breathed it in deeply.

He noticed tiny drops of perspiration beading his wife's pink face and felt a twinge of compunction. She had begged him to install an air conditioner in their bedroom, but he had resisted. "Air conditioning is bad for the health," he had told her. "We need to live naturally." Now he wondered if he was too stubborn, too set in his ways. It was a quality he had disliked in his father, but perhaps he had begun to display it himself.

He was reluctant to rise, knowing he'd be drenched in sweat before he reached the kitchen for his morning coffee. There was no point in showering. In this heat, within minutes of drying off, he would feel as dirty and miserable as if he had never washed.

And there was nothing to look forward to that day. He was the head of the Fujikawa police station but being the top official in the town didn't prevent his being outranked in the prefecture by a man he detested and feared in equal measure.

Superintendent Takenaka was a small, thin man whose pasty face was rescued from insipidity by heavy black-framed glasses. Inoue was wise enough not to expect perfect justice in an imperfect world. Still, it did seem unfair that this puny, shrill- voiced man could order him about. How was it possible that Takenaka had been promoted to the top position in the prefectural police force? Inoue derived a measure of comfort from Takenaka being based in Ishizaki, a good hour's drive east of Fujikawa. But, alas, thismorning, he was due to arrive in Fujikawa to make his annual inspection of Inoue's smooth-running organisation.

Inoue hated the thought of that little mouse having power over him. Takenaka could transfer him at will to another station. He could get him demoted in the case of a perceived minor omission in the performance of his duty. In the worst scenario Takenaka could even lose Inoue his beloved job on the force.

He glanced again at his clock. The deafening cicada chorus was at full throttle. He liked to imagine that the sound represented a kind of musical arrangement and the theme of the piece was an affirmation of existence. A repetition of what sounded like "*Yes, yes, yes, yes*" lasted several minutes, to be followed by an interval of noisy, self-satisfied applause, like tiny hands clapping, before the launch into the "*Yes, yes*" phase again.

Inoue groaned loudly as he realised he should get up. Ellie

stirred. "Sorry I woke you," he said tenderly in Japanese. He could speak a little English and understand a good bit of what he heard, but Ellie had asked him early on in their relationship to speak to her only in Japanese so she could become fluent, a full partner in their life together in Japan.

She turned to look at the clock, too. "Time to get up anyway," she groaned, easing herself from the bed, throwing on a loose cotton wrap and hurrying to the kitchen.

Inoue's daydreams had lasted longer than he'd intended. It was already past 7.00, and his habit was to leave home by 8.00 at the latest to arrive at the police headquarters twenty minutes later. In any case, the need to relieve himself had reached a state of urgency. He threw back his light towel covering and jumped, naked, out of bed.

"What's on today?" Ellie asked him twenty minutes later as she served him his mug of black coffee and buttered toast smothered in a thick layer of orange marmalade. "Anything special?" For someone so plump, she could move with surprising speed. She was still dressed in her cotton robe tied at the waist, her blonde braid hanging down her back. Once her husband was on his way, she would dress properly.

She paused to stand beside him. "Will you be home at 5.00?" she asked. "I'm thinking of getting sushi for dinner. No more meat this week. I think you're putting on a few pounds." She smiled down mischievously.

Nobody else was allowed to tease Chief Inspector Inoue.

But he loved it when Ellie did. He pretended to be angry noticing, at the same time, that he had unconsciously sucked in his stomach.

"Me, fat? Never!" he said in a disgusted tone and with a wrinkled brow. Then he remembered, and his face showed unfeigned annoyance.

"We're having our annual inspection," he said heavily. "You must remember. I was complaining about it last night. I went on and on about it, must have bored you. I bored *myself*. Having to be under Takenaka's thumb all day. Still, it'll soon be over. I'll have an extra beer tonight to celebrate."

Ellie fished out a green handkerchief and mopped her brow. She smiled sympathetically. "Sorry. Of course, you did tell me. In this heat, I can't think straight. That horrible man will be peering and prying into all your affairs. But you run a tight ship. He won't find anything to complain about. Does that mean you'll be late?"

"No, barring any disasters I'll be home at the same time as usual. Probably 5.00 on the dot. That is, if Officer Ando doesn't manage to drop something on Takenaka's foot. Or if Takenaka doesn't set the place on fire with all his cigarettes."

He massaged his creased forehead with both hands. "Apart from that bastard being around to irritate me, it will be just an ordinary day. You know the drill. I'll have to sort out the problem of cars colliding during the morning rush hour. I might get a call about a schoolboy who tried to steal a *manga* by hiding it in his satchel. Or maybe a housewife absentmindedly put a packet of tofu in her handbag without paying. Boring!"

"Okay, that might be *boring*," Ellie conceded, "but what's wrong with boring? It's better than if we lived in Tokyo or Osaka. In the big cities you could be *killed*! I hear the *yakuza* are smuggling more and more guns into Japan. Just think, you could be shot! How awful that would be, waving goodbye every morning, wondering if I'd ever see you again."

Inoue looked up at his fat, pink, perspiring wife gazing at him with tender concern. He knew he couldn't tell her what he was really feeling: *But I want adventure, excitement, challenge. Why do women insist on protecting their men, wanting to keep them like little boys?*

Naturally, none of this could be said, and Inoue contented himself with simply saying, "Of course, but I sometimes long for something more exciting than devising speed traps."

Be careful what you wish for, he would think later.

A Shy Canadian in Japan

Afterwards Andrew Thomas thought of it as a day steeped in blood, its crimson tide rising inexorably and staining every act and thought.

But it was a day that had begun like any other. It was unusual only in that from the start everything conspired to disrupt his daily routine. First, his wife had failed to get him up at the normal time. Alyson woke every morning at 6.00 and got him up half an hour later, knowing Andrew could never wake so early without her shaking him. From childhood, Andrew had been a heavy sleeper.

That morning Alyson, so reliable, who could wake herself at the same time each morning whether she had a clock or not, was still dozing beside him when Andrew woke from a nightmare. Horror! It was already 7.30. Luckily, he'd had a bad dream that had frightened and woken him.

He sprang from the bed, heart still pounding. He hastily dressed, made toast and tea, and set off in his battered old car for the university. As a concession to Japanese expectations of a university professor, Andrew wore a white linen suit. He couldn't quite carry off the look. His suit was wrinkled and even slightly stained, but it fitted and conferred some dishevelled elegance on his tall slim figure. His long, prematurely greying hair was scraped back in a thin little tail held by an elastic band.

Andrew was no longer able to enjoy spring, the season that used to be his favourite when he was growing up in Canada. Since moving to the island of Kyushu, he'd discovered that the Japanese spring was too short. It was nearly non-existent. Like fall, the other transition season, it was telescoped into one or two weeks. The few days of comfortable temperatures only highlighted the hellishness of the boiling hot or freezing cold weather that would inevitably follow.

Still, it was a topic of conversation suited to Andrew's minimal Japanese ability. He was able to exclaim, "It's hot, isn't it?" with an authentic accent and emphasis. He couldn't manage much else in the language, but he had nailed that phrase down, along with "It's cold, isn't it?" It was convenient. Japanese never tired of prefacing their conversations with these remarks made in all eagerness, as though they were trotting out some fresh-minted observation.

In summer, Andrew tended to regard the Japanese around him with envy, thinking they must be acclimatised to the unbearable sultriness. It was different for foreigners like him coming from cool countries.

He pulled into the university parking lot. "Thomas-*sensei*, *ohayo gozaimasu*!"

He was pleased to see it was Michiko Ota, his favourite secretary. She was standing beside a tiny blue car whose rear window ledge was decorated with a menagerie of stuffed toy animals. She was wearing what Andrew thought of as her secretary's uniform: a short black skirt, shiny sheer tights, a crisp white shirt, and black high heels. *Does she not feel the heat?* Andrew thought. Then he saw a small slick of perspiration banding her forehead. She was struggling with a large pink plastic bag held gingerly at her side.

"*Ohayo gozaimasu*," he said. "Good morning. Michiko-*san*, that bag looks heavy. Can I carry it for you?"

She flushed. She was feeling the heat after all, he thought.

"Andrew-*sensei*, always gentleman. No, no, no. I carry this," she said, shifting her bag to the hand away from him as they walked side by side to the campus.

The soldiers at the army camp next door were struggling through their daily morning exercise routine. Andrew stared at the twenty khaki-clad, helmeted figures as they rhythmically moved their arms and legs to a sergeant's shouted commands. He forced himself to look away, not wanting to gawp. He was involuntarily impressed. How did they find the energy, and in these temperatures?

Sweat began to roll down Michiko's forehead to her cheeks, each drop swiftly wiped away with a small pink handkerchief taken from her handbag. She dabbed her plump face, heavily powdered to a uniform whiteness, careful not to smear her makeup.

"You have meeting today?" she asked.

"One, at 11.00 with Nomura-*sensei*. I need to talk to him

about next year's teaching schedule."

"Oh, Nomura-*sensei*." Her sympathy was expressed in a melodramatic intonation of the president's name.

"You know he's planning lots of changes. Rumour has it he's restructuring. I'm worried, to be honest. I hear that many colleges are having to cut back these days, and

getting rid of the resident English teacher is often seen as the easiest way to economise."

Andrew immediately regretted his candour. Of course, as a Japanese member of staff, Michiko would know far more about Nomura's plans than him. Also, he had freely volunteered information when there was no need, an act the Japanese, with their ingrained habits of discretion and reserve, considered a kind of sin.

They strolled on in silence to the administrative office, a small structure covered with a veneer of imitation brick. It occupied centre stage in the campus of grey or white buildings that housed offices and classrooms. Although Fujikawa University was only sixty-five years old, it seemed it could never have been new.

Andrew lifted his feet with difficulty. It was as if the soles of his shoes were melting to the pavement. *Why can I never learn? Why am I so indiscreet?* It was a question Andrew asked himself silently and often – if not hourly, at least daily. Fortunately Michiko was a friend. It wasn't as though he had exposed too much, revealing his vulnerability and his status as an outsider, to someone who would gladly use his weakness against him.

Then Michiko realised she was late. Mrs Noma and Mrs Takagi, fellow office workers, were already outside with their brooms and dustbins, briskly sweeping up litter from the concrete forecourt in front of the brick cube known as Building One. Michiko lifted her free hand, waving at Andrew in an apologetic farewell, and ran towards them, her heavy-looking pink plastic bag knocking against her legs.

A frail middle-aged man wearing white gloves, carrying a plastic bag and a pair of long tongs, stood by the entrance. He saw Andrew and began picking up empty beer cans, discarded polythene cups and snack wrappers from the concrete path in front of the vending machines beside Building Two, depositing them in his plastic bag. His face was the pallor of antique ivory and covered with a network of fine lines, making him look much older than his forty years. Andrew knew Hideo Akamatsu suffered from a heart condition. He was amazed that the poor man, who worked in the second-floor accounts office, had been asked to assist with the daily morning clean-up of the premises. But perhaps Akamatsu had insisted, reluctant to ask for special treatment.

It was a pity if he had imposed this duty on himself. Andrew worried that Akamatsu worked too hard. He always looked exhausted.

"Akamatsu-*san* ... *ohayo gozaimasu.*"

Then Andrew noticed that Akamatsu was wearing a white surgical mask. He gestured towards his own uncovered nose and mouth and said, "Hay fever?"

"Oh, Andrew-*sensei*. You are so lucky. I dread every spring, when it all starts again, and now it just goes on and on, even through the summer."

Andrew silently agreed with the office worker's assessment. He knew he was blessed not to suffer from the allergies that afflicted many Japanese once March rolled around. They would wear masks for months. He sometimes mused on the irony that it was a self-inflicted problem. Cedars had been planted all over Japan in the 1960s as a reforestation project, and it was the pollen from these plantations of trees, now mature, that attacked its population fifty years later causing an epidemic of watery eyes, aching sinuses and streaming noses.

"Do you think they have this horrible pollen in Paris?"

"Sorry, I have no idea," said Andrew, knowing it was Akamatsu's ambition to visit France one day. Andrew liked Akamatsu and hoped he could fulfil his dream, but given the short holidays allotted to Japanese office workers and their reluctance to take even those, worrying their absence might inconvenience co-workers, it was unlikely the poor man would see Paris until he could retire in twenty years.

I'm lucky, lucky! Andrew thought. *I don't have allergies. Even better, I'm not Japanese, always having to work too hard, worrying about what other people think, always putting the group first, and having to think of others before themselves.* He had been stunned when he realised most Japanese wear surgical masks not only to protect themselves but also as a gesture of courtesy in consideration for others.

But then Andrew felt distinctly unlucky. He had just remembered the day's itinerary. *Damn*, he groaned. *I have to see that old bastard today.*

Nomura's Secretary is Surprised

The day was hot and bright. With the academic term nearing its end and the budget tight, the university buildings had become unpleasantly warm. Fujikawa, like most of Japan's small private colleges in the early decades of the 21st century, was unable to attract its full quota of students because of the country's economic downturn and the low birth rate. Toru Kawane, the chief of the administrative staff, had imposed energy restrictions as a cost-cutting measure. The cooling system was turned off in almost all the classrooms and admin offices although the professors had air conditioners in their own rooms.

Akemi Tanimoto's office was not one of the favoured. She was a person of insufficient importance in the university hierarchy, only being the secretary to Professor Nomura. She had to rely on fans positioned around her desk for a tantalising hint of coolness while his office, adjoining hers, was kept icy cool, the way her boss preferred, by an old machine that made a racket he had reconciled himself to, willing to pay this price for comfort. Akemi wondered why her boss didn't splash out on a flash new replacement, but understood he was the type of wealthy individual who could be stingy that way.

It was a day of unpleasant surprises for Akemi. When she

arrived in her office at 8.15, she was amazed to find that Professor Nomura, who usually turned up after

10.00 or even later, was already there and that her boss, usually so calm and carefully dressed, looked worried and his expensive grey suit was crumpled. She wondered if he'd slept in his office the night before. But she put on a face of blank submissiveness to hear his instructions. At his request, she delayed making his morning coffee. He'd just had a can of cold coffee from the vending machines outside. He asked her for hot coffee at 10.00 but wanted her to do some photocopying first, after the compulsory meeting Kawane held every morning for all his clerical staff.

It was most unpleasant and unusual. Professor Nomura looked angry as he handed her the document to be photocopied. It was in a thick file on which he had scribbled the word 'Important'. He said that it was top-secret and wanted five copies of it as a priority.

Professor Nomura usually trusted Akemi's discretion, but on this occasion she felt resentful. He was treating her like a child, cautioning her not to leave the file lying unattended on her desk. After the meeting and the photocopying, she should prepare his coffee and bring him the copies for him to give the five department heads in person.

Akemi filled out a few forms and made some phone calls. She decided it was easiest and safest to take the file with her. She would carry it beneath a notepad on which she could note down Kawane's advice about the most pressing tasks the office staff had to tackle that day. She needed to concentrate carefully. Kawane exercised tough love: reprimands if his orders failed to be obeyed to the letter but compliments if a clerk was working well. At 8.25 Akemi hurried to the half-hour meeting in the administration building. Opening the glass door of the rear entrance, she saw Michiko Ota fetching a broom from the utility cupboard and Professor Yamamoto standing by the pigeonholes in the mailroom, gazing intently at a circular she had just taken from her own box.

Then Akemi had her second surprise of the day. She saw Professor Hunter coming in behind her to collect his mail and sign in. As usual, Gerald was clad in black, but he was clean-shaven. She was relieved he hadn't shaved his head as well. Gerald had a shock of fine ash blonde hair that crested above his brow like a fashionable '50s' quiff. Akemi thought it gave him an air of distinction.

"Professor Hunter!" she exclaimed, "I didn't recognise you without your beard."

He looked in the direction of his mailbox and saw it was empty. He signed the attendance register and seemed anxious to get away. He shifted a big briefcase from hand to hand, swaying softly and saying impatiently, "Sorry, Tanimoto-*san*, I'm in a bit of a rush. I shaved off my beard as a concession to this dreadful heat."

Akemi took her place in the admin office beside Akamatsu,

who looked even paler and more tired than usual, to hear Kawane's instructions and delegation of duties. The office was hot. The air conditioning was on, but with students and professors wandering casually in and out all day asking for assistance and often carelessly leaving the doors open, the room never got properly cooled. There were three clerks, former Fujikawa students doing temporary work, standing in a corner in white shirts and black trousers, their ties askew. They carried pads and pens to make notes, looking eager and exhausted in equal measures.

Akemi was sorry for them but also felt indignation on behalf of her friend Michiko Ota. She was standing beside her desk located just behind the front counter. It was piled high with papers, a small laptop wedged between two towers of documents and the only marker of individual taste, a fat brown cotton dog that encased a tissue box.

She looked demoralised, and it was no wonder. Everyone knew that the placing of desks indicated the office hierarchy. Michiko's position near the front meant that, despite her six years of service at the college, she was at the bottom of the heap. It was still a man's world. The young male Fujikawa graduates, just by virtue of gender, got better places nearer the back of the room, closer to the air conditioner above the rear exit. Kawane naturally commanded the best position. From his desk in front of the screen shielding the back entrance to the office, he was able to oversee the employees working at the desks crowded before him and to keep an eye on anyone coming through the front door.

Akemi liked and respected Kawane, but she wondered if he always needed to look so smug. She toyed with the idea that his big nose gave him a sense of superiority, making him look like a westerner. Looking at him again, she revised her opinion. As he wound up his pep talk, his complacency seemed frayed at the edges. There was even a smear of perspiration on his chin.

No wonder he felt worried, she thought. The end of term was always a difficult time for the office staff, requiring a new slew of duties in addition to all their other responsibilities throughout the year. Things like needing to be on call to field questions or complaints. Or to jump up at a moment's notice to help students and professors. The office workers might be asked to photocopy material for a class, or a distraught lecturer might rush in, asking for help operating a classroom's DVD player or document camera. The staff had to combine clerical skills, technological ability, and a personable manner.

Their plight was only growing worse with all the directives issued by the Ministry of Education. In the past, professors had taught as many classes per term as they thought reasonable; they were even allowed to cancel a few if they liked. In recent years, this easy-going, relaxed regime had been banished. Now the Ministry stipulated fifteen sessions must be taught each term and any cancellations covered by make-up classes. It was the responsibility of the office staff to chase up professors who needed to hold extra class meetings. And, at the end of term, there was so much else: they had to schedule exams and assign rooms for the test taking; they had to input all the

grades in the computer system; and they had to arrange special summer session events, including campus open days to attract prospective students. Everyone in the room that day knew the university was suffering internal convulsions, with some professors and staff strongly against the changes Nomura had set his heart on.

Akemi clutched the file entrusted to her by Nomura more tightly. Surely others could see that even the normally imperturbable Kawane was flustered.

"We are all hot and tired," Kawane said. "But we need to do our best to complete the end-of-term duties. I am counting on you."

Kawane dismissed his staff at 9.00 with a fussy solicitude, his large nose pointed in the air as if sniffing for a breeze. Akemi was surprised to see Michiko Ota's face, under its thick layer of powder, looking nearly as white as Akamatsu's. Her eyes were welling up with unshed tears. Akemi felt sorry for her.

Andrew at Work

After bidding farewell to Akamatsu, still busily picking up litter and depositing it in his plastic bag, Andrew saw the slim figure of Professor Mutsuko Yamamoto. She was loping across the courtyard towards the staff entrance to the brick admin building, a large bag draped over one shoulder, wearing her odd hippie clothes. *She must be going to sign in and collect her mail,* he thought. He needed to do the same but couldn't summon the energy. He'd do it later. There was a cleaner in the courtyard raking the dusty soil and one on a ladder washing Building Two's windows.

He was surprised to glimpse the slight figure of Gerald Hunter rounding the corner of Building Three, also off to get his mail. As Gerald lived on campus, he would usually turn up around 9.00, when he could get to his first-period class in a minute or two at a leisurely stroll. Gerald was carrying a large, bulging briefcase and, despite the heat, was dressed as usual in austere black trousers, black shirt, and black shoes. Andrew wondered if he wore such dramatic but simple clothes because he thought they befitted his vocation as a missionary. The only touch of colour in his appearance was a greying blonde shock of hair standing up like a rooster's comb on his head, turned a gleaming pale gold colour by the bright sun. There was something odd about Gerald's appearance, but at that distance Andrew couldn't see him clearly. Later he realised he had shaved off his beard.

Gerald hadn't seen him. He strode forward, looking intent. Andrew was relieved. He never really knew what to say to him. Gerald was terrible at chitchat. He was impatient with the small change of conversation, wanting always to discuss serious issues. He lacked a sense of humour and perhaps even compassion. Perhaps it was because he had a literal belief in the God of the Old Testament while Andrew was an atheist. He saw the world in black and white, but for Andrew it was all varying shades of grey. He would always be taken aback when Gerald pronounced something or someone as 'good' or 'evil'. Andrew knew he could never have such moral certainty about anything.

Andrew saw Gerald disappear into the brick admin building. Then he pushed open the glass doors of Building Five. A sense of relief flooded through him to be nearly home – that is, his second home, not far from where he had just left Alyson still sleeping.

Andrew laboured up two flights of stairs, feeling unexpectedly happy – he had arrived before his insufferable colleague, Professor Obuchi. What simple joys can brighten one's life he thought as he triumphantly turned on the light switch beside the door to the men's toilets. It gave him a feeling of power to be the one to flood the corridor with the white glare of fluorescent lamps. Only a few more steps. He pushed the key into the lock, entering his office with pleasure and relief. *His* place.

He wanted to wash his hands and bathe his perspiring face in cold water. But once he approached the small, dingy pink basin by the bookshelf, a mirror above it, he found that it was a mistake. How depressing to find that one looks as bad – and as old

– as one feels, peering at his reflection after splashing himself with water. He was only twenty-six, but it was a haggard face that stared back at him: ill-shaven, forehead prematurely wrinkled, discontented lines slanting from the nose to the corners of the mouth. His long, ashen-brown hair streaked with grey was pulled harshly back. Only the eyes, grey-blue, deep set and wide, were unchanged, reminding Andrew of the little boy who had stared out at him with those eyes – that lonely spirit who had lain in the grassy field beside his parents' house in a Winnipeg suburb, looking up at the night sky, absorbed by the wonder of the stars, thinking that everything was possible.

Andrew's office was a sanctuary. Here it didn't matter that he was a stranger in a foreign land, that his Japanese remained rudimentary, that he was an object of curiosity and, he suspected, some derision. Here he was the observer rather than the observed.

He turned on the air conditioner and slid back the paper *shoji* screen that covered the grimy window. The university parking lot was just below, affording him one of his favourite amusements. He liked watching the cars arriving and departing, enjoying the drama in the skirmishing of cars whose drivers were invisible.

The low-slung black cars were driven with reckless speed by young male students; the perky little white, blue, and red models, with stuffed teddy bears crowding their rear windows, belonged to young females; the office staff drove big new white cars while the professors, whether cultivating a reputation for eccentricity or simply economising, favoured old heaps the students despised.

By 9.00, ten minutes before the first classes of the day, the drama intensified. At this point, the parking lot would be nearly full. Andrew relished the spectacle of seeing students rushing to catch the roll call at the start of each lesson. They would compete for the few remaining places, manoeuvring their vehicles with brutal skill. Once the lot was full, late arrivals pulled onto the grass verge where no parking was allowed.

Andrew saw two white-shirted young men striding through the playing field next to the parking lot which was already full. Like Akamatsu, they were picking up wads of paper and empty cigarette packs with tongs and depositing them in the plastic bags they carried. Just beyond, he could see Professor Yamamoto again, striding purposefully across the field toward her office in Building Eight, still carrying her large shoulder bag that looked fuller and heavier than ever. She must have signed in and collected her mail.

He smiled as he watched her figure growing smaller with each large energetic step she took. Professor Yamamoto was one of his favourite colleagues. He liked her for her eccentricity, admiring her as an original in a place that prized conformity. A woman in her mid-sixties who taught feminism and women's studies, Professor Yamamoto was tiny and sexless. She detested the Japanese professional woman's heavy makeup and tailored clothes and the custom for men and women to dye their hair well into old age. She was a law unto herself. She wore her hair in a long grey braid that hung down her back, and faded balloon trousers topped by beaded tunics, and sandals that seemed to have come from a long-ago trip to India.

Then he saw a shiny red sports car pause at the electronic barrier to the parking lot, engine idling noisily. A slim brown arm with a bangle at the wrist snaked from the driver's window and inserted a card into the machine operating the barrier. It rose and the car raced forward in a flurry of gravel, pulling up on the verge beside the nine or ten other cars that had arrived too late to find a designated spot.

Red sports car, attractive female arm; Andrew was gratified to find his prediction confirmed by the appearance of a tall, slim young woman who slid gracefully from the driver's seat, patting her long black hair before adjusting a fashionable little black rucksack on her back.

She glanced up, as if aware of being observed. Andrew hastily stepped back from the window. She had disappeared when he looked out again. He recognised her as Mari Furomoto. She was by far and away his best student: the brightest, the friendliest, and the most eager. Teaching her was an oasis of satisfaction in a desert of

perfunctory instruction to the bored, indifferent female students who used his classes as a place where they could nap, manicure their nails, cut split ends with tiny scissors, or send text messages to friends on their cell phones.

Mari Furomoto. A niggling worry surfaced in Andrew's mind. Hadn't she been the subject of Stephen's gossip two nights before? Stephen was never a reliable news bearer at the best of times, and that night he had been the worse for having consumed four pints of Guinness at the Irish pub beside the train station.

He had related his story with a relish that seemed to guarantee its authenticity. It was something about Mari and, incredibly, Professor Nomura. Even Andrew, a comparative innocent, his ignorance and naivety preserved by his poor Japanese, knew that it was not unusual for Japanese male teachers to take advantage of their positions of authority, flirting with, even seducing female students in their charge at university.

But really! Could it be possible? Mari had told him herself

that her parents were in the process of arranging a marriage for her to take place soon after graduation and that they had already picked out a suitable candidate: wealthy, well-placed socially, not physically repulsive. Yet Andrew couldn't suppress the memory of Stephen, his cheeks unusually flushed, hilarity in his voice as he repeated from an unnamed party the particulars of the so-called affair. Everyone had laughed. Everyone but Andrew.

It was beyond belief. *Mari and that fat old lecher*?

Andrew's disquieting reflections on a possible sexual liaison between Professor Nomura and his favourite student Mari Furomoto were disturbed by a soft, tentative knock on his office door. Andrew knew it must be either a Japanese colleague or a student. Fellow westerners who worked at the university would simply have banged hard and then barged in without waiting for a response. He hastily seated himself at his desk, assembled students' tests in front of him, smoothed down his hair, and tried to look studious, calling out: "*Doozo*, please come in."

The door opened slowly to reveal a gangling figure who could easily have been mistaken for a student. Apart from Yamamoto-*sensei*, the Japanese individuals employed by Fujikawa University, professional or admin staff, male or female, tended to dress smartly, wearing white shirts and dark suits to work each day, But Andrew's visitor was a young man with long unkempt hair and a predilection for jeans and faded polo shirts.

"Ah, Hayashi-*sensei*. Please come in."

Professor Takaaki Hayashi always wore a faintly anxious expression, but on that day he appeared on the brink of nervous collapse. His long, lank black hair hadn't been combed recently. His jeans looked more rumpled than usual, and Andrew detected a small stain on the front of his pale yellow shirt with its emblem of a little red alligator near the left shoulder. Hayashi looked hungry, anxious, and inquisitive, and he smelt distinctly of sweat. He stumbled over a rocking chair Andrew kept in the corner of his office before managing to sit down at Andrew's long worktable.

"So sorry to disturb, Andrew-*san*."

"No problem. I'm just giving a few tests today, and they're all ready. Coffee?"

"No, thank you," Hayashi said. He looked up plaintively. "*Thank you!*" He enunciated deliberately, speaking English in the halting, careful way adopted by Japanese who had studied it half their lives with little chance to use it in daily life even if, like Hayashi, they taught it at university level.

"It's nice to have courtesy. You are so good," Hayashi continued. "But I have bad news. I just came to ask if you heard the latest news about Nomura-*sensei*. I had a meeting with some people last night. They told me he is planning to fire about half of us in the department."

"But you're a tenured member of staff. You can't be fired,

can you? It would only mean that he was planning to shunt you off to another department."

"True, yes, but we don't want that. We have commitment to this department."

Andrew tried to hide his weariness. He liked Hayashi but wondered if he could take more discussion of a topic obsessing everyone at Fujikawa University in recent months: Professor Nomura's proposed changes, rumoured to include dropping its Christian affiliation and dissolving the English department, to which Hayashi and Andrew both belonged.

The campus was situated on a former Army camp, but only one of its original buildings remained, appropriated by the university. Once used as a barracks, this two- storey wooden structure, now known as Building Two, had been converted into classrooms, meeting rooms and offices. Some said the place was haunted by the ghost of a Japanese soldier killed during the Second World War, unable to reconcile himself, even in death, to his country's defeat, but Andrew had seen nothing untoward in this old structure with its creaking wooden floors and nondescript corridors apart from a grenade, presumably no longer functional, stored in a glass box by the upstairs

staircase. He wondered how it had been overlooked when the building was redecorated. Unimaginable that it had been left there on purpose.

Andrew found it typical, if ironic, that of all the departments at Fujikawa, it was the English department that Nomura wanted to obliterate. Fujikawa had once been known locally as the English university, a place that fostered ties with Presbyterian missionary groups in the United States, that had a tradition of employing American teachers and was linked to American colleges by exchange programmes. The institution's emphasis on internationalisation as well as its Christian orientation – unusual in a country where less than one per cent of its population professed that faith – had gained it some renown. And Nomura was fluent in English, taught American studies, and had been married to Liza, a vibrant black woman from New York City who had died only two years earlier of breast cancer.

Yet, even before her death Nomura harboured ambivalent feelings about his wife's native land. Andrew had heard him complain that the English that Japanese students studied as a compulsory subject at junior and senior high school was a covert form of cultural imperialism. Nomura railed against America for failing to show respect for Japan's ancient traditions. After Liza's death his attitude hardened. In the past English support had been offered to all the *gaijin* – the westerners employed by Fujikawa. Now the tacit demand was they should all be fluent in Japanese. Official documents used to be accompanied by simple English translations. Now all paperwork was just in Japanese. When he had become the university president, Nomura made it a point of honour not to hire admin staff with any significant command of English.

Observing Hayashi's hands, closing and opening like fluttery white spiders as he complained about the injustice of closing Fujikawa's English department, Andrew struggled to maintain sympathy while concealing his impatience, digging his nails into his palms. At least Hayashi would still have a job if the department were shut down, but it wasn't certain that Andrew would, as a foreigner on a contract. But they couldn't remove him for seven more months, not until March, the end of the academic year.

"We won't give up without a fight," Hayashi concluded before standing and bowing deeply.

"Should I go to see Professor Nomura, check?" Andrew asked, feeling anxious. He wondered if he should tell Hayashi of his aborted attempt to discuss this topic with

their employer the day before. But Hayashi shook his head mournfully and said, "No point."

At the door Hayashi hesitantly added, "There is a rumour. I ask you to ignore it. It is about Akamatsu-*san*, our valued clerk. Something about money missing from a fund managed by the admin office. Of course, it will be cleared up. It must be some *misunderstanding*." He beamed as he got the long English word right.

That had cleared up one mystery, Andrew thought, as Hayashi-*san* softly closed the office door behind him. It all became clear: the worried-looking clerical staff standing in little knots in the corners of the administration building; their habit of dispersing with guilty haste whenever Andrew appeared; Akamatsu's defiantly cheerful looks at odds with his generally worried-looking demeanour. He had aged years in just the past few weeks, looking frailer than ever.

It was yet another blow to Andrew's peace of mind if it were true that Akamatsu was somehow implicated in financial impropriety and might face dismissal. He was one of the Japanese office workers most supportive members of the university's dwindling band of western teachers. Due to Nomura's scorched-earth policy over hiring staff who would be able to assist the university's foreign teachers, Michiko and Akamatsu, both hired before Nomura's time, were the only people in the admin office able to speak fluent English. Andrew often consulted Akamatsu about documents in his university mailbox – he couldn't imagine him guilty of any wrongdoing.

It was 9.50. Andrew's first class wasn't for over an hour. It was the last week of classes and he would only be handling end-of-term exams, thereby eradicating the need to prepare lessons. He opened his *shoji* screen and saw Professor Yamamoto striding once more in the direction of Building Eight.

Andrew looked out vacantly. Hayashi's news of the rumour about Akamatsu worried him. *What should I do*? he wondered. On an impulse, he decided to try to see Nomura before their scheduled meeting at 11.00. Better to know sooner rather than later if he should look for a new job. If he wasn't to be hired next year, he must polish his resume and send off applications. Even an adverse response was better than this suspense.

Later Andrew recalled having felt he had nothing to lose: Nomura couldn't feel more contempt for him than he already did. And Alyson was depending on him. At the thought of his wife, he felt the usual mixture of dread and anxiety. With unusual energy, he jumped up and set off for his boss's office.

The Body

In his time at Fujikawa University, Andrew had often had to visit Professor Nomura's office. On this occasion he felt fear at the prospect of seeing a man he detested, to beg to keep a job he wasn't even keen on, all to please his wife, who was increasingly indifferent to him. After the previous day's disastrous attempt to see Nomura, Andrew was close to despair.

And curiosity. Nomura was an enigma to Andrew. On his first day at the college over two years earlier, he had met a distinguished, middle-aged, bearded Japanese man in a grey suit who spoke impeccable English. They crossed paths in the dusty courtyard at the back of the admin building in the morning and stopped and chatted at length. The man seemed genuinely interested in Andrew and his circumstances. He asked why the Canadian had chosen to work in Japan, let alone in such a small out-of-the-way place as Fujikawa. The man had charisma. He explained he had once lived and studied in New York. Coming from such a homogenous culture as Japan, he had become fascinated, by way of contrast, in America's multicultural society. He had got his doctorate on race relations in the States. He said he had married a black woman he'd met in one of his classes at Columbia. He drew Andrew out of his usual shy hesitancy, who confided to this man his dream one day to do postgraduate work himself.

Andrew was relieved that he could be certain of one friendship with a member of the Japanese staff at the college. It was reassuring, especially in the light of what an Englishman employed there part-time had told him. Stephen had warned Andrew that the president was a man hostile to westerners although he could speak English well, having married an American woman. Now he refused to use English at all, perhaps in pique at her recent death. Stephen said that, with Nomura at the helm, there was a general attitude of unhelpfulness towards the *gaijin* staff.

When Andrew met Professor Nomura again, he was stunned that the charming stranger he had spoken to was the president of the university. Andrew needed to sign his contract. As Nomura gave a short bow and extended the document to Andrew, he

gave no sign of recognition, no hint of recalling they had already met. Andrew bowed deeply in return, wondering if he had imagined the encounter that had taken place only hours earlier.

He was struck on this occasion and at all their subsequent meetings by the contrast between the Nomura who had sought his acquaintance and the Nomura who occupied the most important position in the college and kept him at arm's length. That engaging individual with whom he had conversed for nearly twenty minutes never reappeared. Andrew was impressed and chilled by Nomura's ability to compartmentalise his personality. At work, he was the intimidating boss. In his private life, he could be approachable, even friendly.

Andrew entered the president's office tentatively, almost on tiptoe, expecting a sharp rebuke for his audacity. He had not only banged on Professor Nomura's door but, even worse, arrived an hour before his scheduled appointment.

Andrew was relieved, no harsh words. He peered in the direction of his boss's desk. He saw that Nomura was seated in his swivel chair as usual, with his head down, the upper half of his body folded over his desk. This was different. He was used to seeing his boss upright and in command, clad in his trademark expensive grey suit, often rising from his chair to strut about the room like a pouter pigeon – proud, a little stout, bristling with irritation and impatience.

Oh god, the bastard's asleep was Andrew's first thought. Nomura's taking a nap was a possibility, considering his visit to Nomura's office the previous day. The president had looked so distraught at that time that Andrew thought he was near collapse.

Nomura had always displayed an aptitude for frustrating Andrew's hopes. *The old devil's playing possum to torment me as usual*, Andrew thought. He had hoped to steal a march by turning up early to see his boss. Maybe it would signal a change of direction, meaning he could wrest advantage out of adversity. Nomura, damn him, was refusing to play ball. He was having things his own way, as ever.

Andrew waited respectfully by the door. He coughed and shuffled his feet. Then he thought about making his presence known more directly. Sleepy or not, surely Nomura could be roused long enough for Andrew to have his say and then go to class.

The president's office was a large room with the desk positioned in the corner furthest from the door. Andrew squinted, trying to get a clearer view of his boss. His myopia didn't help matters; he had been meaning to get glasses.

Apart from Nomura's forty winks, everything was normal. The room was freezing. A large air conditioner on the wall behind Nomura's desk creaked noisily, expelling

blasts of cold air. A big battered old leather sofa was pushed up against the facing wall, wedged between tall shelves bulging with books, files and papers. A decorative folding screen, its four panels covered with the squiggly script of calligraphy, shielded the desk from view from the windows beside and behind it. Two hard-backed chairs were in front of Nomura's desk. The furniture arrangement afforded Nomura close quarters when interrogating some timid staff member. The chairs were positioned to increase the president's potential for intimidation. He could glower threateningly while the victim squirmed in his uncomfortable seat unable to escape. From bitter personal experience, Andrew thought of it as Nomura's private inquisition space.

As he stood waiting for his boss to deign to notice him, Andrew was surprised to feel a twinge of pity for the figure in the swivel leather office chair. *He must be desperately tired to be sleeping like that*, he thought. *So heavily*. Nomura was sprawled over his desk. His head, with its fluffy aureole of white hair, was cushioned on some papers. Squinting, Andrew saw his arms flung out in a protective gesture over files and documents, and there was an object by his left hand that Andrew's near-sightedness reduced to a white blob. Perhaps one of those big white electric kettles people kept in their offices for a ready supply of hot water for a cup of green tea.

As he paused at the office door, he was gripped by foreboding. His noisy rapping should have woken the deepest sleeper.

On that bright morning, his irritation at being kept waiting was replaced by an odd sense of trepidation as he approached Nomura's desk. With each tiptoe towards the desk, he expected the head to lift and growl at him.

Only a step from the desk, Andrew saw that Nomura's left cheek was cradled on a stack of papers as if pillowing his slumbers. But his boss's position looked unnatural, his head tilted up towards the ceiling.

His eyes are open! *There's blood*!

Andrew's mind shut down. He needed time. He sought

refuge in trifles. He saw it wasn't an electric thermos near the clutter of paper on the desk. It was a doll. He had seen such a doll on visits to traditional Japanese farmhouses. In each place there had been a doll like that housed in an ornamental glass box sitting on top of a shoe cupboard in the *genkan*.

This doll was not in a box, glass or otherwise. It was inches away from Professor Nomura's head. It was about a foot tall, a pale, plump, porcelain figure clad in a white kimono with a red decorative border. There was an elaborate topknot on its head. There were slivers of eyebrows over crescent eyes, complete with tiny nose and mouth – a clear representative of the Japanese ideal of feminine beauty. There was a benevolent expression on its face, its thin red lips curled in a smile. But the doll's white cheeks were speckled with crimson dots as if she had been weeping blood from those crescent eyes. There was a curious scrawl, a word lightly pencilled in Japanese on the glowing ceramic forehead, and blotches of red disfigured the gleaming purity of the robe.

A huge buzzing bluebottle made lazy circles over Nomura's head. Its loud humming as it swooped around made Andrew wonder if it had cast a spell on his boss.

He peered at Nomura's face. A trickle of blood oozed from his mouth into his pointed beard. He leaned closer and recoiled. Nomura's thin lips, usually pursed in righteous anger, were mimicked by a second, larger and more voluptuous mouth below them. It was a deep cut across

Nomura's throat: open, red and hungry.

Andrew managed to stand upright but was caught in a kind of paralysis. He could look but couldn't budge. Silent, he observed everything. The stack of paper below Nomura's left cheek. The neat rows of Chinese characters on white sheets obliterated by a widening crimson pool that stained the documents and oozed in a thick red line across the desk, dripping onto the silky grey fabric covering Nomura's thighs and forming a smaller pool on the floor beneath his chair. The bluebottle, still buzzing overhead, looked fat and satiated. The wheezing of the air conditioner sounding now like cries of outrage and horror.

Although part of the left side of Nomura's face was hidden, cushioned on the papers, the left eye was just visible. Both eyes glared up unblinkingly at Andrew standing over the body. Death could not erase their haughty look.

As a teacher at this small, private university, Andrew often felt he was boring his students to death. Seeing them slumped over their desks in the sultry heat of summer, the air conditioner sputtering out a feeble stream of cool air and occasionally pausing to make a sound like a death rattle, Andrew imagined it exuded poison gas accounting for the lifeless bodies of his students sprawled in their seats.

His way of fantasising about his students' apathy was worlds away from the reality of the trickling blood beside his right foot.

How can a body contain so much blood?

Andrew was a fan of murder mysteries and had heard that question in books and films, but he never thought he would ask it himself for real. Suddenly he was one of

those horrified spectators of violent death he used to enjoy watching or reading about. But this wasn't enjoyable at all.

The first thought, theoretical, was quickly replaced by one more personal:

How can I grieve for Nomura, a man I hated? Then he reflected: *It was the Nomura he chose to show me that I hated. The one who thought he needed to act like a pompous ass to ensure his dignity as president. I can mourn the man I first thought he was, who might have become my friend.*

He took a few steps back from the desk. Now he understood he was seeing Nomura's body lying across the desk, dripping red, viscous drops, he thought of an inexpertly wrapped slab of meat. But no butcher's white paper: it was encased in a grey, well-tailored suit with dark crimson spots.

The initial shock over, Andrew gulped. *Is this all we are at the end of life? A bag of bones leaking out the blood that gave us motion and purpose?*

And the place, a book-lined study, and the victim, a university president. It was all wrong. The stillness of the body was upsetting.

Andrew had regarded Nomura as a petty dictator, a man who insisted on being the head *honcho*. But the distaste he felt now was different altogether. It was physical revulsion at the thought that his old enemy was reduced to a state of matter. Nomura was now a thing rather than a person, a *somebody* who had become a *nobody*.

Nomura was completely still. He had once quivered with nervous energy but was now just a heavy lump of flesh. The college president, a fastidious individual, could no longer effect the slightest improvement to his appearance. He was soiled and sagging, a mass of inertness slumped in a chair.

Andrew felt almost embarrassed for him. Coupled with that sensation was shame. And guilt. It was as if he'd caught his boss unawares in some intimate act. He felt like he had opened a stall door in the men's room and surprised Nomura on the toilet.

Then Andrew heard something. Nothing reassuring like a gasp or a shallow breath, it sounded like a papery rasp accompanied by a faint squeal. Andrew suddenly realised the scraping sound was cloth moving slowly across the surface of the desk and the squeal was made by the swivel chair. Nomura's head and torso were moving slightly. The body that was immovably still had begun to tip slightly sideways, towards the right, and the wheels of the swivel chair were moving too. Although Andrew knew there was no hope of his boss reviving, it seemed undignified to allow his corpse to fall and collapse beside the desk. Hoping to anchor the top half of the body more securely over the desk, he put his arms around the man's shoulders, lifting it in a cradling movement as a mother might clasp her sleeping child. Nomura's head lolled forward. The blood stored in his neck wound when he was supine splashed out over Andrew's shirt and trousers when he lifted the head. Nomura was surprisingly heavy. His body lost its precarious balance in the chair, the torso and arms sprawled over the desk, gravity taking it to the floor. The unwieldy bulk took all of Andrew's strength to hold it upright.

What was that smell? One of his boss's personal characteristics, a faint odour of peppermint. Nomura had a scowling, arrogant face but his plump yet trim body always exuded a minty freshness. Then Andrew caught the rusty-iron smell of fresh blood. It provoked him to shout "Help!" over and over, in a distant desperate voice.

Akemi's Final Surprise

After Kawane uttered his last urgings and admonitions, sniffing loudly as he closed the meeting, Akemi hurried back to Building Two, experiencing her usual relief and gratitude that she had her own small annex. This meant she only had to be crammed into uncomfortable proximity with her co-workers half an hour each morning for Kawane's staff gatherings. She passed the door of her office, her refuge away from the relentless busyness of the campus, making her way to the photocopying room. She was relieved the room with its four photocopiers was empty. She could concentrate on making five copies of a document nearly a hundred pages long.

Although the photocopiers were state-of-the-art machines that could collate and even staple the material, it took nearly an hour. There were coloured charts and graphs sprinkled liberally throughout, taking time to copy. The machines groaned as if disgruntled with such a heavy task so early on a hot, summer morning.

Akemi returned to her office. She fished five green files from a desk drawer, neatly labelled each with the name of a department head and placed the copies within them. She got out a large folder and put the five copies and the original document in its own file inside it, laying it on her desk. She would take the bulging folder to Professor Nomura with his morning coffee.

At the small sink behind her desk, she washed and rinsed her boss's favourite cup, drying it carefully and placing it beside the folder. Then she bent down to get the bag of expensive Kenyan coffee beans her boss insisted on from a small refrigerator below the office window, pausing to smell their appetising aroma.

A minute later, at almost 10.00, Akemi heard a strange sound above the racket of the bean grinder preparing Nomura's massive daily caffeine requirement.

It was the third surprise of the morning: something like a strangled gasp but magnified to such a height that it accomplished the near impossible task of being heard above the noise of the grinder.

She had been feeding glossy little black beans into the electric-powered machine, watching as its blades ground them to a fine powder. She turned off the grinder, stopped and listened. No mistaking that it was not a product of her imagination. It was a shout, a man's voice yelling in English, one word over and over, "Help!"

As if in a dream, Akemi watched the bag of coffee beans she held fall to the ground and let loose its contents in slow motion, the beans scattering and bouncing under her desk.

She knew that some response was required, but she didn't want to be the one to have to make it. She walked slowly towards Professor Nomura's office. Holding the doorknob in her hand, debating whether to enter, she found herself filled with reluctance and fear.

Freezing air hit her as she opened the door. Standing in the doorway, she peered across the crowded room. Her feeling of dread was followed by an impulse to laugh. She wanted to giggle at the spectacle that provided her third surprise of the day. How was it possible? Andrew-*sensei*, whom she knew to detest her boss, was crouched beside his nemesis's chair. He had his arms around Nomura's shoulders, as if hugging him. Even at the time, Akemi knew it was a hysterical reaction, but she struggled not to laugh. Andrew saw and looked angered by her smile.

But it was too absurd and improbable not to provoke such a reaction. Then she saw a large white porcelain doll on the desk. Where had it come from? She had never seen it before, although it reminded her of the present her grandmother had given her to commemorate the annual Girls' Day festival in spring when she was a child.

On approaching, Akemi saw that Andrew was preventing Nomura from tumbling to the floor. He gasped and panted as he held the passive Nomura in his grip, his head lolling down, only one eye visible, fixed and staring. Then Andrew shouted wildly, "Help! Call an ambulance! Call the police! His throat's cut!"

Akemi knew of the near-death experiences of people who

claimed that in the moments before they 'died' their whole lives flashed before their eyes with impossible rapidity. Akemi later felt she had had a similar experience, but it was Professor Nomura's death she was trying to register, not her own. She saw him as a child, as a young man, as the university president, and then as a corpse.

Akemi blushed when she later recalled other thoughts she had had in that terrible moment. There was the red patch encircling Nomura's throat that she had noticed on first entering his office. It looked rakish, even jaunty. She had sought refuge in logic, wondering if Professor Nomura had donned a scarlet cravat. She had always admired how well he dressed. Had he decided to try a new look in the role of a nattily stylish professor?

Her mind had instinctively sought to rationalise the impossible. Even though she had never seen her boss wearing a cravat before, this was the only explanation. There were red liquid splashes gleaming on the floor beside her boss's feet, his trouser legs

bore dark stains, and red flecks disfigured the doll's face, with larger patches on her kimono. The word *ikenai* or 'forbidden' was scribbled on her forehead. Drawing closer, she saw a crimson dribble down Nomura's neatly trimmed white beard and a red streak on his shirt front.

Andrew was holding up one red glistening hand while still struggling to support the president's body. Akemi thought of hurrying over to help him, but her attention was taken by a strange noise, loud and piercing. It was a scream, and it was issuing from her own throat. That was her fourth surprise of the day, and perhaps the most unexpected of them all, for she fainted.

Chief Inspector Inoue Has a Bad Morning

While Inoue was driving to work, he briefly managed to forget that Takenaka and his team would inspect his station that day. He even found himself smiling, thinking about the details of setting up a speed trap outside Fujikawa. There was one perfect spot, sited on a narrow farm road used by regular commuters as a cut through.

It was near town. Inoue knew that motorists heading into Fujikawa, frustrated by the heavy rush-hour traffic, routinely turned off the main road on to this quieter one, trying to make up time. Once they'd got through its sole traffic light, they accelerated and drove the three kilometres into town as fast as they could past farmhouses, groves of fruit trees and rice paddies.

But the impatient motorists were not considerate of local residents. There had been complaints – boys and girls cycling to high school felt unsafe and farmers in their little white trucks didn't like being tailgated by menacing drivers.

Inoue planned to position Ando and Kubo in a van beyond a bend in the road. There was a layby that could accommodate three vehicles. Another policeman would be stationed two hundred metres before the bend, concealed behind a tree, aiming a speed camera at the oncoming traffic and waving down those exceeding the limit. This officer would direct the offenders into the layby where Ando and Kubo waited, ready to take down their details, add points to their licenses and administer heavy fines.

Inoue pulled up in front of Fujikawa police station. He had a reserved space, which was just as well. The lot was already crowded with patrol cars, police motorcycles and vans. As he strode into the building, secretaries and junior officers bowed. The hint of a smile curled the Chief's lips as he reflected on the smooth running of the station, but it vanished at the sight of one of his officers. Ando, looking dishevelled and sleepy, sat slumped before a desk littered with scraps of paper, erasers, pencils, pens, and even a broken stapler. There were even two wadded-up tissues, one with red spots on it. *Did the miserable boy have a bloody nose?*

The Chief refused to let a sympathetic impulse interfere with the luxury of frowning at Ando, who looked up sheepishly in his crumpled uniform. Inoue then made a point of bestowing his broadest smile on Kubo, who had sprung up to prepare his chief's morning mug of coffee.

"Clean up your desk immediately," Inoue barked at Ando, who nearly fell over as he unfolded his lanky body from his chair.

"Yes, sir. Sorry, sir," he said snuffling noisily.

Inoue stole a quick glance at Kubo's desk. Of course! Everything was in order. No loose papers cluttered its surface. Everything had been neatly filed away in coloured folders at the back, held upright by two bookends. Even the pencils and pens on the desk had been lined up as exactly as if measured by a ruler.

"Sir," said Kubo, as he entered Inoue's office with his coffee.

"Is everything ready for the inspection?" Inoue said, not bothering to look up from the documents on his desk.

"Yes, sir. We are expecting Superintendent Takenaka at about 9.00." He checked his watch. "That is, approximately forty-five minutes from now."

Inoue struggled to suppress a smile. Kubo was such a keen, diligent young officer, it was a surprise he hadn't said Takenaka was to arrive in forty-five minutes and thirty seconds. But Inoue liked that about Kubo. He took a paternal interest in the young man who, like Inoue himself, was a local boy showing early promise by passing many hotly contested official exams before finally managing to get inducted into the force as a rookie. Inoue sometimes thought that if he and Ellie had been able to have children, he would have liked a son just like Kubo.

Inoue looked at Kubo standing before him, erect, at attention. His shiny black hair was smoothly cropped, his body, encased in a spotless and freshly pressed uniform, slim but muscular. Inoue supposed women found his junior handsome. Better him than me, Inoue thought. Anyway, I've got my treasure, no need to look elsewhere.

Inoue considered Kubo and Ando his protégés. He always took a keen interest in the new recruits who entered the force each year and generally chose one or two to train up. These handpicked recruits would accompany him on his rounds to benefit from his greater knowledge and experience.

Inoue smiled ruefully. This year, the two candidates he had chosen could scarcely be more unalike. How in the world had Ando ever managed to pass the police academy exams? The boy was undoubtedly clever, and Inoue had often been struck by the warmth and kindness he saw in the lad's soft brown eyes, but Ando seemed to carry

confusion and chaos around with him like a second shadow. Whatever had been orderly and clean became messy and dirty. Ando would have ironed his uniform that morning, but it made no difference. It now looked as though it was just out of the dryer, no pressing done on it at all.

Inoue was particularly irritated by Ando's unhygienic habits. There was often a faint rim of dirt under his fingernails, his hair looked unkempt however short it was cut, and in the summer, he sometimes even let off a faint stink.

None of this was acceptable in a Japanese police officer. It was a matter of professional pride and dignity to be clean, well dressed, and properly behaved. Standards must be maintained.

Inoue had chosen Ando out of a feeling of duty. Selecting Kubo as his second protégé was a kind of consolation prize.

For all the work he needed to do on Ando, he would find his reward in the perfect Kubo.

As Inoue emptied his mug, he heard chairs scraping back. He went to the outer office and stood beside Kubo's desk. That bastard had arrived from Ishizaki forty minutes earlier than expected, escorted by an entourage of three of his own officers. Takenaka's beady black eyes glinted under the thick frame of his glasses. His little body seemed to be quivering, reminding Inoue of an eager terrier impatient to tear his prey to pieces. Inoue had to resist barking out: "Heel, you miserable little mutt!"

Instead, he contrived to smile with complacency and pleasure. But did that fool Ando have to bow quite so low, and for so long? It wasn't the emperor himself dropping by their headquarters for a visit. Kubo, on the other hand, behaved impeccably, inkling his head and torso politely but not obsequiously.

Takenaka was obviously under the impression that he was a kind of honoured dignitary. Smiling blandly, he accepted the flurry of office staff standing and bowing at his approach as if it was his due.

"Oh, and Chief Inspector Inoue," he said, fixing Inoue with a startled glance, as though surprised to see him there. "So glad to be able to renew our acquaintance. I trust I will find everything in order."

"Yes, sir," said Inoue, bowing more deeply than he

intended. "We are honoured by your presence, sir." Inoue resisted the urge to slap his superior, managing to extend his hand in welcome. "Please, sir, if you would be so kind as to come into my office." After he had hastily gathered up his papers, he put his empty mug on a cupboard behindhim. He beckoned Takenaka to his own comfortable swivel chair. Naturally, he would occupy a hard-backed chair in front of the desk as though he were the visitor.

"Yes, yes, of course," said Takenaka impatiently. "I'll use your office for most of today while we conduct our inspection. I trust you've got some desks in the outer office for my men."

"Yes, sir, it's all been seen to." "And computers?"

"Of course."

Inoue's secretary came in, balancing a tray as carefully as if it held cloisonné china, not just two sturdy cup-and-saucer sets from the local supermarket, the cups faintly steaming and the saucers garnished with tiny plastic containers of cream, sticks of sugar wrapped in coloured paper, small pale brown biscuits, and silver spoons.

"Thank you, Miss Noguchi," said Inoue. As an aside to Takenaka, he said, "My secretary." The young woman bowed deeply. She was concentrating like an actress in mid-performance, wrinkling her brow as she lifted the cups and saucers placing them gently on the desktop before the two men. Inoue inwardly groaned. Kubo would have brought coffee for Inoue in his favourite mug, but the presence of a guest meant the niceties had to be observed – and that Inoue would get less coffee than he wanted.

"Coffee, sir?"

"Just a mouthful," said Takenaka. "And refreshments for my men, too, please. And an ashtray."

Then, turning to Inoue, as though the secretary had suddenly ceased to exist, Takenaka said, "My men and I need to look at your records: the latest arrests, the state of crime in Fujikawa, and the mundane matters of budgets and accounting."

"Yes, sir. Of course, sir." The coffee tasted bitter in Inoue's mouth. He didn't like the way Takenaka had looked at Miss Noguchi: the politeness overlying indifference, as if she were a piece of furniture, not a human being. It was typical of the man, treating women as servants. Even worse, once she brought the ashtray, Takenaka got a cigarette out and was puffing at it with surprising energy. Inoue struggled not to cough in the billowing smoke.

Inoue felt exasperated. The smoking was an irritant, but so was the behaviour of his staff. Apart from Kubo, everyone had acted with annoying servility. Even Miss Noguchi, usually the most discreet and sensible of individuals, had seemed flustered by Takenaka's presence. Had she needed to play her part of the humble servant so

convincingly? After she had served them coffee, he

wondered if she would kneel down on the floor like an idiotic geisha as she closed the door, smiling and bowing coyly.

The books came. The accounts were looked at in a cursory way. Takenaka kept grimacing as though there were errors. Then Inoue's office door opened abruptly, without even a knock. It was Kubo, looking distraught. Inoue nearly scolded him for his rudeness. But there was a look on his face.

"Sir, if I might just speak with you for a moment?"

Inoue made his apologies and left Takenaka serenely drinking his coffee. "What the hell?!" Inoue blurted.

"A murder, sir. Or at least a suspicious death. At the university," Kubo stuttered. "The president!"

Inoue's wife was a Christian but he wasn't. Still, he involuntarily muttered a phrase he had often heard from Ellie in times of stress: *Sweet God in heaven.*

The Inspector Goes Back to College

At forty, Chief Inspector Kenji Inoue of the Fujikawa police station had seen his share of dead bodies. However much he wanted, he could never efface the first one from his memory. He had been still wet behind the ears, a young rookie nearing the end of his first year in the service when, early one hot morning in mid-June, he was instructed to accompany two senior officers to the site of a suspected suicide.

As the junior, he was appointed chauffeur. He drove his superiors through the sleepy little college town of Fujikawa in the patrol car, sirens blaring. They passed the train station and then got on a narrow road that bordered the railway tracks to the east of town. The tracks were on the right of the road; on the left were rice paddies: green shoots in a sea of mud stretching to the horizon. It was a flat treeless place with few houses, where it seemed nothing out of the ordinary could happen. At a sudden signal from one of the senior officers, Inoue pulled into a layby with a squeal of brakes and stopped. The officers jumped out of the back of the car.

Inoue felt bile rising when he recalled that day, everything indelible on his memory: the glittering rails; the blistering heat; the blazing sphere of a sun like an unblinking eye in the deep blue azure. Three or four black glossy crows swooped insolently above them. They cawed angrily at the car's arrival because their feast had been disrupted.

Then, the *thing* they had been feeding on. A bloody lump on the tracks and, nearby, the trimly suited body it had once been attached to. The stench of death contrasted with the fragrance of emerald green rice shoots undulating in the early summer wind.

The corpse was later identified as that of Yoshifumi Tani, an employee of the Suzuki import and export firm in Shimayama. He had disappeared from his office the previous day after a fellow worker had publicly accused him of embezzling funds. His body and then his head, or what remained of it, had been found by a local housewife walking her dog at dawn, before the heat set in.

The policemen's approach had frightened off the crows but the head, battered to a pulp by the 20.32 express to Onohara the previous evening, was still providing nourishment to flies. Small swarms covered where eyes and mouth had been, sealing

them with a black, pulsating cloth. The man must have lain down in the dark, his neck on a rail; the train's computer would have hardly registered the impact at all.

Now, whenever he heard that a body had been discovered, Inoue again tasted that bitter vomit at the back of his throat, and he would gulp hard.

Since that time, Inoue had come across any number of corpses. Japan's high suicide rate made it highly probable that he would encounter individuals inclined to top themselves. There were office workers who had got into debt, blowing the family savings on horses, boat racing or prostitutes. Or the more recent phenomenon of housewives unable to resist the lure of Internet gambling and who couldn't admit to a costly little habit they had kept secret from their breadwinning hubbies.

Also, to Inoue's chagrin, Fujikawa and its environs were the preferred dumping ground for the Ishizaki *yakuza* – who deposited the dead bodies of gangsters guilty of a serious transgression of the mafia's strict code or those who had been killed by a rival gang. Despite Ishizaki's proximity to the Tsushima Strait, the cement overcoat method of disposal had become clichéd. Ishizaki's criminal syndicates preferred a more bucolic venue. How the victims were conveyed from bustling Ishizaki to Fujikawa was anyone's guess, but Inoue had got used to finding bodies half-buried in heavy woodland, arms and torsos covered with tattoos, hands with missing little fingers.

The most troubling of all for Inoue were the corpses of children who had been bullied or failed to survive the competitive pressure-cooker environment of Japan's secondary schools. Hanging was the preferred way; they often used their own belts as a noose. Whenever Inoue had the misfortune of dealing with one of those thin little bodies twisting in the wind beneath a branch or in the child's own bedroom, suspended from a curtain rail, the bile rose up. He would deeply regret he had not obeyed his father's injunction to become an accountant.

The suicides or casualties of gang politics were usually discovered some time after their deaths. The suicides, as a rule, found some secluded spot in which to end it all – the children, for example, went to woods near the family home or, if they stayed in their bedroom, killed themselves late at night, hours before a mother could be expected to come tapping at the door. The casualties had their killers running around trying to hide their victims. There was usually a time lapse of at least six or seven hours, often days, even weeks, between the death and the discovery of the corpse by the police.

Inoue had never seen a fresh corpse from suicide or murder, discovered within a few hours of the death.

Kubo was deputised to drive Inoue to the university. Ando had been ordered to summon the forensics team and scene-of-crime officers and to drive them and their equipment to the site as quickly as possible. After Kubo had pulled out of the police parking lot in a skitter of gravel and swung onto the main road through town, Inoue noticed his junior officer glancing at him in surprise.

Inoue realised he was cursing, softly but steadily, and that Kubo must be rather shocked, never having heard him swear before. It was one of Inoue's self-imposed rules: no vulgarity, no impolite language. The chief inspector wondered if he had also let his mask slip – that impassive face he self-consciously assumed to radiate calm and authority.

"Sir?" Kubo asked, seeming to wonder if some response was required.

Inoue made a visible effort to pull himself together. He gave a chagrined smile. "Never mind, Kubo. It's just damnable all around. Damnable! The timing, with Takenaka actually in the station when the call came in. The place, our own treasured local university. And the victim, Professor Nomura, the president. Beyond belief!"

As they raced towards the college, Inoue didn't notice the excitement he and Kubo were causing. Cars, motorbikes and trucks pulled over to allow them to proceed at full speed. Women carrying laden shopping baskets and students on bicycles stopped to stare. It was no ordinary spectacle in this little rural community: a patrol car, red lights flashing and sirens blaring, zooming down the dusty streets.

At first, Inoue thought only of how the crime might affect his officers. It was the first murder investigation for his protégés. He had no worries about Kubo, but he wondered if Ando might break down at the sight of the body or if he would embarrass everyone by vomiting.

Their first corpse – it had to happen sometime. He'd ask Kubo to keep an eye on Ando, make sure he didn't do anything stupid or rash.

Then Inoue suddenly realised all the implications of the reported murder. There was the identity of the victim and where he had been found. Professor Nomura, with an impressive record of publications and public works, was probably the highest-profile victim this dead-end place could have produced. And Fujikawa University was Inoue's own alma mater, goddammit!

Inoue was not a religious man, not even a believer in the notion of any deity. So he just muttered to himself that it was a most regrettable mess, the breath-taking fact that the president of Fujikawa University had been killed. *Killed!* Murder was rare in Japan, particularly in a backwater like Fujikawa, and he knew the responsibility for finding the culprit lay squarely on his own shoulders.

The awfulness of it could not be exaggerated. Fujikawa University had long been a flagship institution for the community. It was a source of pride and income for many locals. It employed a quarter of the town's working age population, with residents employed as clerical staff, cleaners, cooks, and guards. A few who had attended graduate school found work as part-time lecturers. Fujikawa children were encouraged to consider applying for this college in their last year of high school.

The town repaid its debt by hiring, in turn, nearly a quarter of the Fujikawa University students. They worked part-time at its petrol stations, restaurants and grocery stores and contributed to the local economy by frequenting the shops and renting small rooms. Although the selection on offer was poor, nothing like what was available in Ishizaki, on weeknights the students often felt it was too much effort to get to the big city. They would eat in Fujikawa's cafes, even if most were just mom- and-pop establishments featuring old-style cooking, browse in the town's sole bookshop, or go drinking in its grubby little bars.

Fujikawa was a middling university, not one of Japan's well-known institutions, but it had achieved a measure of fame as an institution that catered for students with physical disabilities or who laboured under the stigma of belonging to the despised *burakumin* social caste. It even boasted the nickname of *the college with a conscience*.

As for the *burakumin* issue, Inoue hated the fact that this barbaric relic of Japan's old caste system survived in the 21st century. On the other hand, when he was a student at Fujikawa, he couldn't help trying to guess what classmates had *burakumin* ancestry. He would look speculatively about at the figures scurrying around the campus, wondering who might have had a grandfather or great-grandfather who used to work in a trade traditionally regarded as unclean and lower-class: butchers, leatherworkers, rubbish or night soil collectors.

At that time, Inoue's mother was worried about his proximity to *burakumin*, fearing that he might be attracted to a girl whose caste would put her beyond the marriageable pale. It was a stigma that could never be erased. At birth, every Japanese baby's details were recorded in the family register, and when young people announced their

plans to marry, the parents consulted the register to make sure their child wasn't marrying into the wrong sort of family. Inoue knew his own mother, for all her professed liberalism, would have done just that if he'd told her he was thinking of marriage. As it happened, he had married a foreigner, so she couldn't check up on her future daughter-in-law's credentials before the wedding.

Fujikawa had been one of the first post-war Japanese colleges actively to seek out

burakumin and encourage them to apply.

Although not religious, Inoue had a strong moral sense. This aided him in his police work. He liked the fact that Fujikawa recruited students who were physically disabled. Its campus had wheelchair accessibility, and it offered sign language classes and a note-taking service for blind or deaf students. It had been one of the first colleges in Japan to offer specialised studies in social work and social welfare, and it had attracted national attention for the stand taken on the Korean fingerprinting issue by Gerald Hunter, an American missionary employed as a Christianity professor. The university served as Fujikawa residents' single claim to fame, the feature of their hometown they could allude to when they went to Tokyo, Kyoto or Osaka knowing there was at least a chance that the sophisticates inhabiting Japan's metropolises might have heard of it.

Inoue had met Nomura once at a local function – a party held in his honour – five years earlier and instantly disliked him. It was easy to guess, through his accent and manner, where the university president hailed from. Inoue identified Nomura as one of those haughty Kyotoites who consider being born in Japan's cultural capital and old administrative centre reason enough for regarding Japanese from anywhere else with condescension verging on contempt.

On his arrival at the function, Nomura strode hastily through the assembled town dignitaries without bowing or acknowledging greetings. When he was ensconced in his appointed chair by the podium, he sat like a monarch on his throne, languidly surveying his subjects. He acted as though he were conferring an honour on everyone present just by deigning to attend the party they had arranged for him. He glanced at his watch as the mayor made a speech in his honour. Afterwards, he rebuffed individuals who came up to meet him, shielding himself from any unwanted attention with a small clique of the top officials of the town and his chosen circle of university intimates. He was a man who didn't worry about antagonising anyone. Having settled in the sticks, in a quiet part of Japan far away from fellow Kyotoites who might question his status, he could feel superior to everyone about him.

Inoue had never returned to the university since his graduation twenty years earlier. Once he'd left, he had closed that chapter of his life. He periodically received invitations from the college authorities to attend concerts, to participate in class reunions, or even to donate money, but he'd always tossed these letters into the rubbish basket.

Although Inoue passed the university campus daily, it gradually slipped from his consciousness. It was hidden from public view by high cement walls. He would catch a glimpse of its chapel spire or see the outlines of familiar classroom buildings rising above trees, but he was not a man to indulge in nostalgia. He had enjoyed his time there but was glad when it was over, and he was free to pursue his dream of becoming a policeman. But now Inoue's perfect service record was in jeopardy, and from the least likely source: from the place where he had spent four of the most pleasant and least demanding years of his life.

As Kubo manoeuvred the patrol car through the portals of the narrow main gate, Inoue looked at his watch. It was 10.10. Not a bad response time, he thought. The call had come into the Fujikawa station at 9.55, reportedly made by Toru Kawane, head of the admin staff.

Inoue presumed the man waiting beside the main gate on their arrival was Kawane. He was obviously the authority figure on the spot, accompanied by the requisite quota of younger, junior clerical staff.

He was a well-built individual in his early forties wearing a neatly pressed dark blue suit, a spotless white shirt, and a carefully knotted tie. His smug, fat but handsome face was dignified rather than disfigured by a larger than average nose for someone of Japanese origin. He was clutching a large cotton handkerchief.

As Kubo came to a shuddering stop beside a bicycle shed just beyond the gates, the man rushed towards the car to greet them, his subordinates trailing behind.

"Chief Inspector Inoue, I presume," he said, looking terrified and red-faced. He was perspiring heavily and kept mopping his face with his handkerchief. Inoue wondered whether he was one of his compatriots constitutionally ill-equipped to cope with the torrid heat and humidity of a Japanese summer or if he was sweating because of the horror of what he had seen.

Or could there be a more sinister reason? "Mr Kawane?"

"Chief Inspector Inoue?"

Despite the urgency of the situation, neither man was unable to discard a lifetime habit. They each reached for the card case kept in an inner jacket pocket and fished out a *meishi*. On exchanging business cards, they politely scrutinised them before carefully inserting them in the cases, returning the cases to their jacket pockets, and bowing deeply. Then Inoue was introduced to the junior staff and Kawane to Kubo.

Finally, all the niceties observed, Kawane felt he could lead Inoue to the murder scene.

"I should tell you," said Inoue as they set off. "I was a student here twenty years ago. What building was the body found in?"

"Building Two."

It came flooding back to Inoue, how each building on campus was designated by a number. There were eight buildings in all, their numbering representing the time of their construction. Only Building One was the anomaly, having been rebuilt as a brick cube structure on its original site. It now housed the university admin offices. During his time, Building Two, now the oldest structure on campus, had housed the general education office; it had once been a part of the Japanese military base sited there. Nomura had made many changes. Inoue wondered if it was a nod to tradition that he had decided to relocate the president's office from the third floor of the admin building, put up only fifteen years before, to a ramshackle old two-storey building that was over a century old.

As they walked, Inoue asked, "And was it you found the body?"

"No, it was one of our foreign instructors, Mr Andrew Thomas, a Canadian. He's a contract worker here."

Inoue winced. Yet another personal connection. He had often heard Ellie speak of Andrew as her best friend at the university. Inoue liked to preserve a clear distinction between his private and professional life. A murder at the place he thought of as *his* university. A murder discovered by his wife's friend. Inoue wasn't superstitious but he wondered if he'd done something reprehensible in a former life. Was this a kind of karma, past misdeeds coming back to haunt him?

Now a frail-looking middle-aged man wearing a surgical mask that covered half his heavily wrinkled face approached them apologetically and bowed.

"This is Akamatsu-*san*," Kawane told Inoue. "He was with me when I heard that something was wrong with the president. He came with me to the office. I imagine you'll want to talk to him to corroborate details."

As they came nearer the crime scene, Kawane began hurrying them along, his rapid pace forcing them into a jog just to keep up. It was as if Kawane longed to get an unpleasant ordeal over and done with.

Inoue had a chance to look around. There was a student in a wheelchair scooting down one pathway and a few boys loitering behind Building One, puffing on cigarettes. Some cleaners stood under a camphor tree, open-mouthed, at a loss as to what they should do next. One was holding a big bamboo broom. All were wearing the clothes typical of any individual in Japan who worked outside: the broad-brimmed straw hats and comfortable, loose, baggy white trousers and shirts, with cotton gloves that afforded protection from a sun that could be fierce in both summer and winter. Most wore white surgical masks covering the lower half of their faces.

These were familiar sights from his undergraduate days. They were crossing a dusty courtyard. He remembered it well, whiling away intervals between classes, sitting on a bench and chatting with his friends, watching the other students pass by. The courtyard looked the same, but there were changes. Now its benches and tables looked new, a far cry from the battered, splintering old relics Inoue recalled. He could detect the hand of a professional landscaper in the artfully pruned trees and flowerbeds that now formed the courtyard's border. The buildings surrounding the courtyard seemed to have been freshly painted and their windows gleamed in the bright sunshine. The place was immaculately maintained.

He recalled the Fujikawa campus of his undergraduate years as a shabby place with an easy-going atmosphere. Weeds choked its paths. Students sprawled on the old benches smoking cigarettes, and the ground was littered with discarded butts, empty soft drink cans and plastic *bento* boxes.

There was even a pack of feral dogs haunting the campus in those days. Inoue and his friends used to hurl bits of their sandwiches or sweet rolls to the mutts on hot summer days. But the dogs mostly foraged scraps from the bins, leaving behind crumpled polystyrene containers and bits of plastic. In winter the poor creatures looked cold and miserable, ribs prominent, baring their teeth at students in a grisly snarling plea for food.

Inoue had a dim recollection of the former president of the university. He was an elderly, shambling figure with bright pink cheeks who smelt of alcohol and lived on the campus. After graduating, Inoue had heard periodic rumours the university might close because it was failing to attract enough applicants and was in danger

of going bankrupt. Japan's low birth rate produced a demographic crisis affecting Japan's schools for two decades, with too few pupils applying for kindergartens, elementary schools, secondary schools and colleges. Seeing news reports on this issue, Inoue had wondered how his old alma mater was faring.

The campus now exuded an air of prosperity. It was a clean and tidy place with those expensive-looking new benches and tables inviting students to socialise between classes. There were designated areas for smoking. The paths and courtyard had been recently swept. Inoue could glimpse the rippling, gleaming silver roof of the new university library above Building Three. The rumours he had heard were true: things had changed since Professor Nomura arrived and took over as the president. It seemed for the better.

But now Nomura had been murdered and they were off to see his body.

The Crime Scene

Something about the way Nomura had been killed, his throat slit as if he had been slaughtered, made Inoue feel that deep hatred had been the motive in this crime.

However many times he'd seen a murder victim, he never could get used to the sight. When Inoue entered the president's office at Fujikawa University, he took everything in with a practised eye. The body of a well-built individual probably in his mid to late fifties was sprawled precariously over the desk in the far corner. There was blood, seemingly buckets of it, including puddles on the floor and splashes on a decorative screen positioned around the desk, shielding it from outside view. There were dark patches on the man's grey suit, especially on the knees. A large white porcelain doll was standing on the desk near the staring, bloodied face, as if on guard, but there were red stains on it, too. A young man, a foreigner with a white face and a ponytail, clad in a crumpled beige linen suit, was slumped on the floor beside the desk.

Inoue saw and registered it all, noting the odd absence of a computer, that inevitable feature these days of every office desk. He heard rattling old machinery. He felt the freezing temperature of the room. He saw the blood-spattered doll with *ikenai* scribbled on its forehead.

Inoue guessed the foreigner must be Andrew Thomas, his

wife's friend. He looked a sorry specimen, shivers racking his lanky frame. Still, he remembered Ellie telling him her Canadian colleague was a good sort. As he trusted his wife's judgement implicitly, the Chief was willing to give the foreigner the benefit of the doubt. Not that he would rule him out as a suspect. In his long years of experience, he knew that the person who discovered the body was often the one who had deprived it of life.

Inoue then reluctantly turned his full attention to the corpse that once had served as the home of a living breathing person like himself, who had made plans, cherished hopes and dreams, whose future had been brutally curtailed.

Under his father's thumb as a child, Inoue had always been preternaturally sensitive to the use, and misuse, of power. Murder struck him as the extreme in the wide spectrum of its abuses. In this case, someone, for whatever motive – in the grip of
uncontrollable emotion, on a whim, or to exact revenge – had robbed Nomura of all his tomorrows. The victim could seek no justice. He was dead.

Inoue had seen bodies mangled in car accidents or burnt beyond recognition in house fires. It was one of the worst parts of his job: the call in the night disturbing peaceful dreams; the reluctant exit from his warm, comfortable bed, effected quietly so as not to disturb Ellie; the rush to get dressed; the need to keep his wits while driving to the crime scene, and finally to brace himself for a spectacle of horror. Yet these accidental deaths were different from a death dealt out deliberately or a suicide.

Inoue supposed the difference lay in the notion of intent. Car crashes and house fires usually happened inadvertently. Somebody lounging on a sofa or in bed dozing off with a lit cigarette between his fingers; a housewife frying *tempura* in a deep-fat fryer over gas, and the next thing she's trying to extinguish flames with a towel; or a worker having a few drinks before going home, and despite Japan's zero tolerance for drinking and driving, thinking he'd take his chances.

Such deaths were accidental, in most cases the result of human error, weakness or idiocy. But with murder, as with most suicides, there was the clear marker of purposefulness: to deprive oneself or another of life.

Yet Nomura's body wasn't quite so hellish as some Inoue had seen. It was still recognisable as a human being who had lived and breathed only a short time before. A man who, at first glance, could have been napping in his office dressed in the grey discreetly tailored suit of a man of influence and dignity.

Then Inoue saw two things that upset his equanimity. First, he noticed a large bluebottle buzzing around the office that had undoubtedly gorged on the unexpected feast of blood. The second was the sight of blood on the clothes of the foreigner huddled on the floor beside the desk. Inoue suspected that he had committed the unpardonable sin of moving the body. He was a stickler for propriety at his murders. No shifting of bodies. The crime scene cordoned off as early as possible so evidence could not be removed or contaminated. The next of kin contacted. Witnesses identified and their statements taken promptly.

Decorum had to be observed. The victim was to be treated with the greatest respect, whatever one thought of him in life.

The fly disturbed his sense of what was due the dignity of the victim. The sight of that young man in his bloodied clothes affronted him as a policeman keen to secure the crime scene.

At least the room was icy cold, so possibly the putrefaction of the corpse, a problem particularly at the height of a Japanese summer, would be delayed. The president's office was as cold as a morgue. But there was that awful noise from the ancient air conditioner behind the president's desk. Why hadn't it been repaired or replaced?

Inoue was also annoyed by the number of people crowding the room. He noticed not only his own two officers but the foreigner and Kawane, his fat face frowning at this unseemly disturbance of the daily routine and also the sickly-looking office worker wearing a surgical mask who had accompanied them to the crime scene. Inoue searched for his name and remembered: Akamatsu.

Worst of all, faces popped up at the windows, peering in.

There would be no joy for the gawkers, just sore ankles and feet and no gratification of their morbid curiosity. The president's body sprawled over the desk was shielded from outside view by the decorative screen. But who were they? Students? Members of staff? It didn't matter. They shouldn't be there. This wasn't a spectacle, a performance at a theatre, open to the general public. Inoue spoke more sharply than he intended.

"We need to clear the room. Now! Immediately! And cordon off the area around this building. And somebody needs to help that foreigner. Kubo, please see to it."

Ando and Kubo looked at each other with surprise and some trepidation. "*Sorry*, sir. Yes, sir. Immediately," Kubo dependably said.

"And that damned fly. Can somebody get rid of it?"

And then Inoue did something unaccountable. There was a small appointments diary lying on the desk beside the body. He put it in his pocket, stood by the desk, and calmly waited for the forensics team to arrive.

Ando glanced at him before he turned his attention to the fly. Kubo bent over the foreigner solicitously and offered him bottled water he had found somewhere. Ando took out a newspaper from the president's bin, rolled it up and, with satisfying ferocity delivered a mighty thwack that not only killed the bloated fly that had lighted on the desk but cemented its body to the paper. Ando's achievement was undercut by the silly grin he put on as he deposited the paper back in the bin, like a child unsure whether he would be praised or scolded. Inoue knew he shouldn't have allowed his officer to dispose of the fly – after all, the crime scene needed to be preserved intact – but he couldn't help himself.

Inoue quickly issued orders and was gratified to see everyone hurrying about, intent on their assigned tasks. Kubo was dispatched to Andrew Thomas's house to get a change of clothing, Kawane providing him with directions. Ando was responsible for clearing the office of everyone apart from the forensics team. This included shepherding the blood-stained foreigner to an annex within the administration building. Ando then assisted Kawane in setting up an incident room.

On their arrival, uniformed officers were directed to secure the two entrances of Building Two once they had surrounded the immediate premises with yellow police tape to make the whole area off-limits to curious bystanders. Some scene-of-crime officers were on their hands and knees, conducting a white-glove, inch-by-inch inspection of the ground outside the president's office windows, while others were picking up everything on Nomura's desk and putting it in bags. One officer carried off the bagged ceramic doll with exaggerated care, as if terrified it would break with the slightest movement. Another officer ostentatiously retrieved the newspaper with its squashed fly from the bin and enclosed it in a clear plastic bag. There was a whoop of triumph when a knife was found lying on the ground just outside a window of the president's office.

At Inoue's request, Kawane arranged for students to be sent home and for professors and staff to be asked to remain in their offices. He gave Inoue a list of six individuals he had seen in the vicinity of the president's office that morning. Akamatsu was deputised to contact the deceased's family and then to make a list of professors, staff and students known to have been present on the campus that morning. Each was a potential suspect, a sad pity there were so many.

News of the crime had got out fast. Kawane had to field calls from anxious parents. Journalists began appearing in Building One. A photographer loitered outside the police tape fencing off the courtyard and Building Two, busily snapping away. The university guards turned away a television crew that suddenly materialised outside the main gates. Inoue promised to give a statement to the press that evening and an interview to the local news station.

As he delegated duties, he had time to reflect on his juniors' conduct in the case so far. He was pleasantly surprised by Ando's behaviour. He had noticed a crescent of dirt under Ando's fingernails as he pulled on white plastic gloves. He had winced at seeing a small hole in Ando's left trouser leg as he bent to help the foreigner stand up. But these failings were made up for by the fact that his dubious rookie had conducted himself well at his first murder scene. He hadn't got sick.

He'd managed to get rid of that pesky fly.

Strangely it was his favourite, Kubo, who had evinced squeamishness at the scene. Inoue and Kubo had entered the president's office together, and Inoue sensed Kubo's body tensing, heard Kubo's sharp expulsion of breath, and felt his protégé's horror, standing for a moment rooted to the spot, staring at the body and the blood.

But Kubo was a real trooper for all that. He hadn't gagged or vomited. He hadn't requested permission to leave the room. His face white, his eyes staring, Kubo had behaved quite properly after Inoue had nudged him. He had helped calm and comfort the *gaijin* and then rushed off to the foreigner's house, reportedly a twenty-five minutes' drive away, to get replacement clothing for him.

Inoue had the president's diary in his pocket, and he patted it occasionally to reassure himself it was still there. He took Kawane aside and asked him to summon the six individuals he saw that morning near Nomura's office. He wanted to question them personally before any more time elapsed. He dispatched a team of officers to begin interviewing members of staff after learning Kawane had set up a separate interview room in Building Five, and the forensics team was asked to take DNA samples and fingerprints from the six potential suspects.

Inoue was relieved when Kawane, rubbing his large nose energetically, announced he had arranged for a classroom in

Building Six to be the incident room for the investigating team. He said the six witnesses had been told to go to a classroom adjacent to the incident room, to be questioned individually by the police. The interviews would be conducted in the incident room and extra officers from the station would type up and collate all the statements.

Inoue found Ando busy working when he arrived in the incident room a little after noon. The junior officer had arranged tables and chairs in a rectangle and placed a small desk and two swivel chairs and two hard-backed chairs for the interviews. A tangle of power cables and cords writhed on the floor by the two electric outlets. Ando had decided to take advantage of the sink in the room, somehow finding a small fridge and a coffee maker so the team could have hot and cold drinks.

Kubo entered hesitantly: "Sir?" "Kubo."

"I've done as you requested, sir, and got clothing for that foreigner who found the body. I insisted on staying with him as he took off his suit, and I bagged it and delivered it personally to the forensics people."

"That's fine."

"But sir, he seems to be on the brink of physical illness. It may be delayed shock. I wonder if he's in a fit state to be questioned."

"It can't be helped. Miss Tanimoto is in an even worse condition. She fainted on seeing the body. We must question them today! A murder has been committed, a very high-profile one, and we can't give kid-glove treatment to anyone."

"Sir," said Kubo, his eyes widening. "Are they suspects?"

"Anyone and everyone who was on this campus between 9.00 and 10.00 this morning is a suspect, and don't you forget it."

"Even the students, sir?"

"According to Kawane-*san* the professors keep strict attendance records, calling the register at the start of each class, so we should know exactly what students were here, taking tests at the time of the murder, and who were absent," said Inoue. He added, smiling, "Of course, I'll tell the interviewees today that we're only questioning them to eliminate them from our enquiries. No need to alarm anyone."

Nearly an hour elapsed before Kubo appeared once more.

"The six people are in the next room, sir," he said, looking nervous. "You explained why we took their fingerprints and DNA swabs?" "Yes, sir. All done."

"Any resistance?"

"Mr Kawane fretted that it might mean he'd have a criminal record."

Inoue entered the adjacent room to meet the six people for questioning, opening the door softly so he could look at them unobserved for a moment. There was a familiar odour of chalk and sweat and furniture polish and the windows were streaked, having been badly cleaned. He remembered that classroom: the long boring hours sitting in a seat at the back over twenty years earlier being taught Japanese history by an elderly man in a dusty suit who never looked up from his notes, speaking in a soporific monotone. That professor could have been lecturing to an empty classroom for all he noticed or cared. Inoue remembered that the chairs were uncomfortable, the seatbacks bent at an awkward angle. The interviewees wouldn't be comfortable, but they had to be kept together.

They looked sheepish, like six school children kept in for being naughty. Inoue was amused to find that they had voluntarily segregated themselves by sex. Kawane was strolling impatiently up and down by the windows, glancing at his watch. The three Japanese women were huddled in one corner, while the two foreignerswere sitting together. Gerald Hunter had his arm around Andrew Thomas's shoulders, as if comforting him.

It was irregular. It would even seem impolite to a fellow Japanese. But Inoue decided he would privately think of these two, in future, simply as Gerald and Andrew while referring to them publicly as Professor Hunter and Professor Thomas. They were foreigners and, living so long with Ellie and meeting her western friends had got him in the habit of calling *gaijin* by their given names. Unlike the Japanese, they didn't mind and even seemed to prefer it.

Inoue was interested to see that Michiko Ota looked

terrified, that Professor Yamamoto was comforting her, and that Akemi Tanimoto seemed near collapse. He resolved to interview Miss Tanimoto first so she could go home to recover. But why did Miss Ota look so frightened?

If Gerald and Andrew and Professor Yamamoto represented the current crop of Japanese university professors, they were an unpromising bunch, Inoue thought. Had standards slipped so far? When he was a student at Fujikawa, professors dressed in suits and ties, appropriate to their status as demi-gods in the rarefied realm of higher education. At that time Japanese students, whether at primary or secondary school or at university, were expected to stand and bow when a teacher entered the room as a mark of respect. The class then sat in absolute silence, concentrating on scribbling down the instructor's hallowed words.

Inoue now recalled his incredulous dismay when Ellie had once returned home from work tired and demoralised, complaining about the laziness of her own students at Fujikawa whom, she said, she would find sleeping at their desks when she stepped into the classroom or chatting on cell phones or sitting in groups of friends, giggling. The start of the class scarcely altered their behaviour. Some students managed to get forty winks while pretending attentiveness, eyes closed as if in concentration, and others sent text messages on phones they kept hidden beneath their desks.

Inoue took particular exception to Andrew's ponytail. Also,

the change of clothing Kubo had brought back – a t-shirt and jeans – gave the impression the Canadian was a wannabe hippie. But Inoue remembered that Andrew had been wearing a linen suit when he was found sitting in a heap by Nomura's body. And why did Gerald insist on dressing in black shirt and trousers, looking as if he was going to a funeral? His presence, radiating austerity and gloom, would surely intimidate his students. Gerald

looked like the picture of a Jesuit that Ellie had once shown him when they were discussing Christianity.

But Andrew and Gerald were foreigners, and proper dress and behaviour were not to be expected of them. They didn't know any better. No such excuse could be offered for Professor Yamamoto, with her greying hair hanging down her back, looking as though she had just returned from a trek in Nepal.

Kawane stopped touring the windows and, seeing Inoue standing by the door, bowed in his direction. Everyone turned round.

"Ladies and gentlemen," the Chief Inspector said, bowing in return and speaking in Japanese, trusting that Gerald would act as translator for Andrew. "As some of you may know, my name is Inoue. I am the acting Chief Inspector at Fujikawa Police Station. On behalf of my colleagues, I would like to offer sincere apologies for inconveniencing you at this difficult time. We have detained you because we believe you have invaluable information concerning the death of Professor Nomura. You were all seen in the immediate vicinity of the president's office around the time of the murder. I would like to reassure you that you are being regarded as witnesses rather than suspects."

An audible sigh of relief. From all of them? From some? He wondered.

He continued: "We would like to interview you one by one, hoping that you may be able to cast light on the president's final moments."

They stared at him with the same fatal fascination a mouse shows for a snake poised to strike. "We would appreciate any information from you so we can solve this case quickly."

Inoue paused and looked at them each in turn, intently. "I do have one request. I wish I could enforce it as an order, but I can't, so I'll just rely on your discretion and sense of honour. I ask you not to discuss the case with anyone. Please don't mention anything that some of you may have seen at the crime scene. We would like to keep the details as secret as possible. Unfortunately, it has been revealed that President Nomura had his throat cut, but we're hoping to keep further information confidential until we manage to catch the culprit. Please say nothing to anyone, not even among yourselves."

Inoue noticed Miss Tanimoto was holding back tears.

"I would like to ask Miss Tanimoto to be ready to be summoned for her interview in the next few minutes. I understand, Miss Tanimoto, that you collapsed on finding

Professor Thomas with the body of Professor Nomura. Once my brief questioning is completed, an officer will drive you home."

She smiled wanly and stood up, swaying slightly, supporting herself by clutching the back of her seat.

Inoue continued, "I'd like to interview Professor Thomas next, in consideration of the shock he has also experienced in actually finding the body. We'll also send him home with an officer when he's finished making his statement."

Kawane looked at Inoue pleadingly.

"Mr Kawane, I understand you have a great number of pressing duties requiring your attention, so I will interview you after Professor Thomas. As for Professor Hunter and Professor Yamamoto and Miss Ota, perhaps you could decide among yourselves the order for your interviews."

As Inoue exited the room, he heard that soft plaintive noise again, this time collective, as if those left behind sighed with relief from the tension. Inoue then sent for the office worker Akamatsu. Although Kubo had been worried about the foreigner and Inoue about the secretary who had fainted, the Chief regarded Akamatsu, with his lined forehead even whiter than the surgical mask that covered his nose and mouth, as the least hardy of those involved in the case. But concerns about his health aside, Inoue knew that Akamatsu's cooperation was essential. He understood that the clerical worker had gone to the president's office with Kawane when a cleaner had summoned him, alerting him to trouble in Building Two, and he had also accompanied Inoue and his officers there on their arrival. He was the only other person, apart from the murderer, to know what they found there. It was imperative that no details of the crime scene be disclosed to the press or anyone else. Akamatsu should say *nothing* about what he had seen to anyone.

Inoue Finds Akemi Wants to be Helpful

On re-entering the incident room, Inoue was pleasantly surprised to find that Ando had once again exceeded expectations. In an hour, he had located and set up most of the requisite equipment. How had he done it? Banks of laptop computers, a few printers, a scanner and a fax machine were set on the rectangle of tables as Inoue had directed. There was a faint hum of machinery. Once the interviews were completed, it would be a hive of activity, with officers transcribing witness statements and collating data.

Ando had even found a folding screen that resembled the one Inoue had seen shortly before in the president's office; it was intended to hide the interview space from view.

Inoue opened the fridge. It was stocked with bottles of cold coffee, *oolong-cha* and green tea and water, and there was a can of ground coffee beans. There were a few cups and saucers and glasses, some small spoons on a counter by the coffee maker, sticks of sugar and a jar of coffee cream.

Ando stood by the door, looking humble but pleased with himself. Rubbing his hands, he told Inoue that Kubo had arranged the attendance of Miss Shinohara, a discreet individual fluent in English who was regularly employed by the police for interviews with foreigners. Kubo had gone to collect her from her home a half hour's drive away.

Inoue brusquely acknowledged Ando's work and gave him the list of officers whose services he would require after the interviews. As Inoue consulted his interview notes, he felt a grudging admiration. Ando was a diamond in the rough, showing indisputable promise. He sent him off to fetch Miss Tanimoto as the first witness.

**

A slight figure dressed in a white linen tunic top, brown cropped breeches, and stylish brown leather sandals, Miss Tanimoto declined the offer of a drink. Inoue was relieved to see she was coping. She was a pleasant-looking woman with only a light layer of make-up, her eyebrows plucked in shapely crescents. She satisfied Inoue's old-fashioned prejudices. She looked like a good girl: no tattoos, no pierced ears. Her glossy black mane of hair was cut in a bob; she had not succumbed to currentfashion by dying it light brown. There was a small white lace handkerchief in her left hand.

Ando took a digital voice recorder from his bag, placed it on the desk, and turned it on at Inoue's signal.

"Miss Tanimoto, isn't it?" She nodded.

"First, could you please state your name clearly and tell us something about yourself and your connection with Fujikawa University?"

"My name is Akemi Tanimoto. I am twenty-two years old. I live in Fujikawa with my parents just ten minutes from here. I've been employed at the university for several months working as a personal secretary to Professor Nomura."

"You're young for such an important job. Can you tell us about your duties here?"

"I answer the phone. I make photocopies. I keep accounts, and I type up reports. My main responsibility is to act as an intermediary between the office and teaching staff and the president."

"Could you please describe your movements today?"

"Yes, sir. I rose at about 7.00, dressed, had breakfast, and left my parents' home at 8.00, arriving here at a little before quarter past. I rushed to punch in my timecard and then went to my office. To my surprise, Professor Nomura was already there. He usually arrives at the university around 10.00. I even wondered if he had gone home yesterday evening. He looked tired and rumpled. He also seemed worried and angry."

Inoue leaned forward. "I need to be quite clear about this. You say you first saw Professor Nomura today at a little after 8.15?"

"Yes, President Nomura came into my annex just after I stepped in the door. He must have heard me. He knew I needed to attend the staff meeting at half past eight. He told me not to make his usual coffee for him because he'd bought a can of cold coffee from the vending machines outside Building Two."

"Was there anything unusual about Professor Nomura?"

"Yes, as I've said he looked tired and worried. He

is…was…usually the most fastidious individual, his suits always well-tailored and neatly-pressed."

Akemi paused, trying to remember. "And Professor Nomura's behaviour…he was gripping a file so tightly the corners were crumpling. He told me it was confidential, an important document and not to let it out of my sight. I was to make five copies of it."

Akemi paused again.

"Yes, Miss Tanimoto? Something else?"

She looked up apologetically, sighing and pushing a thick lock of hair back from her face. "I understand you need the complete truth. I'll admit it. I was feeling angry with the president. And hurt. I am young to have been given this job, but my relations with Professor Nomura were always good, always professional. He was polite, courteous, but when he gave me that file, he was rude, as if he felt he couldn't rely on my discretion. I felt he didn't trust me to carry out his orders properly."

"Can you tell us more about this document?"

"It was about a hundred pages long. Professor Nomura told me to make five copies, collating and stapling them right after the clerical staff meeting and to bring the copies to him, with his coffee. The meeting is held every morning in the administration building. Kawane-*san* gives us instructions for the day and asks if there are any problems. Attendance by all office staff is compulsory."

"How long do these meetings usually last?" "From twenty-five minutes to half an hour."

"Did you lock your office door before you left to attend that staff meeting at 8.30?" "No, I thought it wasn't necessary as Professor Nomura was in his own office and I

decided to take the document in its file to my meeting. When I arrive each morning, I lock my handbag into my desk so no need to lock my office door and especially not when Professor Nomura is in his office as someone might come to see him. Visitors enter his office through mine."

"Did you see anyone as you left your office to attend the meeting?"

"I left my annex at about 8.25. I saw Miss Ota, from the admin staff, and Professor Yamamoto in the mailroom. Professor Yamamoto was standing in front of the mail boxes, reading a piece of paper. She had a shoulder bag and put the paper in it. I imagine the bag held tests for her students that morning. I think Miss Ota was collecting a broom from the utilities closet there. Then Professor Hunter came in. I was surprised that he had shaved off his beard."

"And did you see Professor Nomura after he gave you that document to photocopy at about 8.15?"

Akemi shuddered. "Not alive." She paused and continued. "Once the meeting had ended, at about 9.00, I went straight to the photocopying room. It took me nearly an hour to make the copies. I then hurried to my annex. I imagined Professor

Nomura

was in his office. I wouldn't ordinarily see him unless he summoned me or came to ask me to do something."

"Any idea why Professor Nomura specified five copies?"

"Yes, he said he wanted to give a copy to each of the department heads, and that he would deliver them personally."

"I'm not very clear about the layout of Building Two. Is there a separate room where the photocopying is done?"

"Yes, it's just down the corridor from my office. There are four machines in that room so it can be used by a number of secretaries at the same time, but I was the only one there this morning."

"If you were in the photocopying room, would you have noticed if anyone had entered your annex or Professor Nomura's office?"

"No, I wouldn't see anyone, even if a person entered the president's office by the corridor. As you have probably noticed, Professor Nomura's room can be entered by the door connecting it to my annex or by a door that leads directly into the corridor."

"You say people usually entered Professor Nomura's office through your annex?" "Yes. The corridor door was always kept locked. Professor Nomura was a stickler

for privacy. He only wanted to see people who had first been vetted by me." "So, nobody used the corridor door?"

"Only Professor Nomura himself. He would leave his room through that door when he visited the toilet down the hallway."

"Miss Tanimoto, do you have a key to that corridor door?"

"No. Of course, Professor Nomura had his own key, and I imagine the head of the ground maintenance crew did as well, in case anyone needed to enter the president's office in his absence to clean the room, repair anything or replace old furniture."

"Did you notice anything amiss when you returned to your office after completing your photocopying?"

"Nothing at all. I put the original document and the five photocopies, each in its own file, in a folder on my desk, planning to take it to Professor Nomura with his morning coffee. Then I began grinding the beans."

"What prompted you to enter Professor Nomura's office before you finished making the coffee?"

"I heard a strange sound. It's amazing I heard anything over the din of the grinder. I turned off the machine and then realised it was somebody calling out. In English."

"Before you describe what you saw when you entered Professor Nomura's office, I need to ask you again about this folder. You say that you laid it on your desk while you made the coffee?"

"Yes."

"Unfortunately, that folder and its contents seem to have

mysteriously disappeared. We have searched your annex and cannot find it. But to return to the events of this morning, you say you went to the president's office because you heard something?"

Akemi's face whitened at the recollection, and she began sobbing. The two officers waited as she regained her composure. She was wiping her eyes with her handkerchief. Inoue was dismayed to see Ando's soft brown eyes were also moist. It was fine being soft-hearted but no need to show it while investigating a murder. Inoue wanted to give Ando a surreptitious kick under the desk.

Ando rose hastily, got a bottle of water from the fridge and poured some into a glass, giving it reverentially to the weeping girl.

She smiled and looked up. She drank deeply and, giving one loud sniff, continued. "As I said, I heard someone shouting in English. Someone was calling for help."

"Did anything strike you as odd when you first went into the office?"

"It was *all* odd. Seeing Thomas-*sensei* in the office was unexpected. Professor Nomura kept his office sacrosanct. As I've told you, I never entered myself unless he summoned me by phone. It was a shock Thomas-*sensei* there, never mind where he was standing, next to Professor Nomura's desk."

Her eyes widened in remembered wonder. "It was like a dream. Not logical, unexpected, strange. Thomas-*sensei* seemed to be hugging Professor Nomura."

She continued in an unsteady voice, "And there were other odd things, like a big white doll on the professor's desk that I've never seen before. I was surprised, too, when I looked at the president. It was as if he had a red scarf around his neck and was sleeping! It was all so strange I became hysterical and actually began to laugh."

She began to cry again, hiding her face in the dainty handkerchief. The thick lock of hair fell over her forehead again, hiding her eyes, but she seemed to prefer it that way this time, and didn't bother to push it back.

Inoue waited until her sobs subsided.

"So you didn't expect Thomas-*sensei* to be in Professor Nomura's office?"

"No. I never saw him come in. He had an appointment for 11.00. I had no idea he would try to see Professor Nomura earlier."

"Do you have any idea why Thomas-*sensei* wanted to meet Professor Nomura? Why did he obviously feel some urgency and not wait until the time of his appointment? Why did he come to see him an hour earlier?"

"No, that is..." Akemi fell silent, remembering the sharp exchange of words between Andrew and her boss the previous morning. She couldn't help hearing. Andrew had been asking about his job, obviously worried his contract might not be renewed.

"Miss Tanimoto, please. This is a murder investigation. Please tell us everything you know, anything at all."

"Thomas-*sensei* visited Professor Nomura yesterday morning. Professor Nomura got quite angry at him for asking about the renewal of his teaching contract here."

"So they argued. And Thomas-*sensei* was the first to discover the body." "I didn't say 'argued'. I said Professor Nomura spoke harshly."

Feeling guilty at the admission, worrying that Andrew, one of her favourite teachers, might get in trouble, she stuttered, "But it was Thomas-*sensei* who called for help. I realise now that he was trying to help Professor Nomura, keep him from falling."

"You mean he moved the body from the position he found it, inadvertently or not?"

The younger officer looked at his superior in surprise. Inspector Inoue was frowning, clearly angry with himself for having spoken so frankly.

Akemi's Take on Her Interview

At the conclusion of her interview with the Inspector, Akemi Tanimoto paused outside Building Six. She tottered slightly and supported herself against a concrete wall. Then she slowly made her way to the university entrance gate where she had been instructed to wait for the patrol car that would take her home.

She had to stand there for several minutes. She stared at the ground, unable to think of anything but the events of the last few hours. The lowest point for her had not been finding her boss dead but wakening from her faint afterwards. She had been surprised to find herself no longer in Professor Nomura's office or even in Building Two. She had awoken in the staff room in Building One, lying on the black plastic couch there. The couch was uncomfortable. It was stuffed too tightly, and the plastic felt slickly cold against her bare skin. The big brown sofa in her boss's room was much nicer, not that she'd ever dared sit on it. It looked soft and was pleasantly creased, as though made of real leather.

Akemi felt sick and began moaning. Her throat ached and she had a vague recollection of having screamed. Then she remembered Andrew holding Professor Nomura's body, and she wanted to scream again.

Keiko Araki was not Akemi's favourite individual in the

world. She was a sharp- featured, sharp-tongued middle-aged woman who worked in the accounts department. Akemi was never glad to see her, but this was different. She was relieved to see Keiko kneeling by the sofa. Akemi knew that Keiko, a trained accountant, couldn't understand her inability to do basic arithmetic. Keiko would often scold Akemi for the receipts and invoices she brought for her approval, complaining they weren't calculated correctly.

Keiko was holding a wet cloth in one hand and a glass of water in the other. Akemi realised that her forehead felt cool and wet and that Keiko must have been dabbing her face when she was unconscious. She hoped she hadn't been moaning.

She drank the water and managed a weak smile when Keiko explained that she had to go to Building Six to wait in a classroom with a few others to be interviewed. Akemi would probably be able to go home soon.

When Keiko helped her up, Akemi staggered slightly and was grateful for assistance. She tried to concentrate on the ground as she walked out, unwilling to face the curious glances from her co-workers who stared, pretended they hadn't, and made a show of being busy.

Akemi was surprised at seeing the other people waiting to be questioned: Professor Hunter, Professor Yamamoto, Mr Kawane, Andrew, and Michiko. What could any of them have to do with the president's death? But then she realised they were the individuals known to have been in the vicinity of the crime. She was not by nature a demonstrative person, but seeing Michiko, or Mi-*chan*, as Akemi affectionately referred to her, looking so terrified and Andrew, like a distraught teenager in jeans and a t-shirt, she wanted to rush over and hug them both.

Professor Yamamoto led Akemi to a chair and sat beside her. Michiko was on the other side, and Professor Yamamoto held first Akemi's hands and then Michiko's as if she were comforting children.

Akemi was grateful to be first to be interviewed. The early part of the interview went smoothly, she thought, and she felt pleased she had held up well, answering the Chief Inspector's questions with some clarity and accuracy. She felt less inclined to make that effort when the Inspector noted his surprise at her getting the job despite her youth and inexperience and when he seemed to be making insinuations about Andrew.

He's heard the gossip about Professor Nomura, she thought, when Inoue began to question her closely about her job. It wasn't surprising. Anyone would have wondered why she had been hired for such an important position. She was young. She was attractive. She had hardly any experience, hired directly after graduating from Fujikawa.

She hadn't even been a good student. She'd often skipped classes and had scarcely done any homework. She hadn't cared for many of her professors, including, for example, her graduation thesis supervisor, Professor Obuchi, who taught social welfare. Akemi had disliked him, thinking him a fraud with his cheery chumminess and for not performing his lectures seriously enough. However, Obuchi was responsible for changing her life. He had put in a good word for her with Professor Nomura when she told him at the graduation ceremony that she had no job yet. It was good timing. Nomura's secretary had just handed in her resignation. Akemi thought it odd she owed her job to a man she despised.

Still, she was a bit wary. Akemi had known Professor Nomura's previous secretary by sight and had heard rumours. It was a hot topic at the college. Professor

Yamamoto, appointing herself the resident feminist, sometimes held evening sessions for interested professors and students on the subject of sexual harassment in the work place in Japan. Akemi wondered whether the attractive young woman who was her predecessor had combined clerical duties with after-hours' activities. She had been seen with Professor Nomura in a few local bars.

If that so-called 'office lady' had been overly friendly with 'management,' it would certainly be nothing new at Fujikawa or at many of Japan's other universities. Akemi suspected that Fujikawa's policy of employing secretaries on three-year, non- renewable contracts had more to do with certain predatory individuals wanting to curtail messy complications rather than that such contracts were designed to offer work experience to young female graduates.

There had been no impropriety, however, in her own relations with Nomura once she started working for him. So long as she was punctual and polite and performed her duties efficiently and quickly, he treated her with the courtesy of a distant uncle. She was grateful. She had heard his explosions of rage, mercifully muffled by the walls that separated her annex from his office, and seen professors and staff staggering past her afterwards, unable to utter a word, intent on making their escape.

Akemi had never really liked Professor Nomura, but knowing that his wife Liza, whom he obviously adored, had died of breast cancer made her feel sorry for him.

Akemi was willing to outline to Inoue the string of events that had led to her becoming Professor Nomura's secretary. She had already told him about the events of that morning and how shocked she had been to enter her boss's office to find Andrew hugging Nomura, then realising he was trying to prevent his body from falling. But her willingness to cooperate dwindled when the Inspector began asking her about the Canadian man she considered her friend.

"Miss Tanimoto, can you give us your impressions of Thomas-*sensei*? Of his life here? Of his wife, Miss Weller? I understand she has kept her maiden name." He paused, at a slight loss, and Akemi could imagine why. Inoue was a typically old- fashioned Japanese. He had no truck with that western fashion that downplayed the importance of the official bond between husband and wife.

He looked at her intently. "We would appreciate your candour."

Akemi didn't feel like answering any more questions. She wanted nothing more to do with Inoue. When she first met the Chief Inspector, she had been surprised. Of course, she knew that he was Ellie's husband. Akemi had met Ellie as a student when Ellie was her part-time English conversation instructor at the college. Once Akemi

had graduated and also got a job at the university, they became friends rather than pupil and teacher. Akemi knew that Ellie's husband was the Chief Inspector of the Fujikawa police but, until this day, she had never met him. Akemi had imagined Ellie would choose somebody more obviously intellectual or refined. She had a faint feeling of dislike for this muscular officer with his short-cropped hair and severe expression. She didn't want to obstruct his enquiries, but she didn't want to be too helpful if it meant casting aspersions on Andrew Thomas. He had won a special place in her heart as one of the few professors at the university who treated her with kindness. He obviously saw her as a colleague he worked with rather than as a lowly employee he could order around.

Two unwelcome thoughts echoed in her mind. *Andrew and*

Nomura had words the day before. It was Andrew who found the body. Impossible to suspect Andrew. It was an odd irony: while Akemi pitied Professor Nomura for the loss of his wife, she pitied for Andrew for having to live with his.

Whenever Akemi met Alyson, she remembered a visit to Matsuo, a town on the Japan Sea her parents had taken her to as a child for a summer holiday. They had stayed three days in a small *minshuku* near the beach, and Akemi and her younger brother Yuji spent all their time exploring the shallow rock pools while their parents sheltered under a large red-and-white striped parasol nearby.

She had been fascinated by the limpets on many of the rocks that jutted like broken black teeth from the lips of the pools. The limpets looked tiny, fragile and helpless, but Akemi couldn't prise them off to put with the other marine specimens in her red plastic bucket. Akemi thought of Alyson as a limpet and felt sorry for Andrew for having to serve as her rock.

Akemi also thought Alyson was like a *hikikomori*. But it was odd. She was a foreigner and a female. *Hikikomori* tended to be Japanese males. The phrase referred to young Japanese who gave up on life, secluding themselves in their bedrooms for long periods, sometimes years on end, surviving on the trays of meals their mothers left outside their door. They spent their time reading *manga*, surfing the Internet, or sleeping.

Akemi sympathised with Japan's shut-ins. She had known the torture of the endless exams administered in junior high and high school in a competitive environment that often led to bullying. She also had stumbled at life's first hurdle in failing to get into a top high school. She had felt the pressure not only to succeed academically but also to

conform to the standards of the group, whatever that group might be: the family, the social circle, the school environment. It was the Japanese way: to bow to the demands of others, including the injunction that children obey their parents until the day they died. Sometimes when Akemi was a schoolgirl and her mother appeared in her room telling her to get up, she had wanted to pull up her blanket and hide under the bedclothes forever.

But what had driven Alyson to her self-imposed exile? Akemi couldn't imagine. She had wanted to ask Andrew but never got up the nerve. For Akemi, the odd thing was Alyson's attractiveness, her having the looks of a professional model. She was the Japanese ideal of western beauty with her slim figure, her blue eyes, and her blond hair. She even spoke Japanese fluently because of a year she had spent on a homestay in Kyoto. She had everything going for her, even a husband kinder than most, but decided to act as if she had nothing at all.

Andrew had once invited Akemi to a meal at their home. A self-confessed TV addict, she had seen many pretty homes featured on American programmes. She had imagined a Japanese house nicely decorated like a western one, but it failed to meet any of her expectations. The little prefabricated house of corrugated iron was tidy inside, but it had the impersonality of a hotel: everything in its place, no personal mementos. There were lots of books but nothing else: no photos, no paintings, no ornaments, no colourful cushions or throws – not an inviting place to spend long periods of time. Yet that was what Alyson had done since her arrival in Fujikawa.

On that occasion, Alyson had made it clear that Akemi was unwelcome. Andrew had answered the door, looking strained.

"Alyson's just in here," he said, ushering her into a room lined with bulging bookcases. It was a dark, damp space, but somebody had relieved the gloom by placing small flickering white tea candles in glass jars on shelves and tables. Alyson was slouched in the corner of an imitation leather sofa. She looked as though she had been there all day and would remain there for the evening.

"I must finish preparing the dinner," Andrew said, "but first, would you prefer red or white?"

"Red, please. But I hope you'll be joining me, Alyson."

"I don't care to drink poison," she drawled contemptuously from her perch on the sofa. "Andrew's a cheapskate. He's got a Japanese red and a Japanese white from the little shop round the corner. From *bitter* experience, quite literally, I know your compatriots haven't got the hang of viniculture. I imagine they supply most of the taste with chemicals."

It was not a promising start to a festive evening, and it went down from there. It was only to be expected when Andrew's friend Stephen rang to say that he had a headache and couldn't make it. This left Akemi on her own with Andrew and Alyson, chattering away doing her best to compensate for those two not speaking to each other. It wasn't easy considering Akemi's rudimentary grasp of English. Alyson seemed to relish her discomfort, refusing to help with Japanese in the awkward silences. Andrew looked nervous. For his sake Akemi ignored Alyson's hostility.

In the incident room in Building Six, Inoue pressed on with his questioning.

"Miss Tanimoto, we need complete openness from you…I think you have actually met Miss Weller on a number of occasions."

"Oh yes, I know her," Akemi said icily.

She noted the look of surprise on the inspector's face. She shook back her hair and gazed at him defiantly, her lips pursed, her handkerchief now balled into her left fist. After her previous evidence, given in a straightforward manner, she no longer wished to cooperate, and it was a relief for her. The policeman was only doing his job, but she didn't care about fairness. It was better to be angry than remain miserable in the realisation her boss had been murdered.

"Thomas-*sensei* and his wife are a charming couple," she said. "And I would trust Thomas-*sensei* absolutely. He is one of the kindest, gentlest men I've had the privilege to meet."

Akemi was amused to hear Inoue's heavy sigh. She saw him look downcast and was relieved when he said, in a subdued voice "Thank you very much, Miss Tanimoto. You've been very helpful." She caught his glance at Ando. "And now an officer will escort you home."

The last straw, Akemi thought, though she was grateful for the offer, feeling in no condition to drive herself. *My parents and all the people who live near us will see me turn up in a police car. The scandal should be enough to keep the neighbourhood gossips going for weeks.*

A Foreigner in Fujikawa

Inoue ushered Miss Tanimoto out of the incident room and was relieved to see the translator standing in the corridor. He had often availed himself of her services; she was trustworthy and discreet.

"Miss Shinohara," Inoue said, bending deeply from the waist in respect and gratitude, "we are indebted to you for helping us at such short notice."

Miss Shinohara, a diminutive woman in her early forties, black hair in a bun, smiled at Inoue and bowed in return. Inoue thought of her as one of those shy middle-aged Japanese women who try to hide in plain sight – make-up unobtrusive, clothes discreet and appropriate. She spoke softly, reluctant to look at anyone directly. Her looks and manner achieved her goal of being nearly invisible.

Inoue knew Miss Shinohara had spent several years in California with an American husband who had proved unsatisfactory. On returning to Japan after an acrimonious divorce, she had turned tragedy to advantage, making a good living from her English proficiency. She was sought after for her skill in translating and interpreting, often asked to help at social functions at the city hall in Ishizaki. And she was valued for her discretion. In recent years, with the influx of foreigners into Fujikawa unable to manage more than basic

Japanese, many of them ignorant of Japan's traffic rules and getting involved in minor accidents, she was routinely employed by the Fujikawa police. They knew she would never reveal details of any case.

"I imagine you have heard of the president's death," Inoue continued. "We are now questioning several individuals known to have been in the vicinity at the time of his murder. Professor Andrew Thomas, a Canadian, was the individual unlucky enough to discover the body. He knows little Japanese, and it is his interview we require your assistance with."

Miss Shinohara bowed once more.

Inoue had instructed Ando, after he had escorted Miss Tanimoto to the patrol car to take her home, to check on the interviews of the university administrative staff in Building Five and also to liaise with the scene-of-crime officers still conducting their

search for clues in the president's office and the environs of Building Two. Kubo sat down beside Inoue to operate the recording equipment.

Andrew Thomas shambled rather than strolled into the room. Like Miss Tanimoto, he looked near breaking point but without the advantage of her fine dress style – Inoue was baffled as to how the young Canadian's wife could have supplied an old t- shirt and ragged jeans for a police interview about a murder.

He looked at Andrew closely. That awful ponytail! Apart from his darling Ellie, foreigners could be incomprehensible. Their disregard for their appearance in public was disconcerting.

Inoue was impassive as he stood and bowed slightly. "Professor Thomas, thank you for agreeing to be interviewed at this difficult time. I would like to make this questioning brief and then you'll get a lift home. You must have had a terrible ordeal."

There was a short pause as Miss Shinohara, seated beside the foreigner, relayed the gist of the police inspector's words to him. Andrew slumped in his seat, his head bowed, hardly heeding.

Kubo looked enquiringly at the bubbling coffee maker. Andrew and his translator were offered hot coffee but only Andrew accepted. While Kubo stood and busied himself in pouring him a cup, Inoue shuffled papers on his desk and out of the corner of his eye noticed a group of schoolchildren heading home on the sidewalk skirting the campus. They were laughing and chattering, their black and red satchels bouncing up and down on their backs as they ran with not a care in the world. He envied them knowing nothing of death, let alone of murder. Once Andrew had his cup of coffee, Inoue said: "Please tell us your name and occupation."

Thomas replied: "My name is Andrew Thomas. I am Canadian, from Winnipeg, and I have been employed as a contract teacher of English at Fujikawa University for the past two and a half years."

Miss Shinohara had a pad and paper on which she made notes before conveying the foreigner's words to Inoue in Japanese and Inoue's to Andrew in English.

"Could you please tell us your movements today?"

"I got up a little later than usual, at half past seven. I live in Akane-cho, a little town thirty minutes' drive to the east of Fujikawa."

"And do you live there by yourself?" This question for the tape. "No, I came to Japan with my wife, Alyson Weller."

Inoue couldn't help enquiring, with a tinge of distaste, "Weller? Not Thomas?"

Inoue saw Andrew smile as Miss Shinohara relayed his words. He took a final swallow of his coffee and carefully placed the cup and saucer on the floor by his chair. Had Andrew heard the disapproval in his voice? He answered soberly, "My wife has preferred to keep her maiden name. Miss Weller and I have been living together for the past four and a half years. We married just before I was to take up my job here. It was a matter of expediency. She would otherwise have found it hard to get a visa to enter Japan. We went through the official service, but she refused to take my name, and I quite understand her reasons. We were as good as married before. It's just a meaningless piece of paper..." Andrew trailed off, sensing Inoue's distaste.

"And is *Miss Weller* also an employee of Fujikawa University?"

"No, she generally stays at home. She gives the occasional English lesson to neighbourhood children by appointment."

"I see. Thank you for your frankness. Now, if we could return to your movements this morning."

"I got up at half past seven and left home about eight. I drove to Fujikawa University, arriving about 8.20. You can verify I'm sure by checking my parking card. I happened to meet Miss Ota, who works in the university administration office, and we walked together to Building One. I left Miss Ota there. She stayed to help some of her co-workers sweeping up the courtyard, and I went up to my office. Professor Hayashi came by at about 9.00 and stayed around forty-five minutes. My next class was at 11.10. In fact, I had an appointment with Professor Nomura at 11.00. On impulse, I decided to see him earlier. I went to his office as soon as Professor Hayashi left me."

"And that would have been … ?" "About 9.50."

"Can you please explain this sudden decision to see Professor Nomura? You already had an appointment with him for an hour later."

Andrew looked down at his empty coffee cup – there was no offer of a refill. He frowned and sighed. "In fact, I was worried about whether my contract here at the university would be renewed, and I panicked at Professor Hayashi's visit. He said that he knew people were to be fired, *let go*...and I wondered if I would be one of them. Then he said something strange about Mr Akamatsu. It was upsetting." Andrew paused.   "Also, Alyson made a point yesterday evening of asking me to see the president as soon as possible."

"Miss Weller wanted you to see Professor Nomura?"

Andrew sighed again, this time more deeply, held out his hands looking at them carefully, as if checking his nails.

He suddenly blurted, "Hands! They can paint the Mona Lisa or they can cut somebody's throat."

Inoue looked at him impassively.

"Sorry," said Andrew, tucking his hands under his thighs, as if to restrain them. "Just a thought. To answer your question, yes, Alyson had been nagging me to find out if a decision had been made about the renewal of my contract."

Andrew wiggled slightly in his seat, settling more heavily on his hands, and continued. "I visited Professor Nomura's office yesterday morning about the same matter. No answer from him then meant that I was desperate to have a decision. As I say, Professor Hayashi's visit to my office this morning added a sense of urgency because he mentioned the English department would be possibly losing staff."

"Tell me about your visit to the president's office yesterday."

Andrew gave a bare outline. "I was surprised not to find

Professor Nomura's secretary, Miss Tanimoto, in her annex when I arrived," he said. "She is usually in the outer office. Perhaps she was at a meeting. I admit, when I found her annex empty, I thought of turning back, but desperation pushed me on."

Inoue looked puzzled. "But *was* it so desperate for you?"

"Not for me, personally. I like it well enough here, but I know I could probably get a job at some other college in Japan. If the worst came to the worst, I could return to Canada, of course. However, Alyson has told me often quite forcibly she wants to stay in Fujikawa for at least another year or two."

Inoue sensed Kubo's impatience as he shifted in his chair, operating the digital voice recorder. He must be wondering why he was going into such detail about the foreigner's wife when it was the thin Canadian himself who was the *de facto* chief suspect in a murder enquiry, having found the body.

Inoue would explain his method later to both Kubo and Ando as part of their training…that it is important in any police case, especially in a murder enquiry, to understand the circumstances and motives of anyone involved. Or at least the ones they professed in initial interviews, whose implications they might not even grasp.

The recordings meant the police could check on inconsistencies in subsequent statements when the individuals they questioned might get tripped up by their own words.

"I see. So you were trying to get your contract renewed mainly to please your wife. Can you explain why she finds it so agreeable here? It does seem slightly strange. Fujikawa, after all, is just a rural backwater, and she's not even working at the university herself."

Andrew smiled. "To be honest, I don't know. As you say, she has no real job. There is no kind of bustling cultural life in Fujikawa to attract her, let alone in our even smaller town of Akane-cho. She has made few friends here unfortunately. But she once spent a year in Kyoto as an exchange student and is fluent in Japanese, so maybe she feels comfortable here."

Inoue made a steeple of his hands at his chest. He seemed to be brooding over Andrew's words. "Did you see anyone on your way to Professor Nomura's office this morning? After you'd decided, on impulse, to see him an hour earlier than originally planned?"

"Just before leaving my room, I looked out my window and saw Yamamoto-*sensei* walking towards Building Eight. As I left my building, I noticed a stepladder propped up against the wall of Building Two. I think there was a cleaner near the ladder. Andrew paused to reflect. "In fact, once I'd left my office in Building Three, I ran quickly to Building Two, not wanting to risk reconsidering. There may have been a student sitting on one of the benches in the courtyard. I was in such a rush...just thinking of my dreaded interview with the president."

"You say you were surprised not to find Miss Tanimoto in her office."

"Mostly disappointed, to be perfectly honest. I thought that in the worst scenario she could act as a buffer between me and Professor Nomura, who would surely be angry I was an hour earlier than arranged." Andrew smiled ruefully. "He was often angry in my dealings with him."

Andrew paused and added, "As I'd come that far, I didn't want to go back. I walked through the annex and knocked on Professor Nomura's door, gently at first, harder when I didn't hear anything. Then I simply opened the door."

Andrew released his hands and looked at them as if they could help him to continue. "When I saw Professor Nomura slumped over his desk, I thought he was having a nap. I just stood there, hoping he'd wake up."

"But you didn't call out from the doorway, to attract his attention?"

"I'm just a contract teacher here," Andrew said. "I'd got used to thinking of Nomura as a god. Everyone does here…did here. Can you understand? Nomura was like some deity, pulling the strings, deciding our fates. He was mysterious and powerful."

Tugging at his ponytail, Andrew added, "To be perfectly frank, I was terrified. I thought he'd yell at me if I woke him. I wish I *had* walked off when I thought he was taking a nap, gone back to my office, waited until eleven. Then somebody else would have found him."

Andrew rubbed his eyes wearily. "After I'd stood there a bit, I began thinking how unlikely it was that anyone could sleep through my banging on the door. Then I began to notice other things. Like the president's unusual position at his desk. That he hadn't moved at all. Then I went closer and saw…and saw… "

Inoue leaned forward and interrupted Andrew's stammering. "Professor Thomas, we are coming to yet another point that baffles me. Why did you disturb the body? Try to lift it?"

Andrew covered his face with his hands. "He seemed completely still. But once I was quite close, I realised his body was slowly changing position, shifting, that he might even fall on the floor."

There was a long pause. The Chief looked at a spot on the wall behind the young Canadian's head and moved not at all. When Andrew uncovered his face and continued, he blinked as if the lights had become too bright. "As I say, once I got near the president, I could see he was *unnaturally* still, not even breathing. I saw blood. But I couldn't believe he was *dead*, that was too far-fetched a notion."

Andrew took a deep breath. "When I noticed the body *was* moving, that it might slip down, I wanted to stop it, to raise it up, perhaps even to help Nomura breathe, although I knew, deep down, that he couldn't be revived."

Andrew had delivered this explanation in a staccato rush of words, leaving Miss Shinohara looking bewildered. She gazed distractedly at the words she had scribbled on her pad.

"I'm sorry, sir," she said to Inoue in a hushed, apologetic voice. "I'm not sure I can translate his words. He spoke too quickly…"

Inoue said: "Can you give me the general idea?"

"He realised the president was dead but noticed the body falling so he thought he would try to catch him. But he knew there was no point, the man was dead."

"Foreigners!" Inoue involuntarily exclaimed, and then felt bad, as if he had betrayed his wife with that word.

"I know, sir, it's hard for me to understand, too."

Andrew looked at their puzzled faces. He couldn't blame them. He had been surprised, too, by his impulse to hold the body. Possibly a misplaced sense of helpfulness. But the prospect of seeing the poor man slump to the floor was unbearable.

"And what happened after you clutched the president's body?" Inoue continued.

"It was heavy, I nearly fell over. I shouted for help again and again. Finally, Akemi – Miss Tanimoto – appeared."

Andrew looked more confused than ever. "It was so strange. At first, she seemed to be laughing as I struggled to keep the president's body upright. Then she came a few steps forward and, seeing he was dead, she began screaming."

Andrew closed his eyes briefly. "I think I'll hear that sound in my nightmares for the rest of my days. She went on and on, then passed out. I got his body back leaning over the desk; I was exhausted in a kind of daze. A cleaner appeared in the room. Then Mr Kawane and Mr Akamatsu came and carried Miss Tanimoto away. Then you and your officers turned up."

"A cleaner?"

"Yes, he was just suddenly there, a man wearing one of those big broad-brimmed hats and a mask. I assumed he heard the noise, came into the office and saw us, and went for help."

"Can you describe him?"

"No, just one of the cleaners." Andrew shook his head and gazed at the floor. "I was in no state of mind to be more observant."

Andrew looked up at Inoue. Of course, he knew Inoue was Ellie's husband, and he wondered about their marital relations, even wondering what they did in bed. He could not imagine her being sexually attracted to this bullet-headed, muscular, middle-aged Japanese man. Did he have a scrap of sensitivity? How could Ellie bear sharing her life with him? How could there be any intimacy?

"Chief Inspector Inoue," Andrew said. "You have been asking me many questions, but I'd like to ask you one. Have you ever done something that was illogical or out of character?"

Miss Shinohara relayed Andrew's words, looking anxious at

their impertinence.

"Never," he said in a firm voice. "I only act as the result of thought and deliberation. I don't let emotions into my decisions." Andrew meekly apologised.

Questioning was over for the day, and Miss Shinohara led Andrew out. A junior officer gave him a lift home.

Inoue turned to Kubo. "I want you to find that cleaner. Get an officer to begin interviewing the maintenance staff. Then tell Kawane-*san* we'll be questioning him next."

"Yes, sir," said Kubo, "right away, sir." Inoue sensed Kubo wanted to salute to evince his eagerness. Inoue reflected that he had not told the whole truth. Falling in love with Ellie and marrying her: those were events at odds with his earlier life and inexplicable.

Kawane Explains

Inoue knew Kawane wouldn't want to be kept waiting in the adjoining classroom a moment longer than necessary. He would be pacing up and down, checking his watch, a busy man, no time to spare. He'd occasionally rub his large nose, his smug, florid face full of impatience.

There was a light tap at the door. Kubo, impeccably turned out in his short-sleeved blue shirt under his tunic, came in and bowed. "Shall I call the next witness, sir?"

"Yes, please bring in Mr Kawane."

Inoue could see that Toru Kawane was accustomed to being able to cut quite an important figure at the university. He was a man in his early forties dressed in a black suit, perfectly clean and crisp white shirt, and a grey-striped tie, looking upset and struggling to retain his composure.

Kubo started the recording equipment.

Inoue said, "For our records, please tell us your name and occupation."

"My name is Toru Kawane. I have been employed as a clerical worker at Fujikawal University for twenty years. For the past four years, I have worked as the head of the office staff."

"Can you outline some of your duties?

"To do that, I think I need to give you a basic explanation of the workings of the college." Kawane gave Inoue an unexpected smile. "I imagine you know much already. You graduated from here twenty years ago. I came just after you left."

Inoue noted again the unwelcome intrusion of the personal in this investigation. "I can see much has changed since," he said calmly.

"Well, the student numbers are about the same, unfortunately, even though we've added a few departments. I suppose you know Japan's low birth rate has meant some colleges can't attract enough students. They have declared bankruptcy and closed down." Kawane rubbed his nose and looked anxious.

"I'd be sorry if the university folded. It would be a blow to the town," Inoue said. "Well, at present there are around fifteen hundred students, including fifty graduate

students doing Master's degrees in sociology, social welfare and English. There a r e

one hundred and forty-two professors, including full-time professors as well as associate and assistant professors and part-time teachers. There are ninety-five clerical staff. Fujikawa University also employs ten men and women, mostly in their sixties, who perform menial chores such as collecting and disposing of the rubbish from each building and the outdoor bins, cleaning the windows, floors and blackboards, scrubbing out the toilets, raking leaves, mowing grass, trimming bushes, and sweeping paths."

"And the person at the top in charge of this huge hierarchy of students and staff is the president?" Inoue asked.

"Professor Nomura was very good at the job. Since his election five years ago, President Nomura took a close interest in the day-to-day running of the university. He was fully involved." Kawane spouted the facts and statistics with an ease born of experience, but now he paused and looked blank.

Delayed shock, Inoue thought, and looked silently at him, waiting.

After a few moments, Kawane gulped and shook his head. "I simply can't take it in, what's happened today. I'm stunned. You must excuse me." Perspiring, he took a handkerchief from his jacket pocket to wipe his face and rub his large nose.

"In fact," said Kawane, swallowing hard, "I am a beneficiary of Professor Nomura becoming our president five years ago. He was impatient with the old employment system, with seniors automatically promoted over juniors. He wanted a system based on merit. There was a man in his late thirties in charge of the office staff in Building One when I first joined this organization twenty years ago. He should have kept that position until retirement at sixty, but Professor Nomura liked my work, and he demoted him and gave me his job, even though I was ten years younger."

"That brings me neatly to my next question. Did Professor

Nomura have any enemies? The man who lost his position was probably not terribly pleased."

"Indeed, he was furious. Did the professor have enemies? Yes, there were many who liked the way things were and hated change. Some were angry because the president's new policies meant they had to work harder. In Professor Nomura's defence, I would say that he asked a lot of everyone, but no more than he asked of himself."

"Were you one of those opposed to the changes?"

"No, I welcomed them. Under the leadership of the former college president, dead these four years now, the place was falling apart. Student numbers were down. The staff, both teaching and clerical, was demoralised, lazy and ineffective. The campus looked a mess. The buildings weren't looked after and there were no plans for the construction of new ones. No new courses were being proposed to attract new students. It was just the status quo and hoping for the best."

"I recall a pack of wild dogs," Inoue found himself murmuring. "We had them rounded up and taken to the local pound."

"They were gentle enough, too weak and emaciated to be threatening," Inoue said, in a regretful tone.

"President Nomura thought they had to go, that they gave out the wrong signal. He wanted a perfect place. Even his enemies agreed he worked hard. Most important, he had vision. He turned everything upside down. His key words were change, efficiency and accountability. Students were encouraged to assess their professors and their classes and the professors' bonuses were adjusted according to satisfaction ratings for their teaching. Clerical staff was transferred from one section to another to reduce complacency. You may have noticed our new library. It's just one of a number of buildings recently constructed on campus. We even have a purpose-built archery range! New courses have been initiated and new professors recruited, often well- known ones, to advertise to the world that Fujikawa is trying to escape the second- rate."

"And was his grand scheme working?"

"Yes, after a significant dip in enrolment under the previous president, student numbers have been rising, although this disaster may reverse that trend."

Kawane wiped a forehead dripping with sweat. He looked gloomy. "I don't know if you know, but Nomura graduated from Fujikawa himself. He was from Kyoto, from a wealthy, well-connected family, but he set himself the task of saving his alma mater. I for one will be eternally grateful."

Inoue said, "I need to pursue all lines of inquiry, and so I require your complete honesty and frankness. Can you think of anyone in particular who was opposed to Professor Nomura's reforms, who felt personally harmed by them?"

Kawane shifted uneasily in his chair and wrinkled his large nose thoughtfully. "I think you will hear this from somebody else, so I'll be frank. I've told you about my predecessor.

After losing his job as chief of staff, he opposed Professor Nomura's changes so vocally that he was asked to quit. That was four years ago, when I took his place."

"He was asked? And did he comply willingly?"

"No, he and one of the professors, a physics lecturer also angry about the changes, sued Professor Nomura in court and, with typical bravado, Professor Nomura sued them back."

"And the result?"

"I'm surprised you don't know about it. It was a big scandal in Fujikawa and was even on national news. The court decided in Professor Nomura's favour, finding the two individuals in question to be unreasonably and unhelpfully obstructive of changes that were necessary, given the demographics and current economic climate in Japan and their effect on the private universities."

"What happened to these two men?"

"It's rather odd. A private settlement was reached between them and Professor Nomura. It's common knowledge. They could continue to draw their salary until retirement age so long as they did not set foot on campus again. I think his main concern was to stifle negative publicity that might have put off prospective students."

"Were they told not to talk to the press about the case?"

"Yes, I think there was some such proviso in the agreement." "Could you please give me their names and whereabouts?"

"My predecessor was Mr Akiyama. The physics professor's name is Horii." "Where are they now?"

"They still live in Fujikawa, one in an apartment near the campus, the other in his family home. Both are from Fujikawa originally, you see. I bump into them sometimes at a local restaurant, but we just bow to each other, nothing more."

"Thanks for explaining this to me," said Inoue. "Your insider's knowledge of the workings of the college and the people here is invaluable. Now, please tell me about your movements this morning."

"The teaching and clerical staff are encouraged to live as near the university as they can. My home is just fifteen minutes away by car. I got up as usual at 6.00, watered my garden, had breakfast, and left for the university at 7.30. I was at my desk by 8.00."

"Please tell me who you saw on campus this morning."

"Professor Nomura generally arrived after 10.00, so I didn't expect to see him. I was surprised his car was in the parking garage when I arrived, and then I actually bumped

into him as I was entering the admin building. We exchanged a few words. Everything seemed normal. He was normal, maybe a bit tired."

"Did you meet anyone else?"

"As I get to the university a good hour before the first class, I rarely see any students. I passed several cleaners as I was walking to the administration building. One was sweeping the path between Buildings One and Three and one was collecting rubbish from the bins in the forecourt with his trolley. I had been at my desk for perhaps ten minutes when two of our clerks, Mrs Noma and Mrs Takagi, appeared. Mrs Noma vacuumed the office area while Mrs Takagi went outside to begin sweeping litter and to collect bottles or cans dropped by students. After Mrs Noma finished cleaning inside, she joined Mrs Takagi outside. The students can leave a terrible mess. They like to meet on the campus at night, particularly in the summer, and they sit chatting on the benches, drinking beer and eating snacks."

"Kids today!" Kawane hissed unexpectedly. "I don't know if you have children, Inspector Inoue, but sometimes I wonder what parents these days are thinking of. When I was a child, I was taught manners. But our students just throw empty bottles or plastic bags on the ground, even though the bins are in plain sight."

"No, I have no children," Inoue said, "but I've noticed that some young people are careless and selfish. It's regrettable."

Kawane nodded and continued. "I saw Professor Hunter and Yamamoto-*sensei* enter the administration building. I assumed they were there to sign in and collect their mail. A member of our clerical staff, Michiko Ota, also entered the building around that time."

"And that time was?" Inoue interposed.

"It must have been about 8.25. Miss Ota generally helps

Mrs Noma and Mrs Takagi in sweeping the concrete forecourt in front of Building One. I saw her come in to collect her broom, but she was running late. She had to return to the office within minutes as I hold a meeting of all the employees under my supervision at 8.30."

"What happens at these meetings?"

"I assign chores, remind the clerks and secretaries of the work I expect them to complete each day or check on the tasks they are working on."

"And everything went as usual?"

"Yes. There was no new business to discuss or matters to get sorted. Everyone knew what was expected of them. I just had to offer a few instructions. The meeting lasted half an hour. Afterwards, I returned to my own desk."

Kawane looked worried, and he wrinkled his nose as if scenting danger. "This is a busy time for us, the end of term." He looked anxiously at his watch, obviously hoping the interview could finish soon.

Inoue felt he needed to bring him back to the matter at hand. "And how did you learn that Professor Nomura had been murdered?"

"I was sitting at my desk looking over class attendance files when I realised someone was standing right beside me. I looked round and found one of our cleaners. He was snuffling, a bad cold maybe. I didn't recognise him: a stocky looking man, overweight. He had his hat jammed right down.

He was wearing a mask and mumbled something indistinct about trouble in Building Two and gestured in that direction. I hurried to Miss Tanimoto's annex. She wasn't there. I went into Professor Nomura's, where I found her lying on the floor."

There was another long pause. He continued in a softer voice, speaking in a monotone, looking at the wall behind Inoue. "It was all so *odd*! No other way to put it. I'm used to things going to plan, but everything was out of order. Miss Tanimoto appeared to have fainted, lying on the floor in front of the president's desk. He was sprawled over it at a strange angle. Thomas-*sensei* was sitting on the floor. It took me a minute or two to see the cut across the professor's throat." Kawane gulped. "And lots of blood everywhere. It was clear that the professor had been *murdered*!"

"And then?"

"I used my cell phone to call the police. Then I was relieved to find that Akamatsu- *san*, the clerical worker you met at the gate, had followed me to Building Two. I gestured to him to help me with Tanimoto-*san*. We picked her up but she revived only a little. We wanted to get her away from the scene. She couldn't manage to walk. We took her to the admin building, carried her, really."

"You left Thomas-*sensei* alone with Professor Nomura's body?"

"I didn't know *what* to do. Apart from calling the police, of course." Kawane stopped, wanting to look at his watch. Resisting such a discourtesy, he looked up and said, "There's no protocol I'm aware of for such a situation."

Inoue wondered if Kawane was making a feeble attempt at humour.

"As we were lifting Tanimoto-*san*, Professor Thomas said nothing at all. He was in a kind of catatonic state. I couldn't ask him for help or information."

"I'm sorry," Inoue said. "I need to ask you one more question. You may find it strange, and I'd appreciate if you keep it to yourself. Do you know if Professor Nomura had a large white porcelain doll in his possession, the kind given to young daughters for Girls' Day? You must have seen it on his desk."

Kawane reflected. "Yes," he said. "I saw it and was surprised. I have no idea where it came from, have never seen it before. Professor Nomura was a widower. His wife died about two years ago. They had no children. Professor Nomura has a brother, also childless."

"Thank you very much for your assistance, Kawane-*san*." He seemed visibly relieved the questioning was over. Inoue imagined he was jumping from the frying pan into the fire – there must be a million things to do if your boss has just been murdered.

Michiko's Fear

When Michiko Ota was led into the incident room, Inoue saw the same look of terror in her eyes he had noticed earlier. He couldn't imagine she had killed the president or was in mortal danger herself, so he couldn't account for it.

He pretended he had seen nothing, smiling pleasantly while gesturing the young woman to a seat. He noticed she was attractive if unfashionably well proportioned, a fact accentuated by her tight clothes. She had applied make-up lavishly, a common fashion but one he personally found off-putting. She dabbed with a pink cloth at the rivullets of perspiration trickling down her forehead. Her mascara was smeared.

Kubo handed her a glass of water that she gratefully accepted. Kubo seated himself and switched on the recording equipment. Inoue began his questioning. "Please tell us your name and occupation."

"My name is Michiko Ota. I have been employed as a clerk at Fujikawa University for the past six years."

"Please outline your duties."

"Because I know a little bit of English, I was put in charge of administering the professors' research budgets."

"Sorry, I don't see the connection."

Michiko Ota sighed, took a sip of the water, and wiped her

face. She was trying to collect her thoughts. She spoke slowly and deliberately. "Each professor, full-time, associate and assistant, is allocated a certain amount of money annually that he or she can spend on attending conferences, buying books, or on new office equipment. This money is known as research money. It's on top of the monthly salary. When Professor Nomura became the president, he insisted on greater accountability, wanting to know exactly how professors spent this money and whether their expenses were justified. Professors are now required to submit documents and receipts and even, at the beginning of each academic year, a plan for the use of this fund. A few of the foreign professors here speak very little Japanese. Naturally, they can't read or write it either. I explain the rules of their research budgets to them and help to fill out their forms."

"I see," Inoue said. "Thank you. May I ask about your movements this morning?"

"I live in Fujikawa. I'm from this town, and I attended this university as a student majoring in English. My parents died in a car crash when I was a child. I live at my grandmother's home, only ten minutes by car from the campus. My grandmother woke me at 7:00 as usual. I showered, got ready, had breakfast, and then I drove to the university, arriving at about 8.20. I happened to meet Andrew-*sensei*…Thomas-*sensei*, in the parking lot, and we walked together to the administration building."

"Did you notice anything out of the ordinary this morning, about Mr Thomas, or anything else?"

She took a moment before saying, "No." Her tone reminded Inoue of Miss Tanimoto when he had questioned her about the Canadian.

"Tell me what you and Mr Thomas talked about as you walked."

Miss Ota took her time again, then answered hesitantly, "Thomas-*sensei* admitted that he was worried about his job. He said he was meeting Nomura-*sensei* today."

"Was that all?"

There was a note of defiance as she spoke rapidly and emphatically. "Thomas- *sensei* is a kind person. I can't think about what happened to Nomura-*sensei*. It is unthinkable! I know Thomas-*sensei* had nothing to do with it."

"And what happened when you got to the administration building?"

"I was upset I was late. Two of the office women were already sweeping the court in front of the administration building. I hurried to get my own broom. I saw Professor Yamamoto briefly in the mailroom and, as I was leaving, Professor Hunter was coming in. I saw Miss Tanimoto approach the building to attend the morning meeting."

"Did you see Professor Nomura at all?"

"No, but that's normal. His office is in Building Two, and he'd arrive after ten."

"Thank you for your assistance, Miss Ota. You may go now but I may need you for questioning again."

Ando came in and told him the interviews of the administrative staff were finished and were being compiled. Professor Nomura's body had been taken away, the scene-of-crime officers had returned to the station, and they hoped to submit a preliminary forensics report within a few hours.

"We need to check several other matters now," Inoue told Ando. "First, I'd like you to interview a Professor Hayashi and ascertain that he visited Andrew Thomas this morning at the time Thomas said." Inoue consulted his notes. "Hayashi says he visited him at 9:00 and left at about 9.45."

"Yes, sir," said Ando, noting his instructions in a well-worn little notebook.

Inoue's face became stern. "Ando, you've been performing quite well during this investigation. Above expectations, I'd say. But your clothes are disgraceful. Please make sure you report for work tomorrow properly dressed, properly groomed."

Ando looked abashed. "Yes, sir. Sorry, sir."

"Okay, one more assignment. It's important. Get the addresses of two individuals who had a grudge against Professor Nomura. They lost their jobs here because of him four years ago, shortly after he became president. As for their names," and he consulted his notes again, "the two individuals in question are Akiyama, a former head of the administrative office, and Horii, who had worked here as a physics professor. You can get more information about them from Kawane. They both live in Fujikawa now."

Inoue looked at him and Kubo meaningfully. "I hope you know this murder investigation is a training opportunity. I am evaluating both of you. I am watching how well you do your work."

Inoue continued. "Once you have tracked down this pair, interview them separately and find out if they have an alibi for this morning or if they could have had anything to do with the president's death. Requisition a voice recorder from the station. Kubo, I need you here to record my interviews."

Kubo looked at him with surprise. There was even a hint of resentment shadowing his handsome young face. Inoue realised his favourite must wonder why he had entrusted Ando with the important responsibility of interviewing suspects while Kubo had the undemanding task of operating machinery.

But Inoue had no chance to offer consolation or explanation. The door flew open and a paunchy man in his fifties rushed in. He was wearing a three-piece wool suit and smoking a cigarette. Kubo and Ando tried to stop him, but he threw them off and marched straight up to Inoue. Admiring the man's nerve, Inoue bit back a reproach and instead greeted the unexpected visitor, all the while wondering how he could bear the heat wearing such an outfit.

"Chief Inspector Inoue," the man said in an agitated voice. "My name is Obuchi, I've been working as the deputy head here at Fujikawa University for several years. And in Professor Nomura's…regrettable absence…I'm in charge, temporarily at least."

Inoue felt he needed to observe the formalities as far as possible even if Obuchi was overexcited. He stood, bowed, drew out a business card and said, "I'm pleased to make your acquaintance, sir."

Obuchi did not reciprocate. He didn't bother reading the card but crumpled it in one hand and stuffed it in his pocket. He was distraught, breathing hard. He took a deep drag of his cigarette, knocking the ash on the floor. "We've no *time* for all that. I have parents on the phone. Some are even turning up on campus. They wonder if their children are safe. Of course, we've sent everyone home for the day. At least we're mercifully close to the summer holiday..." He threw up his hands in melodramatic despair. His cigarette fell on the floor. Ando picked it up, pinched out the flame with his fingers, and threw it in a bin.

Professor Obuchi suddenly fell silent. He got out another cigarette, lit it, and took a deep puff. He was having trouble breathing. His weight and heavy clothing made matters worse. The professor's ruddy face paled as he gasped out: "It's a *disaster*!"

Inoue put up a hand to reassure him. "Sir, we have officers

stationed around the campus. We can reassure the parents about the students' safety. We will have officers on campus for several days. I think the exams will be finished by the time we are ready to leave."

Professor Obuchi was still breathing heavily but continued puffing on his cigarette. His other hand clutched his chest. Inoue said gently, worrying the man might have a heart attack, "It must be a terrible shock to you, sir."

"Yes, yes, yes!" Obuchi said impatiently. "A great shock. Horrible!"

Obuchi managed to get a grip on himself. "I've scheduled a special chapel service for our president for tomorrow afternoon. Classes won't resume until the day after, out of respect for the dead. We just have to get the students through their end-of-term exams."

Now Obuchi looked angrily at Inoue, as if blaming him for the crisis. Blowing smoke in Inoue's direction he demanded, "How are your enquiries? Any leads?"

"We are questioning people seen around the crime scene. We've had forensics in the president's office and at Building Two. We're expecting their findings and the post- mortem report soon, and we are following leads."

Obuchi pressed his lips together in a sour expression, turned on his heel to leave, before pausing at the door to fire off a parting shot: "I'm sure you're doing your best, Inspector. I'm confident you're able to handle the petty crime we get in little

Fujikawa. However, this might be out of your league. I'll be frank – I've contacted the prefectural governor to ask if Superintendent Takenaka can head this investigation."

Obuchi saw Inoue's angry look and turned sharply away. Then he stubbed out his cigarette in the ashtray on the desk, and immediately lit another. He took a puff or two and, emboldened, looked at Inoue again. "The governor rang me an hour ago to say that he would consider my request. It's such a high-profile case! It must be solved quickly. You'll need all the help you can get."

Obuchi took a deep drag on his cigarette and remarking, as a final shot, "You'll hear from somebody about this matter soon," sped out of the room.

Ando and Kubo studiously looked away. Inoue's face was mottled with rage as his right fist hit the desk in front of him, hard, and he gave a gusty angry sigh.

The Feminist Professor

Professor Yamamoto was put out. She looked thin and unhappy as Kubo escorted her into the incident room. Inoue flexed his aching right hand. He thought she looked like a bird, a heron perhaps, with feathers dyed in purple, yellow and orange. He half expected her to fold wings rather than arms on her chest as she perched on the edge of a chair.

Once she was seated, it all came out. "I'd expect a policeman, at least, to keep his word," she accused Inoue sharply. "You told Gerald, Miss Ota and me that we could decide which of us would be interviewed next. We'd decided it was to be me, but then you called for her."

It was obvious this ageing hippie had a temper. "I'm sorry, Professor Yamamoto. Please forgive us for that oversight."

"One reason I wanted to go before Miss Ota was to ask you to treat her gently. She doesn't have an easy life. She's caring for a grandmother in the early stages of dementia, an old person who can barely walk let alone remember what she did an hour before, not surprising as she's ninety-two. Poor Miss Ota must wait on her hand and foot. Community volunteers look after the old woman while Miss Ota is at work."

"I hope Miss Ota won't complain of our treatment of her. We only had a few

questions to ask. We offered her a lift home, but she wanted to drive herself."

Miss Yamamoto settled back in her chair, wrapping her long, purple tasselled scarf around a withered neck. "Well, I do like to have promises kept," she said. "I think truth-telling and promise-keeping are the foundations of a moral life. I make a point of telling my girls in their women's studies classes that they should never tell lies, never pretend, or else it will come back to haunt them."

Inoue was intrigued. "And your male students? I think, historically, they have a poorer record of keeping their word than females."

"I seldom get any boys in my classes. Perhaps I intimidate them."

Inoue was beginning to understand that. This wrinkled old woman with her long grey braid was a force to be reckoned with.

Professor Yamamoto smoothed her yellow beaded tunic and crossed her legs clad in billowing orange material. A foot in an ancient sandal of cracked black leather jiggled up and down.

"Well, let's get on with it," she said, "I have marking to do." She was peering at Inoue. "Wait! I think I remember you. Weren't you here decades ago? I never forget a face. You hung out with the boys majoring in baseball. It was odd because you were bright, but your friends weren't. They could handle a ball and bat and run fast but they weren't academic. I wondered why you bothered with them. I also wondered why their parents sent them to college. They didn't want to study. This place isn't cheap."

Kubo's enjoying this, Inoue thought. The note of the personal. Again! Time to reassert control over this interview. "Yes, I was once a student here, Professor Yamamoto, but we need to focus on the matter at hand … the murder of the college president," he said.

"Oh yes, sorry," she said, a little defensively.

But Yamamoto-*sensei* had rattled him. It suddenly came back to him: an attractive female professor at Fujikawa University who had taught sociology and women's studies. He'd never taken any of her classes, but as a young man he was attracted to beauty and had admired her lovely face and figure. He'd stare as she strode rapidly about the campus in unconventional dress – jeans and plaid shirts, if he recalled correctly – her long black hair swinging. Had that been *her*? She must have been in her late thirties or even early forties at the time, but she had looked much younger.

"If we could get back to the matter at hand," said Inoue sternly. "We need to ask you about your movements this morning."

"Oh, yes," Professor Yamamoto said, suddenly sitting up and smiling, her eyes shining. "I'm a great fan of murder mysteries – not Japanese ones, they're too gory, too concerned with social realism – but the amusing puzzles set by western writers like Agatha Christie. A very important bit in Christie's stories is taking people's statements, catching them out with discrepancies."

"I'd like to remind you, professor, this isn't a game. Somebody has been killed."

She looked apologetic, and he continued in a softer voice. "Well, I'm sure we can rely on the truth of your statement, Professor Yamamoto, particularly in light of your beliefs.

Was there a hint of anxiety in Professor Yamamoto's eyes? She pursed her lips and sat up in her chair before saying, "I will answer questions to the best of my ability."

"How long have you worked at Fujikawa?"

"I got my job here about thirty years ago now. Impossible to believe it's been so long."

"Please tell us what time you arrived at the university this morning?"

"I live in a small flat just ten minutes' walk from the campus. I tend to get here early. I get my daily exercise by walking round the boundary of the campus for about twenty-five minutes. Then I go to the administration building to collect my mail and sign in before heading for my office."

"And what time did you arrive today?"

"I must have got here about 8.00 and, after doing my circuit of the campus a few times, went to get my mail. I saw Miss Ota looking for a broom. I got a few official documents out of my mailbox. Then Professor Hunter came in to collect his mail. Miss Tanimoto rushed in before going to the main staff room…that settles the time. She was on her way to her 8.30 meeting, so it was before then."

She glanced out the window. The trees bordering the building were motionless, their dusty leaves hanging limp, bathed in a bright yellow light. "In the summer, I try to get up earlier than usual to catch the cooler temperatures. After finding the usual boring official documents in my mailbox, I went to Building Eight, where my office is. I remembered that I hadn't signed the attendance book. I went back to do that. I was irritated at myself. I felt I was getting old, forgetting things! But I was also glad to get out. I was restless, I didn't want to be in my room."

"I'm not sure I understand," Inoue said.

Professor Yamamoto looked wistful.

"I'm getting old," she finally went on, looking at him almost shyly. "More and more, I feel I have to make every moment count. Once I would have plonked myself down at my computer to read stories on the Internet about people I've never met, living in places I'll never visit. Now I want to keep more active. Can you understand that at all?"

Inoue asked another question. "Did you see anyone else on your first visit to the administration building, apart from Miss Ota and Professor Hunter, Miss Tanimoto and Professor Thomas?"

"No. Professor Hunter and I happened to leave the building

at the same time, and we stopped and chatted for a few minutes. There were cleaners about, students lounging around, but I took their presence for granted, hardly noticed them."

"So you went to your office but then remembered you needed to sign in."

"Yes, I did. Another of our president's innovations. We used to be trusted to appear at the university every day, but now we have to prove we're here, have our attendance checked, like children, by writing our names in a book in the admin office."

"And did you see anyone then?"

"I had tests to prepare. I rushed over, signed in and hurried back to my room." There may have been a cleaner in the courtyard. My powers of observation aren't what they were."

Inoue looked at the birdlike woman. She was a shrewd judge of character and he wanted her thoughts on the deceased. "Can you tell us your own personal feelings about Professor Nomura? Was he a good president?"

"I can't see how my opinion of him is relevant."

"Please humour me, Professor. I'm trying to draw a picture of Professor Nomura, get some idea of him, of how he was regarded by others."

"People always say we mustn't speak ill of the dead," she said, "but I can't hold to that. If you couldn't stand somebody in life, why not say so after the person dies?"

"And your opinion of Professor Nomura?"

"I hated him," she said flatly. "I didn't kill him, but I'm glad he's gone." "And the reasons for your dislike?"

"He was a sexist pig," she said angrily. "He was abusing his power and privilege with some of our young female undergraduates. One in particular, a bright girl named Mari Furomoto. I sometimes saw her going in and out of his office. He needed the company of a compliant woman, any woman, after Liza died. She was a good friend of mine, like a sister, but I never understood what she saw in that man. She knew how I felt. We tacitly agreed never to talk about him."

Professor Yamamoto was staring straight ahead, absorbed in her memories. Now she looked directly at Inoue, glaring. "I had been here for many years before that upstart came. Wretched man. I watched his rise to power, saw him inveigling his way to the top. He cared nothing for the university's original mission: to give hope to those who were outcasts in society and to train social workers who would help such people. Maybe he didn't care. I was hired at a time when the whole staff had to be baptised Christians. Nomura was supposedly a Christian, but in name only. He saw the university as a little pet project. He wanted to rescue the college and make it a paying concern. He also liked the sense of power he got from being its president."

"Is there anything else?" "It's just…"

"Yes?" Inoue said brusquely, still prepared to listen.

"I have what you policemen call 'form'." She blushed.

Now Inoue could trace the outline of a youthful, beautiful face amid the lines and sourness. "Once your charming young officer insisted on taking our fingerprints, I knew I must 'fess up. Curious but I never thought my past would catch up with me."

She leaned back, a dreamy look in her eyes. "When I was in my early twenties, in my senior year at Tokyo University in 1968, I got caught up in the student demonstrations."

Her features softened and she smiled.

"May I ask what you were protesting against?"

"The Vietnam War, apartheid in South Africa, the grip of capitalists on the world economy. We couldn't bear the injustices: the rich getting richer, the poor getting poorer. Being young and educated and privileged, we felt we had to right the world's wrongs."

"And were you arrested at that time?"

"My boyfriend and I were attending a big demonstration in Shinjuku and somehow we got the idea to help in turning over a police car that was parked there."

"I see. Then you were both taken to the police station and fingerprinted."

"Yes, yes, that's right. We were both from well-off families. We felt we were striking a blow for those who had been born less fortunate."

"I can imagine your parents were horrified."

"Of course. I got packed off to America as soon as I was released from jail. I finished my first degree by correspondence from there and then did a postgraduate course at Harvard. But all my parents' efforts to make me a normal, law-abiding member of society came to nothing. While I was in Boston, I was caught up in the feminist movement sweeping the States."

She smiled again and her eyes brightened. "It was all so exciting! I was thrilled to be a part of it. I felt I was making the world a better place. At least for the half of its population that wasn't male."

It irritated Inoue to see the younger woman, radiant with the happy optimism of youth, shining out in fits and starts from the wrinkled old woman before him. It was a reminder of mortality. It gripped his heart with pity, and the easiest way to deal with soppy emotion, he had learned, was to react with anger.

"Yamamoto-*sensei*! I must ask you again to consider the gravity of the occasion," he said harshly. "This is a *murder* investigation."

His tone surprised her and brought her back to the ugly little room with laptops lined up on the tables, shiny whiteboard, stained walls and scuffed tile floor.

"I'm so sorry, Chief Inspector Inoue. I got carried away, reliving old memories." She looked down at hands that resembled bird's claws but also looked surprisingly strong.

"My father was a wealthy businessman, influential in high places. He pulled strings. I got off with no criminal record, but my fingerprints must still be on file."

"I imagine so. Professor Yamamoto, please give details of your life and career for our records."

"My name is Mutsuko Yamamoto. I am from Tokyo. I did my first degree at Tokyo University and then a Ph.D. at Harvard in women's studies."

"So you graduated from Tokyo University, got a doctorate from Harvard, then settled for our mediocre local college."

"I'll be honest with you," Professor Yamamoto said. "It's all laughable and pathetic, but I had my heart broken, first by that fellow revolutionary in Tokyo in the late '60s, and then by an American in Boston. Fujikawa, a little place off the map, offered me a place to lick my wounds and recover. I didn't want to be near my parents, who tended to reproach me with my youthful indiscretions."

The old woman straightened and looked serious: "Also, Fujikawa gave me more freedom to teach what I really want to teach than I'd have been given at a prestigious university with more rigorous standards."

"I'm sorry to hear heartbreak brought you to our little rural corner of Japan, Professor Yamamoto."

She glared defiantly at him. "I don't want your pity or sympathy. I want your understanding. I'm not a victim. It was a blessing in disguise, and I decided to liberate Japan's farmers' daughters by teaching them women's studies – telling them their rights."

"Forgive me, but isn't that a bit of a cliché? A woman gets ditched by a man and becomes a man hater?"

She picked her bag up from the floor ready to go. She was angry, with herself as much as with the good inspector. "I don't hate men," she snapped. "I hated *that* man, Nomura, a predator and a cad, however efficient he might have been at turning this college's fortunes around. But I didn't mean to confide such personal details. I have told you my movements this morning. If you have any further questions, I'd like to have the services of my lawyer."

She stood up. Inoue got up too. "My apologies if I have offended you, Professor." He bowed as she left the room. She banged the door behind her.

A Professor with a Mission

"Only one more interview, sir," Kubo said, cheerily. Usually Kubo's enthusiasm pleased Inoue. Today it was only one more irritant.

"Please summon Professor Hunter," he said sharply. A slight, black, even funereal figure entered the room. This was their first proper meeting, but Inoue felt he already knew Professor Hunter in the way he 'knew' any celebrity. Five years earlier, Professor Hunter had contested the national policy of routinely fingerprinting second-generation Koreans resident in Japan.

Gerald's advocacy of this cause resulted in his picture's being regularly featured in the Fujikawa newspapers. Inoue had even seen Gerald's thin angular face on national news programmes as he explained, in perfect Japanese, his dislike of a policy that treated those Koreans as if they were aliens even though they had been born and raised in Japan, thought of Japan as their home, didn't speak Korean and had probably never even been to Korea.

Inoue knew Gerald's action had won him the gratitude of Koreans throughout the country. He also knew it had attracted the enmity of right-wingers, outraged that a foreigner should dare to criticise Japan. The university became a focus for their anger, and the police had to be on the alert each spring and autumn when it was a ritual for large black vans decorated with nationalist slogans to circle the campus slowly, blaring out patriotic slogans and songs from loudspeakers.

Inoue had heard rumours that Professor Nomura hated Gerald for bringing notoriety to Fujikawa and worried that the right-wingers' campaign against him might give the university a bad reputation and frighten off students. Complicating matters, given the close links between Japan's right-wingers and the armed forces, was the fact that the president had a brother based in the army camp next to the university.

Inoue thought Gerald looked different from the photographs or his television appearances. Then he realised Gerald had shaved off his beard, and quite recently by the looks of it. Also, that striking quiff of bright blonde-grey hair looked flattened. There was a thin, scarcely perceptible red line across his forehead. He had lately worn a hat.

Inoue bowed and beckoned Gerald to a seat. "No need for an interpreter, Professor Hunter?"

"No, I feel Japanese has become my first language. When I return to the States, I make mistakes in English!"

"Please tell us your name and occupation."

Gerald shifted in his seat saying, "I'll never complain again when my students sprawl at their desks. I had no idea those seats were so uncomfortable! I must have been sitting next door for two hours while you were interviewing everyone else. I used to feel it a hardship having to stand up to lecture. Now I realise how lucky I am."

"We apologise, Professor Hunter, for making you wait. Again, may I have your name and details of your work here?"

"But you know all that…Oh, I see, you are making an official transcript of our conversation. My name is Gerald Hunter. I am an American, and I've been a resident in Japan for thirty years, working at this college since my arrival. I teach English and Christianity, also helping with events at the chapel as I am a Presbyterian missionary and minister."

"Please account for your movements this morning." "Am I a suspect?"

"We must ask these questions of everyone."

"I live on campus." Now Gerald rose and walked to the window. "You can see my home from here, that two-storey, blue, wood-frame house."

"It's one of the largest of the professors' homes on campus, I believe."

"Yes, when I first arrived and began working here, the teaching staff at Fujikawa was much smaller than it is now. We were strongly urged to live on campus so our students could visit us on an informal basis. Accommodation was provided. I think I enjoyed some preferential treatment in housing because of my links with the American Presbyterian mission board."

"Did this cause any resentment?"

"I'm sure it did, particularly among younger members of the staff who were expected to settle in the smaller houses on campus regardless of how large their families were. I live on my own in a huge house. But I didn't get murdered for it."

"And this morning?"

"As I'm on campus, I can easily get to first-period classes on time even if I rise at

8.00. That's what I did today. I got up at 8.00, had breakfast, and then sauntered to my

office. I wanted to get the tests ready for my second-period class, the end-of-term exam for religious studies, a compulsory course for all the first-years. I had to make sure I had enough copies."

"Was there anything unusual about this morning?"

"No, apart from deciding to make an early start. I usually sign in after nine, but I was at Building One today before 8.30. As I entered by the back entrance, I could see Kawane-*san* at his desk. Another professor, Yamamoto-*sensei*, was there, collecting her mail, and we exchanged greetings. Miss Ota, one of the office workers, was around. I think she was looking for a broom. Miss Tanimoto came in on her way to the staff meeting. As I approached the building, I saw two office women whose names I don't know outside, sweeping up litter, and the clerk Mr Akamatsu picking up rubbish with tongs. I also saw a cleaner, emptying the bins. And maybe another cleaner on a ladder washing the windows of Building

Two."

"Anyone else? Did you see Professor Nomura at all?"

"No, but I briefly met him last night. I was walking round the campus at about nine, saw his office windows lit, and exchanged greetings with him."

"How did he seem?"

"I imagine you've heard this from other people. He had been under a lot of strain lately. I thought he was losing weight. There were signs of ageing such as his hair turning grey, but the change in the past week was extraordinary. He looked terrible – gaunt, stooped and white-haired. When I saw him yesterday evening, he was in a foul mood. He complained he'd have to spend the night in his office to finish off some important work."

"Did he give you any idea what that work was?" "No. He didn't confide in me."

"Now to the events of this morning…"

"After I'd signed in and collected my mail, I chatted briefly with Professor Yamamoto and then went to my office in Building Five. As I've said, I was to give a test during the second period, from 11.10, to a class of over a hundred, so I needed to make sure I had a sufficient number of copies. I was in my office until a little after 10.00, when I heard a commotion outside in the courtyard. I looked out to see you arriving with an officer, accompanied by Kawane-*san* and Akamatsu-*san*, hurrying into Building Two. It was obvious something was amiss."

"And then?"

"It's human nature to be curious about untoward events; I was compelled to rush down and find out. I saw officers sealing off the courtyard and Building Two with yellow tape. Then I heard the president had been murdered. I returned to my office. Within an hour, I was summoned to Building Six by one of your officers for interviewing."

"Can anyone vouch you were in your office from, say, 8.35 onwards?"

"No, we're not a very sociable bunch on my corridor. We keep our office doors closed and see each other by appointment. I tend only to see my fellow lecturers if we pass each other in the corridor going to the toilet or to classes."

"Can you tell us anything that might be of assistance? What was your impression of Professor Nomura? Would you say he was a man who had enemies?"

Gerald considered for a moment. "It's no secret that he did, and that I might be considered one. We hadn't seen eye to eye since his arrival fifteen years ago, and relations between us got steadily worse when he was elected president five years ago."

"You've been employed a long time here, twice as long as Professor Nomura; you must have felt some resentment of him and his power?"

"Yes, but I was not the only one with reservations about his changes."

"Yes, of course. Can you tell me about the two staff members sacked four years ago? And taking their case for unfair dismissal to court."

"They lost, oddly enough."

"They are both still resident in Fujikawa. Doesn't that strike you as odd?"

"Yes, I used to meet them sometimes, but not recently. Akiyama-*san*, was Kawane-*san*'s predecessor as the manager of the clerical staff and the other was Professor Horii, who taught physics. He had an office near me; we managed a kind of friendship."

"But you hardly see them now?"

"They were so traumatised by events that I think they cope by keeping to themselves. They were both forcibly expelled from the campus. Professor Horii collapsed when a guard came to escort him away. He was in hospital for about a week."

Hunter sighed. "Poor bastards. They weren't even allowed to return to their offices to collect their belongings. Somebody boxed up their things and sent them on. I suppose you've heard that Nomura employed two guards for a year expressly to keep these two individuals out. They lost the initial court case but lodged an appeal."

"I didn't know that," Inoue said.

"Well, they lost that too. It's understandable they're

reluctant to see anyone related to that unhappy period. I occasionally run into them in local coffee shops, but we pretend not to see each other."

"Why on earth have they stayed in the area? I should think they would like to forget this place altogether after suffering such humiliation."

"Unlike Nomura they are Fujikawa born and bred, as well as being graduates of this university. Their parents are here. They are both eldest sons, and in a rural community like this, are expected to make their homes with their parents and take care of them in old age."

"One last question, please, Professor Hunter. Have you heard anything about Akamatsu-*san*?"

"The college is a cesspit of gossip. That spiteful woman in accounts – what's her name? Oh, yes, Araki-*san*. Well, she's been hinting some money's gone missing and is pointing the finger at Akamatsu-*san*, one of the more decent members of staff in my opinion. It's wrong of her to accuse him, causing him stress considering he has a heart condition."

"So there's no foundation to this rumour?"

"I can't imagine Akamatsu-*san* being involved in anything criminal. He's nothing like the recently departed. I'm not one to speak ill of the dead, but have you heard the rumours that Professor Nomura acted inappropriately with some female students? It may well be malicious gossip, but I think you should know."

Gerald stood up to leave.

"Sorry, Professor, but I have just one more question, please," said Inoue. "It's been a long day. I'd like to go home."

"Were you surprised to hear that Professor Nomura had been murdered?"

"It was a *yappari* moment," said Gerald. "I somehow always expected it. He attracted enemies like a long-haired dog gets covered with burrs."

"How did you feel when you heard of his death?"

"That's a second question, but never mind. Although I'm a Christian, when I learned he'd been killed, I thought of the demise of an irritating fly."

Inoue recalled the bloated specimen that had gorged on Nomura's corpse. "Thank you, Professor."

After Gerald had walked stiffly out, Inoue stood, scratched his belly, and then said to Kubo, "Please get these interviews typed up and begin computer checks on everyone we've questioned. And chase up those rumours of the president's hitting on young girls. There may be someone spurned, who decided to have her revenge. 'Hell hath no fury like a woman scorned.' I'm off to the station."

Inoue was glad he had managed to memorize some famous English quotes and could use them aptly from time to time. He doubted if students bothered learning such things today. It was good to put the crime scene behind him. This relief was offset by the reflection that the station that he considered his home away from home had been transformed by the presence of the detestable Takenaka. It was no longer a desirable destination. Could it be that Takenaka would still be there in Inoue's own office, filling the air with his damnable cigarette smoke, gimlet-eyes behind thick black glasses, waiting to interrogate him, to find out if he'd made any progress?

The young officer driving them back there felt Inoue's frustration when the Chief barked out, "Get a *move on*. I would like to get to the station before nightfall."

Inoue's Blonde Wife

Ellie Marshall Inoue had just stepped out of a shower and into a beige linen dress when she got a call from her husband. It was not the voice of the Kenji who shared their home. It was the brusque, official voice of the Chief Inspector of Fujikawa police sternly informing Ellie her husband would be late and telling her he'd like sushi for dinner. Only when ringing off did it return to familiar tenderness, a soft whisper, with Inoue promising to explain everything when he got home, whenever that might be.

Ellie had tried numerous diets, but she stayed obstinately fat. She tried to eat the right food and didn't drink alcohol. It was no use. She remained almost clinically obese. She had a pretty doll's face with porcelain skin, china-blue eyes, a rosebud mouth and thick blonde hair worn in a braid curled on top of her head. But the doll's face was attached to a stout figure.

Inoue often told his wife she was his moral compass. She would sniff in apparent disbelief when he said that, but she was pleased to be of use to one person in Japan. She had arrived in the country twelve years earlier, in her early twenties, to serve as a missionary, inspired by an article in a church bulletin bemoaning the fact that less than one per cent of Japanese were Christians. She was full of evangelical zeal but quickly found that the polite nice Japanese had no interest in anything she wanted to teach them about religion.

Naturally, as a fellow missionary living in the same town, Professor Gerald Hunter made her acquaintance. She found him slightly intimidating in his black attire with his bearded, intent face, but he was friendly enough. She was grateful for his promise to find her some work teaching English at his university.

Then, out of the blue one Sunday morning, Ellie no longer believed. The service lasted three hours, the sermon taking over half that time. The Japanese congregation showed no sign of impatience. They listened with bent heads and downcast eyes, sang the hymns loudly and knelt by their pews in prayer.

Ellie usually relished Sunday services, but this time it was different. She was bored. When asked to confess her sins, she could find no words. The connection between her

and a personal deity was suddenly severed. When she tried to pray it was as if she was addressing empty space. Somehow, at a stroke, she had lost her faith.

She was able to keep up appearances. She couldn't express her true feelings to Gerald Hunter. She never doubted the sincerity of his own religious convictions, but he was an individual who seemed to have little understanding of or sympathy with human weakness. Ellie continued to attend the tiny church near the city centre with its congregation of twenty. She read the Bible every morning and evening, trying to renew her faith. But it was a charade. There had been no nagging doubts. Her faith had simply evaporated as mysteriously and completely as it had appeared when she was converted as an adolescent at a revival meeting at her school in the American Midwest. She stayed on in Japan, hoping it might reappear.

Gerald had been as good as his word and found Ellie part-time work at the local university on the strength of her American BA. Teaching English conversation classes three times a week helped to supplement her meagre allowance from the mission board. She didn't much care for the president, who would sweep by without returning her greetings, but that didn't matter – the staff and students treated her with solicitous affection. She was friendly with two of the secretaries. As a Christian, albeit a lapsed one, she admired the college's policy of recruiting students who were disabled or who suffered social discrimination.

When Gerald Hunter heard Ellie had been invited to a summer festival, he encouraged her to attend. "It's all pagan ritual, of course," he said disparagingly, "a mix of Buddhism and Shintoism, but they seem to believe in it." He'd sighed, "It's such a pity to be so delusional."

Ellie met the man who would become her husband at this festival.

Along with the other westerners resident in Fujikawa, Ellie

had been asked to join a foreigners' dance troupe that would parade down the town's main street. Their participation had been arranged by a local cultural centre keen on helping the city to promote international relations.

Ellie had to attend weeks of practice sessions at the centre. On the night of the performance, staff at the cultural centre put her hair up in a bun, applied heavy make- up, and swathed her body in a light kimono lent especially for the occasion.

The evening had not got off to the best of starts. Not only was she the object of stares, but the sweltering heat of a Japanese summer night in the tightness of the kimono made her uncomfortable before she had even begun to dance. She felt ridiculous and fat.

While her friends were jumping up and down in excitement, awaiting the signal that would send them off to join the parade, she sat down on a large rock by the roadside, flapping her hands in an attempt to cool her red, perspiring face.

A muscular, bullet-headed man in police uniform approached and gave her a paper fan. His English was minimal, but he managed to ask if she was all right. Then Mr Tani, the cultural centre's organiser, came up. They had been high school classmates, and they chatted briefly. The policeman went off to set up barriers on the road for the procession.

Mr Tani said, "Inoue-*san*. He's one of the best. After we graduated from high school, he went to a local university and

I went to one in Tokyo, but we've always kept in touch. He fulfilled a childhood dream, becoming a policeman."

As he and Ellie went to join the parade group, Tani added, almost as an afterthought, "Oh, Inoue-*san* has a hobby, learning English. He would like to meet you again to give him a few lessons."

Ellie had been reluctant. What could she have in common with a policeman? Back home they were called pigs. She decided to meet him again though.

Ellie Marshall and Kenji Inoue were married within the year.

In the early months of their relationship, before Ellie became fluent in Japanese, the language barrier didn't matter. Kenji was a man of few words. Their real form of communication was non-verbal. Kenji had eloquent eyes.

Uxorious. It was a word Ellie had known as a high school student tackling the vocabulary section of the university entrance exam. In knowing and loving Kenji, the word had changed for her. No longer an abstract in a dictionary, a word in Scrabble. It was real, and it was how her reticent, burly husband felt about her.

Ellie and Kenji settled in a small, prefabricated house near his mother's farmhouse. Kenji's mother was a widow, her husband dying four years ago. She was a small elderly woman with the exquisite politeness of a bygone age. On Ellie's first meeting with her future mother-in-law, she was shocked when the tiny figure not only knelt in the *genkan* but then prostrated herself on the floor, uttering words of welcome.

Ellie loved her husband's mother. It didn't matter when Kenji admitted one night he couldn't remember ever being kissed or held by her as a child.

"It's not our way," he had muttered. If God had blessed them with children, Ellie was sure she would never have stopped kissing and hugging them. But they were not blessed with children, a considerable sorrow, requiring all their love to overcome it.

In marrying Kenji, Ellie felt she had entered into an agreement that was all the more powerful and binding for never having been verbally expressed. She would keep her side of the bargain with loyalty and trust. Their love was special, a sacred pact that could not be broken. Whenever Ellie and Kenji were with other people, and particularly with Japanese, they acted with reserve towards each other as though they were strangers, despite being married and sharing a home.

On the rare occasions when Kenji invited a colleague or a friend back to their house, Ellie knew the part she was expected to play. She would bow, offer slippers, and disappear to the kitchen. She would brew the coffee and serve it with all the paraphernalia and custom expected. She would enter the front room with the deference of a servant, placing cups and saucers carefully before Kenji and friend, bowing before she left them to return to the kitchen.

When they were with his mother, Kenji regarded Ellie with bemused indulgence, as though his affection for her were a weakness. To help her become fluent in Japanese, her husband didn't translate for her. In the early years of her marriage, as she struggled to communicate with her new mother-in-law, Kenji would look away in embarrassment as if she were performing a trick badly.

Apart from her husband, Ellie made only one other true friend in Japan. At the university, Gerald was too intimidating. One colleague at the college, Ben, was too much of a pompous know-it-all who saw himself as an old Japan-hand, and another, Stephen, was always finding something to moan about.

Only the Canadian Andrew Thomas, who had arrived two years earlier, an unpromising partner in tow, offered her genuine companionship. She could tell him anything and he would listen with warm, uncritical attentiveness. She thought him unusually mature. He told her how, after leaving high school, he'd spent two years working at a ranch before going to university. She confided in him her loss of faith. He simply accepted it all. He never tried to change her mind about anything, and he could keep a secret.

She often wondered what Andrew saw in that ice queen, Alyson, who shared his home and presumably his bed. It was incredible that he had asked her to be his wife. As if by mutual consent, the one topic Andrew and Ellie skirted was their partners. He never asked about Kenji, and she never mentioned Alyson. But Andrew was surprised she had married a policeman while Ellie pitied him for being with Alyson.

The day Professor Nomura was murdered was a typical day for Ellie. After getting her husband's phone call and learning he wouldn't be home till late, Ellie settled

down to her usual routine. She didn't ask questions of her husband about his work and never complained. She knew he had to keep irregular hours – and secrets. She filled her time by doing the laundry and ironing, gardening, and cleaning the house. She rarely listened to the radio or watched television and they didn't get a paper. That afternoon she cycled to the nearest grocery store and bought vegetables and the sushi she had promised her husband for their supper. It was only then that she allowed herself the luxury of settling in front of a whirring electric fan with a good book to await his return.

The heat made Ellie feel uncomfortable. She often put her book aside to rise and look out the window. Twice she ventured to the front gate, gazing down the road, hoping to see Kenji's car. The bright blue of the morning sky had given way to a mottled layer of white. Soon thick grey clouds hung overhead like the roughly plastered ceiling of a sauna. She felt rivulets of sweat streaming down her legs and between her breasts. Her light dress clung to her back and thighs. She wished she were at least a stone lighter. She hated being so fat. A large black crow on a telephone pole beside her house cawed derisively. A helmeted man on a red motorbike screeched to a halt beside the front gate and, as he delivered a bundle of letters and a small parcel, he and Ellie bowed to each other.

When Inoue got home after 10.00, Ellie wondered, after her long hot day, whether she looked as tired as he did. She had learned to wait for her husband to speak first. She rushed to the entranceway as she heard the front door open, taking his jacket to hang up as he silently stepped into the slippers she had laid out for him. Three bottles of beer were cooling in the fridge, and the rice in the rice-cooker was freshly made. He usually had only two. She had put in an extra bottle to comfort him after his long day with Takenaka. With the beer was an assortment of savoury rice crackers criss-crossed with glossy bands of seaweed and bundles of asparagus wrapped in bacon and then fried in butter. A pan of miso soup was on the stove, needing only to be warmed up, and plates of sushi and stewed vegetables lay on the polished low table.

Kenji had given Ellie the surprise of her life ten years earlier, when he had asked her, in halting English, to marry him.

She never thought he would top that, but tonight he did after she poured his beer.

Taking a long drink nearly emptying the glass, he said,

"Some fool of a foreigner stumbled across a dead body at the university."

Ellie knew her husband well. He liked spring news on her. He also loved teasing her and knew it pleased him to add, "It's that even greater fool of a president there, Nomura, who's got himself killed."

Then he took another swig of beer and grinned at his wife as he delivered the knockout line. "It was your friend Andrew who found him."

A Country Girl

Michiko Ota entered the house she shared with her grandmother with a sense of dread. It was late in the afternoon. She had rejected a policeman's offer of a ride home. She wanted to go by herself. She needed to be alone. She would use the time in her car to compose herself. The journey was only ten minutes, but that was enough.

She drove carefully up a narrow road like a tunnel with its high walls of cement breezeblocks on either side. Some parts of the road retained the old mud walls that used to separate family compounds. Michiko manoeuvred the steering wheel carefully. Even though she had bought the smallest type of car possible, it was easy to scrape its sides on walls crowded inches from the road.

Near the top of the hill, she steered the car through a narrow gate and parked it in front of the house. She noticed her grandmother had managed to hobble from the house and hang out the laundry, draping it on metal bars beside the outdoor toilet to flap in the sultry breeze. No fabric softener for this old woman, who had such an ingrained thriftiness she used linen until it was in rags. The towels and sheets felt like cardboard Michiko thought as she gathered the stiff pieces in her arms before going inside.

She slid back the glass front door to be assailed by the

familiar choking fug: a mixture of cooking smells, mould and dust. She sniffed at the lingering odours of all their recent dinners: stewed pumpkin, boiled spinach, Japanese hot pot, curry, *miso* soup and cooked rice. These were traditional dishes whose odour had become part of the very fabric of the house.

Even with all the windows thrown open on this hot July afternoon and despite Michiko's zealousness – scrubbing, spraying deodorizers, using cleansers – there was also a faint scent of decay, the mustiness of age. Dust particles floated in the air and a streak of mildew on a panel of the shoe cupboard in the *genkan* looked like a wisp of pale cloud painted by Monet.

Michiko and her grandmother lived in a traditional Japanese farmhouse over a hundred years old. It was a squat black building with a heavy tiled roof fronted by a small garden. A dusty courtyard bounded by a mud wall separated the house from the road. Adjoining the house were sheds that held the equipment once used by Michiko's grandfather when he had been one of the largest orange growers in the area. There

were cupboards of white gloves, broad-brimmed straw hats, and pruning scissors. Shoulder bags used for harvesting hung from nails on the walls, above stacks of cardboard boxes and piles of the twine, tape and scissors needed to pack up the oranges to take to the market by truck.

One room was filled with small wooden boxes to store the

fruit until the market price was deemed good enough to pack it for sale. An ancient conveyor belt that polished and sorted the oranges by size was abandoned at the back, covered with dust and cobwebs. A portable spraying machine kept it company, its shoulder harness rusty and the plastic container for spraying preservatives against disease was wrinkled with age and even cracked in places.

Unless Michiko ended up marrying a farmer, unlikely because few local young men wanted that job, none of that equipment would ever be used again. Her grandfather's death ten years earlier had meant the death of the farm as a going concern.

Michiko closed the glass sliding door, kicked off her sandals and lined them up beside the three pairs of her grandmother's impossibly tiny slip-on shoes in the *genkan*. She called out "*Tadaima*, I'm home" as she stepped up into the hall and deposited the stiff bundle of laundry on the floor.

A thin, reedy voice called out from the kitchen: "Mi-*chan*! *Okaerinasai*. Welcome home. You're back early today, aren't you?"

Her grandmother was seated as always at the cluttered kitchen table, picking desultorily at a heap of papers, books, magazines and newspapers and tattered old photographs. A cardboard box that once held stationery now served as a medical chest. It was filled with aluminium-wrapped pills doctors prescribed for the old woman. There was a teapot half full of green tea, a matching cup with a chipped rim, and a pair of scissors and a tissue box. A black velvet box housing a hearing aid had a pair of wooden chopsticks across it, and there were three pairs of reading glasses. Michiko's grandmother looked smaller than ever, a miniature figure wearing a blouse above baggy polyester trousers bent over the table. She picked up a piece of paper and scrutinized it, holding it close to her eyes.

Michiko checked the plastic lunch box that had been delivered in her absence by a city social worker and was relieved to find all its individual compartments were nearly empty. From the tiny remnants left she could see her grandmother had had a portion of rice with a pickled plum on top, a piece of bonito, boiled spinach cooked with tiny white fish, and some stewed pumpkin. She had eaten well.

"Mi-*chan*, have you seen my glasses?" the old woman asked plaintively as the girl carried the box to the sink to wash.

Michiko turned back to the table, picked up one of the three pairs and held it out to her. "Are you writing some more *haiku*?"

"I was looking for those!" her grandmother exclaimed triumphantly, taking the glasses. "I wondered where they'd got to!" Despite her advanced years, the delicate features of her nearly unlined face meant she was still attractive. She held out a thin sheet of onion-skin paper covered with her flowing old-fashioned script, indecipherable to Michiko but as beautiful as a work of art.

"There was another competition announced in the paper and I wrote something for it. I'm looking it over once more before sending it. I'm not pleased with it, but it's the best I can do. The deadline is today. Mi-*chan*, can you take it down to the convenience store before 6.00 for the last post? I've got the envelope ready here."

It was only 3.00, plenty of time.

Her grandmother began carefully putting the crinkly paper into the envelope and then looked up. "Mi-*chan*," she said tenderly but firmly, "you haven't paid your respects to your parents or grandfather yet."

"Sorry, *Obaachan*. I'll do that now. Then I'll post your letter."

"Please take two of these *o-mochi* cakes with you. Auntie Kyoko brought them this morning. She remembered they're your grandfather's favourite."

Michiko picked up the two pink rice cakes filled with sweet *azuki* bean paste that her grandmother had wrapped in a tissue. She went down a passageway leading to her favourite room, a large airy space separated from the western-style rooms by sliding paper doors decorated with paintings of flowers. It had an elaborately carved wood lintel. Its only furniture was a large low table with cushions for kneeling on. A vase filled with purple hydrangeas stood below a calligraphy scroll in an alcove.

No cooking smells in here. Just the grassy fragrance of the *tatami* matting of the floor and the incense burning at the family altar in the corner, an elaborate wood and gilt structure serving as the household shrine. Wisping smoke spiralled above the bundle of four incense sticks. There were also two small white candles, their orange flames motionless in the heavy heat of the room. Her grandmother must have just come from there, and Michiko imagined the bent little figure making her laborious way there and back to the kitchen, using a little trolley that aided her progress.

Michiko knelt before the altar. She reverently laid the cakes on a special platter in front of grainy old memorial photos of her parents and grandfather. Her parents had been killed in a car crash when she was ten. Her grandfather had died seven years later of a heart attack on a mountainside overlooking the sea as he picked oranges

one December morning. The slightly blurred black-and-white faces stared at her impassively. She clapped her hands together, closed her eyes and bowed, saying a prayer to them.

"I'm home," she said. "*Tadaima.*"

Michiko followed this ritual three times a day: on first rising, on returning home from school as a child and now from work, and every night before bed. Her grandmother observed the communion with her dead more frequently. Despite her inability to walk unaided even the shortest distance now, reliant on the trolley that she pushed in front of her, her grandmother had put fresh flowers in the vases flanking the photographs which shone as if freshly polished.

Michiko could scarcely remember her parents and her grandfather only faintly, but her grandmother kept their memory alive by constantly talking about them and talking to them. Seated before the altar, she would confide in the photos, untroubled by the one-sided nature of the conversation.

Her grandmother often laid out the treats she claimed had been their favourites on the purple cloth on a small table in front of the memorial photographs. It was in this way that Michiko learned that her mother had had a sweet tooth, that her father liked Asahi Super Dry Beer, and her grandfather was partial to delicate pink rice cakes filled with sweet red bean paste.

As a child, Michiko had been irked by her grandmother's insistence that she pay obeisances to the dead. On returning home, she had only wanted to throw down her heavy school satchel, change into comfortable clothes, and go out to play with her friends. She had obeyed with a bad grace, pouting and sulking.

But now Michiko was grateful. These rituals kept her parents and grandfather alive to her, as if they still played an important part in her life. Michiko had got in the habit of sharing her thoughts and troubles with them in her prayers; it was a kind of contact with the dear departed.

Today the ritual was unpleasant because Michiko didn't have a clear conscience. She didn't want to talk to the dead because it would mean telling them her guilty secret. It was fortunate her grandmother had an errand for her. She couldn't dwell on it now. The busier the better. That was the only way forward until time effaced the bad feeling and the bad memory.

She shook herself, casting off a burden, rose and returned to the kitchen, where she caressed her grandmother's hunched shoulders and then took the envelope to post.

Cycling down the hill towards Lawson's, the nearest convenience store, she was again rapt in thought. She hardly saw the familiar scenes from childhood, the

neighbourhood nearly unchanged from those days. Most of the inhabitants of the ancient family compounds were old. Men and women here worked as farmers. There were orange groves, vineyards, kiwi fruit and fig greenhouses, and plots of carefully tended flowers and vegetables wedged between the houses and the road. The neighbourhood had a distinctive smell, a compound of dust, machine oil and a hint of drains. It was a rural area not yet connected to a modern sewerage system. Little blue 'honey' trucks were still a common sight, dropping by each month to use hoses to vacuum out the contents of full cesspits. Michiko would hold her breath until her lungs ached on seeing one of these trucks. If she were on her bicycle, she would pedal away quickly. Anything to avoid that stink!

Approaching Lawson's, Michiko woke from her reverie and reluctantly re-entered the modern world...the world where university professors could be killed in their offices. She wanted to go back to the past, where her grandmother lived, preserving the old ways. Michiko's grandmother cooked traditional food. She gave boxes of towels, canisters of coffee or packages of smoked meat to family and neighbours at the prescribed gift-giving seasons. She wrote haiku and loved watching *rakugo* on television, staring in rapture at the storytellers in kimono who used as props only a paper fan, a small folded cloth and a repertoire of stylised gestures as, sitting cross- legged on a cushion, they related long, complicated, comic tales.

Michiko's grandmother was old and so were most of her neighbours. The young had fled to the cities. The old farms and the life they represented, with rites and rituals stretching centuries past, were fast disappearing. Down the hill from the grouping of ancient farmhouses was a brightly lit shop open twenty-four hours a day selling products Michiko's own mother would have marvelled at, whose purpose she would have struggled to guess. Lawson's, like the thousands of convenience stores that appeared in Japan in the 1990s, was open all day and all night and seemed to sell a little of nearly everything – from hosiery and rice balls, to beer and cell phone covers.

Michiko bought a stamp and then pushed the envelope into the post box at the store. She also bought her grandmother some sweet buns flavoured with beans as a treat, hoping to tempt her. Her grandmother had always eaten sparingly, but lately she didn't eat much more than the contents of the lunch box provided daily by the city.

It was a strenuous ride back up the hill and Michiko wanted to get off the bike and walk. She found peace of mind in the exercise. "If I can just make it to the next house, my troubles will go away," she told herself. And then, once there, "Just on to the next

farm, and then I'll get off." She got to the top exhausted and wheeled her bike into the courtyard.

"Michiko-*san*!" Her grandmother called as soon as she stepped inside. Not "Mi- *chan*," the affectionate diminutive of her name. It always meant trouble when her grandmother addressed her by her full name. Michiko's heart sank.

Sometimes she wondered if her grandmother was in the early stages of dementia. At others, she was surprised by the shrewdness in her grandmother's eyes when the old woman showed an acute grasp of facts or vestiges of her old phenomenal memory.

Her grandmother had moved. It must have required a great effort, but she was now in the western-style room with its carpet, curtains, television, sofa, and easy chairs.

Michiko settled into a chair opposite her grandmother.

Her grandmother looked stern and sad. She was holding the remote control in one hand, tapping it absent-mindedly on the arm of the sofa.

"Michiko-*san*, I just saw the news on television. I heard the terrible news about Professor Nomura, who's been so kind to you at Fujikawa, who helped you find work there. I can't believe it."

She groaned and added, "What is our country coming to? This casual violence! It's beyond comprehension. And at a *university*! An institution of higher learning."

Michiko agreed with her grandmother's dismal sentiments, and her eyes filled with tears. She wondered who she was crying for. Certainly not for Professor Nomura, although Michiko keenly regretted the manner of his death. He had always been obnoxious and proud, she thought. And he reprehensibly preyed on vulnerable women. *I can't think of that just yet*. She dimly became aware of her grandmother still speaking.

"I understand now why you came home early. And I'm wondering, child, is it safe for you to return to work?"

"A memorial service for Professor Nomura will be held at the university chapel tomorrow afternoon. I must attend. All classes are cancelled until the day after when some students take end-of-term tests. I'll go back to work then."

"I see. But please be careful, Mi-*chan*. I can't imagine you'll come to harm but then I would have said the same of

Professor Nomura. He was one of the leading lights of our little community. I shudder to think of the consequences."

"*Obaachan*, I must make dinner. Are you comfortable? Shall I turn on the fan?

As she began to slice vegetables and heat fish stock for soup, she allowed herself to reflect on the events of the momentous day. But only for a minute or two. Then she tried to close off her thoughts, recoiling from the horror of it all.

She skimmed the top of the soup with a ladle. Nearly done. She sliced some tomatoes and *shiso* leaves for the salad and then fried a few eggs.

But her mind was too active for her to control. She gripped the counter. *What was going on*? Somebody had killed the president! And there had been so much tension before in recent months, uncertainty and resentment hanging over the university like a black cloud.

Michiko had heard the rumours of Professor Nomura's far-reaching reforms. She had seen the groups of clerks in corners, whispering to each other, and sometimes even professors huddled together, speaking in low voices, looking worried. She had heard gossip but had little idea what the changes would mean for her. It was possible she could lose her job despite her ten years' service. She didn't have a permanent contract.

She was also worried about her co-worker, Akamatsu. He was a gentleman like Thomas-*sensei*. Some Japanese men treated women as second-class citizens, but since she had begun work at the university, Akamatsu had always shown her the utmost courtesy. His kindness touched her. Michiko's gender rendered her dispensable, but Akamatsu should be safe as a man. He also had a tenured position. So why was he always so anxious these days? It was a mystery that niggled at her.

"Mi-*chan*."

She turned off the gas under the skillet and went back to the front room.

Her grandmother laid her hand on her arm and looked up with a puzzled expression. "Mi-*chan*, it's odd. This morning, while I was on the phone to your uncle in Tokyo, I noticed the porcelain doll I got as a child for Girls' Day is gone from the cupboard in the entranceway. The glass case is there, but it's empty. Do you know where the doll is?"

Andrew and Alyson

"You can't be serious, Alyson," Andrew gasped. "You can't tell me you were having an affair with that creep!" He shuddered. "You were fucking that old man?" The images of it filled him with disgust. "You touched him? He touched you?"

Alyson and Andrew faced off in combat in their dark and dank front room, now less inviting than ever. It looked as if there had been an earthquake. There were books scattered on the floor, shabby chairs overturned, and the kitchen floor was covered with smashed plates and glasses.

The devastation was Alyson's way of coping after Officer Kubo turned up with the news that Andrew had found the president murdered, had blood on his clothes and needed clean ones.

For Andrew it was a day of shocking discoveries. First there was the murder of his boss, but now he had to contend with something even worse. The slim and pale elegant blonde he'd loved, the woman he'd shared everything with for the past four years, whom he'd tried to love, had gone. She had been replaced by a frightening creature with a face twisted in wrath and grief, her chignon tumbled down, her rage uncontrollable and destructive.

Could this red-faced, screaming harridan really be Alyson?

Blurting out the news that she had been sleeping with Professor Nomura for the past six months?

What a nightmare! He had no idea of her being unfaithful. She had been uninterested in sex for a long time, but Andrew had blamed that on a low libido caused by depression.

Had Alyson suddenly gone mad? She was always a bit reclusive, but this was a double life, a secret existence, with her sneaking off at night when he was sound asleep.

"What a way to hear the news!" she spluttered angrily when he entered the front door. "From a damned cop!"

Exhausted, Andrew had sat down in the entrance hallway to take off his shoes. As she continued, he felt paralysed, unable to get up.

"Masaki was my lover," Alyson said. "I loved him! He loved me, too!

He got to his feet in astonishment and anger. Speechless, he followed Alyson into the front room.

Finally he said, "*Masaki*?"

"You're so useless! Everyone says you're so *nice*! To me, that means you don't do anything. Why I ever married you is beyond me."

Tears streamed down her cheeks. "I saw him only last night. When you came home yesterday afternoon, saying you still hadn't got your contract confirmed, I felt like hitting you. I couldn't stand the limbo. I rang Masaki on his mobile and we arranged to meet at 10.00 at a little dump of a bar half an hour away. I knew something was wrong when I saw him, he was in such a state. He'd just seen Professor Hunter. He said he'd kicked up a hell of a fuss about the changes Masaki was going to make at the university. He said he couldn't concentrate on *us* just now, that perhaps we should end it. That was just the worry talking, he didn't mean it."

Andrew was battered by her words. He wanted to retaliate. He adopted a contemptuous tone. "Was Nomura the new Bill, your latest sexual experiment?"

Alyson lunged at him beating her fists on his chest. Andrew nearly lost balance, leaning against a wall. He was so filled with hatred, he wanted to beat her to a pulp.

He caught her hands and drew her in tightly to stop the blows. It was an embrace, an ironic parody of passion, as he squeezed her in fury. She relaxed, he released her, and they stepped back, glaring at each other, seeing clearly for the first time. He realised she must have tired of him long before.

Maybe it was because she intuited his simmering resentment born long before, when she had betrayed him by sleeping with a college friend. Alyson and Andrew had met in a French class at a university in Winnipeg in their junior year. Andrew wondered if they were attracted to each other because both had had experiences broader than those of most of their fellow students. Andrew had worked at a ranch for two years after high school trying to 'find himself'. Alyson had spent one year after high school in Kyoto, learning Japanese. In any case, Andrew was grateful for the attention of the attractive girl with long blonde hair in a French roll and dressed in black clothes like a trendy goth. It was apparent she was a born language-learner. By the end of the term, she could easily converse with the instructor in French.

But there was a paradox about Alyson – she was gorgeous and clever but morbidly shy despite her exotic experience of having lived in Japan. Her confidence deserted her outside the classroom.

In the first months of their relationship, Andrew wanted to protect and cherish her. Several months after they had become lovers, Alyson gave up her dorm room and moved into the house he shared with a friend. Perhaps that was their fatal error. When

they had had to arrange meeting places and times, their get-togethers had been invested with drama and sexual urgency. This dissipated when they started living together.

Gradually they began to behave like siblings, not lovers. They were good friends who could about everything – except how their romance was unravelling.

Andrew got the chance to go to Japan out of the blue because a professor who liked him had connections there. He knew Andrew hadn't yet decided what to do after graduation, and he suggested he try teaching English in a foreign country for a year. Andrew jumped at the proposal, realising that rather than a career opportunity or an adventure, the job at a small, private university on an island in western Japan was most desirable to him as an escape from Alyson. He told Alyson nothing until it had all been arranged. He eventually had to reveal his plan, preparing for her hurt and anger. What happened was even worse. To his horror, she had looked up brightly from her book saying she'd love to see her homestay family again and practise her Japanese.

Andrew had not anticipated this. He wondered if she'd guessed what he was up to and was deliberately subverting his plan. Could it be possible she did not realise it was over between them?

"It is alright my going with you, isn't it?" she had asked, suddenly doubtful.

"Of course, I wouldn't go without you. I kept it secret as a surprise."

Had he needed to lie so blatantly? He hadn't the heart to tell her the truth and Alyson was obviously content to be deceived. She had visibly relaxed and embraced him, winding her hair around his neck as if tying the two of them together. All he could feel was a sense of captivity, that their relationship was a ball and chain he couldn't cast off. The bleak ceremony in the city office where they exchanged marriage vows a week later had felt like confirming a life sentence.

Andrew enrolled in Japanese language classes before their departure. Alyson tried to help, but he couldn't manage even elementary phrases however much she coached him.

Alyson had few occasions to demonstrate her own fluency once they arrived in Japan. She became almost a hermit. If Andrew didn't insist on her presence at official university functions, she wouldn't go out.

She was punctilious about the household chores – waking him, preparing meals, keeping their home spotless – but what he wanted was unlimited, adventurous sex or at least companionship. But she was passive, silent, a mystery. He had first learned this about her when she slept with Bill, a mutual friend at the university.

One night shortly after Alyson had moved in, Andrew found that a writing assignment due the next morning meant doing an all-nighter. He had already bought tickets for a play and asked Bill to take Alyson in his place. They didn't come home that night. He later learned they'd gone off to a motel after the show.

Bill was ashamed but Alyson showed no remorse. She didn't understand why Andrew was so angry. She'd just been curious. Andrew had been her first lover, and she simply wondered how sex would be with someone else.

Andrew couldn't go on being outraged when he realised Alyson saw it as a trivial offense. Somehow, they began sleeping together again. It was routine. Then they married and moved to Japan.

Now, hearing about her affair with Nomura, Andrew was

revisited by that terrible feeling of betrayal he'd had after finding out about Bill. For a moment he clutched her in fury. Then Alyson shook herself free and they sprang apart to sit in silence at opposite ends of the room. They were hostile strangers.

Then Alyson's anger gave way to grief. She buried her face in her hands and rocked back and forth in her seat in agony. "My God, you actually found him? Tell me he didn't suffer. Who could have done this?"

"He was dead. That's all I know about it. *Dead*!"

Alyson began beating her palms hard against her thighs as if physical pain might offer mental relief. "Oh, my god, my god, my god! When I rang Masaki last night, I heard craziness in his voice. I needed to see him, and he needed to see me. It was ten o'clock. You were dead to the world, of course," she added sarcastically.

Andrew vengefully said, "And now it's Masaki who is."

Alyson winced but remained sitting slumped, hands in her lap. "*You* were the one who introduced us. *You* insisted on my going to those horrible university functions. I never wanted to go."

Andrew silently agreed. It had always been a lengthy procedure, persuading her, painful to them both. She would agree and then demur. She would be ready, but then say that it was impossible, her clothes weren't suitable.

Andrew got up and went over to the pale figure, resisting

the urge to hit her. "I can't take this in," he said. "It's impossible! How could you have been carrying on with Nomura week after week without my knowing it?"

Alyson tried not to look amused. "I don't think you know me at all."

Andrew recalled when he had introduced his new girlfriend to his parents. His father had looked astonished that his gawky son had managed to pull such a beauty.

His mother had got along well enough with Alyson, but sometimes Andrew caught her looking at his girlfriend with puzzlement. He remembered his mother once saying, "Alyson's a dark horse. Be careful."

"Why have you always acted as though you were a recluse, unable to leave home? Were you just play-acting?"

"No, it was real enough. I hate the people always staring at me."

She stopped pacing and sat down. "Masaki told me he'd felt the same way in the States. He felt like an oddity. People were always asking him if he was Chinese or Korean."

"Masaki!" Andrew shouted. "Was I, or am I, so bad in bed that you have to look for it with someone else?"

"I don't think I've ever had an orgasm with you. If it's any comfort, I didn't have one with Bill or Masaki. I suppose I might be frigid."

So, it was all a lie. He remembered her naked body twisting below his, heard her gasping and moaning…at least he had experienced pleasure when they'd had sex. In the beginning of their relationship, the lovemaking had been rapturous. It was like he no longer existed. There were no thoughts or fears, just simple ecstasy. Seeing Alyson standing before him, dishevelled and vulnerable, he felt a flicker of the old passion and started to feel an erection coming on. He remembered how he had once loved her.

"It started four or five months ago," Alyson said, in a sad voice, still sniffling. "Do you remember taking away a novel I was reading? I was desperate to get it back. It was a murder mystery. I was on the last chapter. I rang you at work and you promised to bring it home, but you forgot it. You fell asleep. I felt lonely and bored. I drove to the university to collect the book from your office."

Alyson's eyes clouded and her face relaxed. "That's how it began. The campus was deserted but I ran into Masaki. He'd been working late in his office and was on his way home. Of course, at first, I tried to hurry away, but he stopped me. He knew who I was. We were the only two people around. He asked me about you. Then, somehow, he began telling me about his experiences studying in America. He'd heard how shy I seemed about being in Japan. It was a cold night and uncomfortable to be standing outside. He suggested we go for a coffee at a place nearby."

"Why did you keep it a secret? Surely you could have told me about that!"

"He and I agreed not to say anything about it to anyone. I think we knew that something was going to develop."

"How did you manage to keep it under wraps? You went to cafes and bars?"

"Only to the one bar, owned by a friend of his. That is, except for last night, when we went to another place. He may have asked his friend to keep quiet about it. It was always late, the bar in such an out of the way place, it was usually just the two of us."

"But why all the pretence? Why were you worried I'd be fired? Surely your *lover* would want to keep me on!"

"It *wasn't* a pretence. I *was* worried. Masaki said it would look suspicious if he retained you when he had to fire other foreigners who had better qualifications or had been teaching longer. He kept saying he wasn't sure what to do. That's why I wanted you to visit him, to make a personal plea."

Andrew was furious. "I think your Masaki got tired of you, just as you seem to have got tired of me. Maybe this whole business of getting rid of the resident foreigners was his roundabout way of getting rid of *you* – through my losing my job."

Alyson trembled. "Masaki was tense and upset. Something was bothering him." "Do you know what it was?"

"He was getting threatening phone calls but gave no details."

"Face it! He was on the point of dumping you. He'd had his

fun and decided he wanted you out of his life. What amazes me is you're not sorry in the least."

Alyson looked at him in stony-faced silence.

My wife: the infuriating enigma, Andrew thought. He felt that bracing sensation of anger rising again. "And on that note, we have to think of what to do next. First, I want you out of this house as soon as possible."

"You know I have no close friends, no family here. I have no money. Where can I go? What can I do?"

"You're the one who can speak Japanese, the one who betrayed our marriage vows. You figure it out."

Alyson jumped up, went to their bedroom, and slammed the door.

Inoue Must Bear the Unbearable

Inoue had been schooled in stoicism from his earliest years. Even as a toddler, he was taught never to complain, never to cry. When he fell from the playground swing as a first grader, the school nurse rebuked him for his tears as she wiped up the blood and bandaged the deep gash in his left leg. When his father died, he could not weep at the funeral. However much pain he suffered, whether it was mental or physical, he was expected to grin and bear it and get on with life. He was Japanese.

Takenaka's presence in his own police station – lording it over him, sitting at his desk, ordering his officers around – strained his endurance. But bear it he must.

The nightmare had begun when Kubo turned up to announce that the university president was dead. On hearing the news Takenaka had dropped his cigarette. Inoue had picked up the burning stub from the carpet and placed it pointedly in the ashtray, hoping his superior got the point. New health and safety regulations prohibited smoking in all government buildings and offices.

Inoue was angry that this didn't stop that fool Takenaka from flouting the rules. Takenaka was the senior officer for the whole prefecture, which meant he could get away with it. There was nobody in a position of greater authority who could complain. It rankled with Inoue, who always took great care to go by the book and saw smoking in public places as an offence on a par with able-bodied drivers parking in handicapped spaces – a sight that always made his blood boil.

When they got the news from Kubo, Takenaka at least had the courtesy to pretend to accept that Inoue would be the chief investigating officer. His eyes behind his thick-rimmed black glasses were bright with excitement, but he told Inoue that he understood he needed to proceed immediately to the crime scene and that he and his team would continue, in their absence, with their routine check of the Fujikawa police station.

"Naturally," Takenaka had said, just before Inoue could rush from the room, "your performance on this case will reflect on the report we make."

There was menace in Takenaka's eyes. "In fact, it would be no exaggeration to say that your success – or failure – will have an impact on your future and the prospects

of your team. We have had our eye on you and your officers, Inoue. Questions have been asked about slackness."

Inoue's face had reddened. He'd clenched his fists. No doubt there was some ill feeling. He was well aware the officers at the Ishizaki station were hard-pressed to cope with the crime endemic in a large city. Although Inoue sometimes wished his job had more challenges and excitement, he was lucky not to have to deal with the problems his colleagues faced in the prefectural capital, a hotbed of prostitution, gambling, and organised crime.

But little Fujikawa was a model community. Sure, it had its problems – the half- hearted hookers who loitered late at night on street corners near the old temple, the occasional undergraduate who did some casual shoplifting, and there were even a few gangsters who'd found modest houses in the town and commuted to Ishizaki – but it was mostly a law-abiding community with its students, small shop owners and residents co-existing in peaceful harmony. He hoped to god the murder wasn't the start of an unfortunate turn in Fujikawa's fortunes.

Inoue had listened to the superintendent's words in stoic silence, replying, "Yes, sir. Thank you. We'll do our best" before turning to hurry to the crime scene.

What made it worse was that he had allowed himself the luxury of hope. On returning to the station on the night of the murder, after conducting the interviews, Inoue was told that the prefectural police chief had gone back to Ishizaki. Gone and good riddance! He tried to forget Professor Obuchi's remark about asking for Takenaka to take over. He hoped that, with his unblemished record, he would be allowed to lead the murder investigation.

That meant he returned home the night of the murder in high spirits. He enjoyed springing the news on Ellie and relaxing with three beers.

In retrospect, Inoue conceded that his hope to be allowed to lead the investigation had been a result of wilful blindness. It was absurdly optimistic given the high-profile status of the victim and the site of the crime. Naturally the students' parents would be spooked and clamouring for the culprit to be apprehended quickly. There was also economics to be considered. Fujikawa University was an important source of income for the whole community.

When Inoue went to the station the following morning, Takenaka was already installed in his office and the room was thick with smoke. Professor Obuchi rang me last night," Takenaka said airily, beckoning Inoue to a seat in front of his own desk. "He's been talking to the prefectural governor and I've been prevailed on to take charge. The consensus is this case is too important to entrust to the local authorities."

He blew a smoke ring in Inoue's direction and added, "Not that I don't have every confidence in your abilities. But did you see little Fujikawa featured on the national news last night? Violent crime on the rise in rural Kyushu, that was the line they took, though I'd admit one murder doesn't constitute a crime wave."

Inoue bowed to his new boss and to the inevitable. "Grateful for your help, sir," he said, staring at Takenaka's eyes and thinking they resembled wet beans. He wished he could squash them between his fingers.

"I'll be bringing in my own team," Takenaka added, "but

relegating certain tasks to you and your top two officers, Kubo and Ando."

Takenaka stood and extended his hand to Inoue. "This will be difficult for you, Chief Inspector. We all must make sacrifices for the common good. The sooner this case is wound up the better."

Takenaka settled himself back in the swivel chair. "I knew you would insist I took your office for the duration; I've arranged alternative accommodation for you."

Inoue turned to leave and Takenaka added, "I've heard from the president's brother. He has requested we delay our interview with him until after the memorial service. The poor man sounded distraught."

Inoue wanted to insist the police had the right to override that request given the urgency of the situation. But he was now a subordinate in his own police station.

His new office was down the hall. Inoue closeted himself there for an hour, unwilling to see anyone after his "demotion". He set about helping his officers collate the witness statements. Later he took Ando to search the president's house, a handsome modern concrete building surrounded by azalea bushes and bonsai trees sited a short walk from Fujikawa Temple.

Nomura was that rare beast, a house-proud single man, keeping his place immaculate if impersonal, filled with expensive western furniture and paintings but no personal mementoes. Inoue was disappointed. He had hoped to see at least a photo of the president's late wife, Liza, but any traces of her existence had been tidied away. The place had been checked the previous evening for fingerprints. The president was unsocial. There were none apart from Nomura's. Despite ransacking the man's desk and cupboards, Ando and Inoue could find nothing to shed light on why the president had been, according to so many witnesses, agitated in the weeks up to his death.

Inoue went on to the memorial service in the university chapel. A huge black-and- white picture of the late president dominated the wall above the altar. The place was filled with flowers. Kubo and Kawane, positioned behind one of the chapel pillars,

noted the names of all attendees. From force of habit, Inoue assessed the sincerity of the mourners' grief. Nomura's fellow professors looked grim, the office staff were anxious, but a surprise was the contingent of weeping female undergraduates.

One person Inoue had expected to see didn't turn up. Andrew was there but not his wife.

Finally, two days after the murder, Takenaka told Inoue to report to the army camp next to the campus to interview Professor Nomura's younger brother.

As Kubo drove Inoue down Fujikawa's streets lined with shabby little shops, apartment blocks and stunted trees, he thought of the uneasy relationship between the university and the army, so close in physical proximity but poles apart in their world views. The university's mission was to help those discriminated against or disabled. Inoue respected this. The chapel, one of the largest buildings on campus, had a tall spire topped by a cross visible from afar. To Inoue, it was a symbol of hope. Services were held each morning between the first and second classes. Locals had become accustomed to the pealing of bells every morning at 10.45, signalling the start of the twenty-minute service. Inoue used to attend as a callow undergraduate, savouring

seeing his professors nervously standing at the pulpit giving sermons.

But Inoue wasn't sure what to think of the army. For one thing, there was the link between Japan's military and the country's vocal right-wingers. The latter included prominent politicians who made visits to the Yasakuni Shrine in Tokyo to pay their respects to deceased soldiers some considered war criminals. Conservatives petitioned for Japan to write a new constitution, one that wouldn't include the renunciation of war as a means of settling disputes. They felt this clause, known as article nine, had been unjustly inflicted on them by the Americans after Japan's defeat in the Pacific war. Others continued to view the emperor as semi-divine and indignantly rejected Korean and Chinese recriminations about alleged Japanese atrocities during the war. They chafed at Japan's dwindling role on the international stage and felt indignant at seeing China, its traditional rival, rising in power and influence.

These right-wingers gave Inoue the creeps. He hated their arrogance. As a student, he used to watch the big black vans emblazoned with their crude depictions of rising suns circling the campus broadcasting loud patriotic songs and slogans. And the army seemed another branch of the same 'disease'. There were bases dotted about the town, and the trucks and jeeps that crowded the narrow streets, filled with helmeted and uniformed soldiers, made it sometimes feel as though Fujikawa was under military occupation.

Before he joined the force, Inoue wondered if there was some collusion between the police and the nutcases who spent their time driving around in those sun-stencilled vans. Surely the police could keep those loonies off the street. He later learned that the police were simply trying to keep a low profile and not worsen the situation by pointless intervention. It was a policy of damage limitation that seemed to work. For some years after Inoue joined the police, there was a lull in this type of harassment. Then, with Professor Hunter's championing the rights of Koreans born in Japan, it began again. *But the vans haven't been around lately* Inoue realised with a start.

As Kubo pulled into the headquarters of the Japanese Self-Defence Forces in Fujikawa, Inoue felt a kind of dread. He wasn't looking forward to questioning Professor Nomura's brother. He knew he'd need to be sympathetic about the man's loss while trying at the same to time to dig up dirt, to find out if Nomura's younger sibling had anything to do with the murder.

Kubo and Inoue were led to the office of the presiding officer of the base by a cadet. Inoue had seen army barracks clustered around the environs of Fujikawa all his life but had never been inside one before. The keynote of this building was austerity: bare corridors, shiny floors, sparkling windows, a lingering smell of gunpowder and antiseptic. Inoue wondered if the cadets had to polish the floors of the buildings of the base the way schoolchildren cleaned classroom floors: on hands and knees, pushing a large cloth up and down, rinsing it out in a bucket of cold water.

The chief officer of the Fujikawa base, seated behind a huge mahogany desk, introduced himself as General Murasaki. Inoue thought there was another officer standing in the corner. Then he realised it was a dummy of a Pacific War soldier clad in a single-breasted tunic, pantaloons, puttees, ankle-length boots, and a peaked cap with the skirting of cloth that shielded one's neck from the burning, tropical sun.

The general smiled, "It's a way of paying respects to the brave men who gave their lives for us fifty years ago. Reminding us of our *honoured* dead. We respect the sacrifice they made for us."

Lieutenant Nomura came in. Murasaki beckoned Inoue to three chairs at a small table set out in preparation for the interview and left the room. Army officers had attended the memorial service, and Inoue had seen Nomura's younger brother

there, a fit muscular man in his late forties. Inoue motioned to Kubo to put the recording equipment on the table. Before sitting, Inoue bowed. "I would like to offer my condolences for your loss. I'm terribly sorry I need to question you at this time."

Nomura rose and gave a small bow.

A demure-looking young woman in a pink pussy-bow blouse came in and bowed. Small porcelain cups of green tea on wooden saucers were set on the table. As she left Inoue noticed Kubo ogling her legs, shapely under her short black skirt, and suppressed an urge to hiss at him.

Instead, he began his questioning. "How did you come to live in the same town as your brother? Surely that was not coincidental."

"My name is Teruo Nomura. My elder brother and I grew up in Kyoto. We belong to an old Kyoto family. Our father was a soy sauce manufacturer. It's a family business dating back over two hundred years. We were well off. We lived in a large gated compound in an eastern suburb of the city. I think my brother took perverse pleasure in disappointing any hopes our parents had for him. He could have gone to a top-class place like Tokyo or Kyoto University, but he suddenly announced he was going to attend the college in provincial Fujikawa. He said people there had so- called 'values'. It was one disappointment after another. Once he graduated, he told us he wanted to study race relations at Columbia in New York."

"I would like to get as full a picture of the victim as possible. Please tell me what kind of person your brother was."

"Masaki was a rebel. Ordinary enough as a primary and junior high school student, but once he'd got into a top high school in Kyoto he changed. My parents said it was to do with associating with undesirables."

"At one of the best high schools?"

"Remember that my brother entered high school in the late Sixties, when there was student unrest throughout the world, even in Japan. It was a sickness that affected all classes of people."

"I take it you didn't agree with the student protest movement."

"Of course not, I was disgusted when its poisonous philosophy infected our country, with young people selfishly turning their backs on thousands of years of history, questioning the old order of society, even daring to ask whether the imperial system was necessary."

Nomura sighed. "I'm ashamed to say my own brother

harboured such revolting views. He rejected our Father's dearest wish of keeping up the family business. He

washed his hands of us, ignoring family obligations by flitting to America to do postgraduate work. He broke our parents' hearts. He became a Christian here in Fujikawa, before he went to America, then he topped that by marrying a black woman and bringing her back." He spat out the word "black" with evident distaste. "I hold my brother responsible for our parents' early deaths."

"There was no love lost between you?"

"No, but I didn't murder him. I want to find the bastard who did and finish him off myself. But I don't feel devastated he's dead. The Masaki I loved died long ago."

"Did you never think of stepping into your brother's shoes and taking over the family business once he had shown no inclination?

"No, to my regret. I was so angry with Masaki when he went to the States that I impulsively joined the army. You could say I wanted to make a public statement, to show where my allegiances lay. Anyway, my taking over the company would have been disastrous. I have no head for business. Mind you, I felt relieved when Father told me I needed a life of authority and order, self-discipline, and sacrifice. Just the sort of life in I could lead as a member of Japan's armed forces."

"How did your brother feel about you? You lived near each

other. Were you reconciled?"

Nomura said angrily, "He called me a fascist, a reactionary, a relic of a period of Japan's history best forgotten – as though the Pacific War didn't represent our finest hour, the time when we showed the world our bravery and determination. There could never be any forgiveness between us."

Inoue looked puzzled. "Given this mutual dislike, why did you end up in Fujikawa, living next to where your brother worked?"

Nomura smiled grimly. "As you surmised, it was no coincidence. I arranged it on purpose."

"But why?"

"I wanted to follow my brother, to remind him of his forsaken duty and make his life difficult."

"When you say, make his life 'difficult,' are you referring to Fujikawa University's being targeted by right-wing elements?"

Nomura's face was impassive. "I sympathise with the aims of nationalist groups. Those patriots include some of my closest friends. But I'm not to blame if there are individuals who take matters into their own hands and go too far. It's understandable some Japanese got upset when that *gaijin*, Hunter, meddled in Japanese affairs. I'm sure you agree the Koreans are lucky to live here."

Inoue looked puzzled again. "But aren't you aware your

brother was not a strong supporter of Professor Hunter or his efforts to help second and third-generation Koreans in Japan?"

"Masaki allowed that western busybody to work at his college and sully the minds of young students. That was guilt enough. That *gaijin's* position of authority made them susceptible to his nonsense."

"But recently those right-wing lorries aren't seen much in Fujikawa." "Their activities have nothing to do with me; I can't account for them."

Inoue had got some background information. It was time for pertinent questions. "I need to ask where you were yesterday morning between 8.30 and 10.00."

Nomura replied in a jeering tone. "Am I a suspect? I may have hated my brother, but I did not kill him. I wouldn't risk my future getting rid of that bastard, just as I wouldn't go out of my way to step on a cockroach. And I've heard he had his throat slit. Not my style at all. If I had wanted him dead, I'd have challenged him to a duel, a sword fight, perhaps. The proper way, the Japanese way."

"We ask these questions of everyone to eliminate them from our enquiries."

"From 8.00 to 8.30, we had our usual calisthenics in the army grounds. From 8.30 to

11.00 I was in my office here doing some paperwork." "Can anyone vouch for that?"

"I saw nobody from about 8.40 to 10.30."

Inoue stood and bowed formally. "Thank you for assisting us with our enquiries. Though you and your brother weren't on the best of terms, I offer my condolences again."

"Sir?" Kubo asked tentatively once they had left the office. "Yes, Kubo. What is it?"

"May I ask your opinion of that witness, sir?"

"I was a young, impressionable man when Mishima Yukio committed *seppuku*. He espoused the same views as Lieutenant Nomura. I thought Mishima way over the top and I feel the same about Nomura. The damnable thing about this case is hardly anyone has an alibi and almost everyone speaks ill of the victim – they all seemed to want him dead."

Inoue and Kubo were looking at each other in exasperation when Ando appeared. "Sir, there's been a development. Superintendent Takenaka has made an arrest. You

must return to the station immediately." "Who's been arrested?!"

"Andrew Thomas. They've learned his girlfriend was having an affair with Professor Nomura."

"Damn!"

The Boys Go Out to Play

The bars of Fujikawa were usually crowded every Friday and Saturday evening with western males employed at language schools or at the college. Some spoke little or no Japanese. Surrounded by their friends, they could imagine they were back home, with the Japanese setting an exotic backdrop to their partying.

The Friday night Andrew was arrested was no exception. His absence made little difference to the gang's festivities. He had only nominally belonged, hardly ever joining them on their nights out. They snickered at him going to bed by nine most nights. But the news that he was suspected of murder elevated him to celebrity status, and his arrest was a diversion for the bar crowd.

That night they were in a pub called *Izakaya*, one of the oldest drinking places in Fujikawa. With its dark walls and a sawdust floor, it was impossible to imagine the place had ever been new, clean, or inviting. Its dingy walls were covered with tattered posters of pop stars from twenty years before. Its scuffed chairs and tables smelt of beer, sweat, cigarettes and cooking oil. Smoke billowed from an open kitchen where the cooks in long blue aprons and caps fried noodles, chicken, and fish.

The gang's ringleader, Stephen, a weedy young man with

sandy hair and a small mouth concealed by a wispy moustache, was the first to arrive, and he chose to sit in his favourite booth, close to the toilets.

Only the core members turned up. They were Stephen from Birmingham and his closest friend, Ben, a red-haired Irishman; Billy, a habitually drunk computer whiz from Canada; a moody American named Karl, and Dave and Pete Carrel – brothers with matinee idol looks – from Los Angeles. The Carrels were seated on a bench between Ben and Stephen, strategically positioned to prevent the arguments the two best friends had on such occasions. The brothers liked to attract gullible young Japanese girls who held fantasies of dating a westerner. The Carrels had an impressive tally of conquests.

"So the old reprobate got himself killed," Billy mumbled into his beer.

"And our Andrew's been arrested. Didn't think he'd have the balls. He couldn't have chosen a better victim," said Stephen, stroking his moustache.

"You only hated Nomura because he wouldn't give you a full-time position at the college," Ben laughed.

"That's right, rub it in, you jerk," said Stephen, angrily. "God knows why he gave one to you. And only a contract job to me."

"Maybe my doctorate in linguistics had something to do with it," said Ben sarcastically.

"At least the memorial service was fun," said Stephen. "But it was disappointing there was no food on offer. Where were the baked meats for the funeral?"

"I can't get my head around it," said Pete. "A murder! Here! The old man had his throat cut and Andrew was covered in blood when they found him with the body, like something out of a Hammer film."

"But did he do it?"

"The million-dollar question."

Stephen had never liked Andrew's wife, who had always treated him with icy contempt, so he was enjoying being nasty. "Maybe he did. Rumour has it that bitch Alyson was having it off with Nomura. I always had my doubts about her, a little ice princess. Butter wouldn't melt in her mouth. Now it turns out she was just a slag."

"But I can't believe she'd have anything to do with him. Nomura must have been over fifty. Ancient!" Ben said, incredulously.

Stephen said, "It was all very well for sweet little Mari Furomoto to get close and personal with him. She was worried she was going to fail a few classes. He could help her get the right grades to graduate. But Alyson? I fail to see the attraction. Poor Andrew."

"And poor Gerald. I hear Alyson is sponging off him, using his place like home." Stephen said, "Of course it was very good of Gerald to take her in, but he *is* a

Christian missionary. I think self-sacrifice is part of the job description. I still find him one of the most irritating people I know. Heaven preserve me from people with principles. He's frighteningly moral."

"Gerald always treats me with maddening forbearance, as if he knows something bad about me he's too kind to mention," Ben observed.

"We all know something bad about you, you fool," said Billy, "and not just one thing."

"Ah, the difference is kindness. Gerald has it but you have none."

"I disagree," said Stephen. "That's just what Gerald doesn't have. He has principles but no tenderness at all. He reminds me of those obsessed religious types who still go around killing people thinking their convictions justify everything."

Ben wanted to deliver his theory. "Remember that Gerald is a missionary and a teacher, a fatal combination, jobs that produce professional bores, droning on and on."

"Speaking of bores, why must you always sound so damned pompous, Ben?" Stephen complained.

The group's table was covered with empty glasses and chopsticks on small plates smeared with red, yellow and brown sauces. There were many empty sake decanters with matching cups. The ashtray was full.

Billy sat with his hands placed meditatively in front of him, looking dazed. He was notorious for his seemingly limitless capacity for alcohol and had been responsible for emptying most of the beer glasses and sake cups. Fool or genius? He could drink his friends under the table and repair computers. In the ex-pat community, Billy was known as the only westerner who earned his living not doing language teaching. He designed websites for clients in Europe, America and Canada, communicating at all hours with his employers by Skype.

Billy was seated beside Karl Matthews, a strapping, swarthy man in his mid-thirties from Chicago. Karl said he was a quarter Cherokee. He also said he had served in the U.S. Marines for six years and had worked as a paramedic. Nobody knew whether any of these claims were true, but nobody dared question them. A number of subjects were off limits when Karl was around. The others were afraid of him, and with good reason. Large and lithe, he resembled a fierce creature ready to strike and exuded menace. His eyes had a wild look, darting about in a swarthy, impassive face with thick black eyebrows and a full moustache. Karl said he was a true American, a throwback to the rugged pioneers, a loner, a survivalist, a hunter and trapper – he even made his own bows and arrows in the tiny, cluttered apartment where he gave private English lessons. He said the weapons were to tackle the exploding population of wild boars inhabiting former orange farms, abandoned as unprofitable, in the surrounding mountains. But hunters in Japan required a license. The group was silent when Karl boasted about his hunting expeditions in the mountains outside Fujikawa. Did he have a gun license? They knew he probably hadn't bothered with such formalities.

There were lots of amazing stories about Karl. Although he had a Japanese wife and a small boy, he was rumoured to be a sex addict, hiring prostitutes from as far afield as Osaka. He was famous for cowing his classes into a stunned compliance. Ben joked, when Karl wasn't around, of course, that his students were probably afraid he'd pull out a gun if they hadn't done their homework.

Many members of the gang had been resident in Japan for ten years or more. Some had beautiful young Japanese wives. A few, like the Carrel brothers, were still unattached. They were much envied, questioned eagerly about their latest conquests.

These male ex-pats liked to call themselves 'the boys'. More worryingly for those who were married, that's exactly what their wives thought of them. As brides, the young Japanese women had dreamed they'd committed to the type of western husband they had seen in Hollywood films, a gentle kind man who changed diapers and did the washing up.

The reality was different. These hopeful, beautiful young girls usually found that the prize they had landed was a foreign husband who felt living in a strange land entitled him to behave like a child. They were like big babies, dependent on their wives because many had failed to acquire enough Japanese to manage everyday tasks like the renewal of a driver's license or making a dentist's appointment. To them, it was natural that their wives see to these chores.

Apart from Billy, the boys taught languages in Japan: mostly English, but there was also a demand for French and German. The English teachers had been recruited in their home countries on three-year contracts to work as assistant language teachers in primary and secondary schools. Others had less prestigious jobs at language schools where they laboured long hours for a pittance. The more enterprising had established their own small private schools, usually in their own homes.

The prize position was a tenured post at a Japanese university, but these were harder to find nowadays – a doctorate and a command of Japanese were essential.

Andrew, Stephen, and Ben had struck lucky. Ben had tenure at Fujikawa University; Stephen and Andrew had two-year renewable contract positions there. Ben had a doctorate in linguistics; Stephen had an MA in teaching English as a foreign language; and Andrew had been the beneficiary of good timing, his letter enquiring about a post

at Fujikawa coinciding with a retirement. Karl worked part-time at several of the language schools in Fujikawa and the Carrel brothers were employed at a local cram school.

Stephen was gay; Ben's wife was a gorgeous, self-assured

woman named Keiko; Karl was married to Junko, a shrinking sallow-faced woman; Andrew was now separated. The conservative nature of Japanese society legislated against Stephen's being open about his sexual orientation although it was speculated about by colleagues and students. His small flat near the town centre was cluttered with books, and he held an important position in the social life of its male ex-pat community. He was seen as a bit of a wag.

"You have a waspish nature, Stephen," Ben informed him.

"Yes, I know I can sting," said Stephen with a satisfied grin on his face.

"Gerald, on the other hand, is so straight he would make an arrow look crooked," said Stephen.

"Not a problem you suffer from, Stephen," said one of the Carrels with a smirk.

As if to confirm his words, Stephen threw his hands over his heart dramatically and stared at a handsome young waiter in a white shirt and bow tie and a long blue apron who was serving a noisy crowd of girls at an adjoining table. "What a beauty! What a dainty morsel!" Stephen gasped in a comic stage whisper to his friends.

"I beg your pardon," said Ben. "He's a first-year student in my communicative English class. I have high hopes he'll choose English as his major and that I'll be chosen to supervise his graduation thesis. I'd appreciate if you'd stop eyeing him up."

"But he looks so delicious," Stephen enthused.

Karl drained his glass, and following their gaze, said, "You talking about our order of fried chicken? It's taking forever to arrive."

"Idiot. Our Stephen is drooling over the local talent."

Karl looked uncomfortable with the turn of the conversation. The boys thought it advisable to change the subject although, when Karl went to the toilet, Stephen hissed "Those macho types with their aggression. It's all a front. My bet is Karl plays both sides."

"AC/DC?"

"Well, it's a distinct possibility. He's so interested in sex, why should he limit himself to women?"

Karl's return ended this speculation. Ben turned to him saying, "Karl, how about if I hear of any work going, I send it your way? Heard you might need some."

The gang had only that day heard about Karl's latest escapade. He had forbidden his students at a certain school to use cell phones in class and, on catching one young man texting, had thrown his phone out the window. The school was located on the second floor of a building but, landing on thick grass, the device hadn't been damaged. However, the elderly woman who ran the school was not amused and had told Karl his services were no longer required.

The Carrel boys admired Ben's nerve in bringing up the subject.

Karl looked momentarily put out but then settled back in his seat and said, "Oh, don't worry, Ben, my little man. I have other things going you have no idea about."

The gang looked at each other. Was he selling wild boar meat on the black market?

Karl lifted a glass filled to the brim with beer and emptied it in one gulp. "I'll let you in on one thought though. As a military man, I'll be sticking with my own kind."

"Are you getting chummy with the Japanese army people here?" Ben enquired innocently.

"Never you mind, Ben. Let's just say I have prospects other than teaching. Other

irons in the fire," and Karl tapped his finger against the side of his nose.

Nobody had the nerve to ask what he might mean. In any case, Billy was tired of all the chat. He'd been dazed by the amount of booze, but now got his second wind. "Let's order one last round of drinks here and then head to the Irish bar. I hear they've got a new dart board, an electronic one."

The Girls Go Out to Play

On the night Andrew was arrested, Ben's wife Keiko, Karl's wife Junko and a wannabe wife Misa, Billy's girlfriend, were out with Ellie Inoue for a meal at an upmarket establishment, a modern building on the shore. Situated to the east of the ferry port, it was a place of glittering plate glass windows with spectacular views over a bay crisscrossed by ferries, tankers, and container ships. Beyond were the tiny mountainous islands dotting the Seto Inland Sea like a scene on a picture postcard.

The restaurant had polished wood furniture, and candles and vases of freshly picked flowers adorned the tables. It served a vegetarian and a meat option. In the daytime it was the preserve of ladies who lunch: attractive, well-dressed women married to men who pulled such big salaries they didn't need to work themselves. These lucky trophy wives had time and money on their hands. They met after morning lessons in tennis, English, aerobics or yoga. At night, apart from a few adventurous groups like Ellie's, that included foreign women, or were comprised of Japanese women married to foreigners, the restaurant became a mostly male enclave, transforming itself into a classy bar frequented by the big spenders married to the lunching ladies.

The western boys liked to call the Japanese women in their

lives 'the girls,' but to Ellie they were mature women. In fact, she thought of them as being older than their years. Most had the weary air that age and experience confers on some adults, especially on those in marriages less than happy. They were glad to be away from their *gaijin* spouses. The wives with children coerced their mothers or sisters into babysitting.

Ellie had met Keiko many years before, through Ben, and she imagined Keiko had engineered the invitation to join them. She hadn't wanted to accept but her husband told her to go, saying that he wouldn't be home till late and there was no point fretting about her friend Andrew's being detained for questioning.

Ellie was uneasy. She knew her company would be more desirable than usual because of her husband heading an exciting murder investigation. She wished she'd refused. She felt she was straddling two enemy camps: the foreign husbands and their Japanese wives. Ellie knew the boys, inevitable in such a small place, and had used to go out for a drink or two with them before her marriage.

Ellie didn't care much for any of the boys apart from Andrew. She knew she would never have been friends with them in ordinary circumstances. But living in the same rural area of Japan meant they became acquaintances of a sort – the foreigners latching hungrily on to each other, longing to talk with somebody, needing the companionship in a place where they were so out of the normal flow, particularly if they weren't fluent in Japanese.

But the foreigners' novelty value had its pluses. Ellie would never have got such a lucrative, albeit part-time, position as she had at Fujikawa at any university in America, given her lack of postgraduate qualifications. She also felt the boys would never have acquired such gorgeous capable wives.

Ellie felt sorry for them – these lovely girls who often were disappointed in the marriages they'd entered into with such high hopes. Although the number of international couples in Japan was gradually growing, they tended to be contracted between Japanese women and western males, and they often ended in separation or even divorce. Ellie thought their dismal success rate was due to the different cultural expectations of marriage entertained by Japanese and westerners. She wondered if poor Misa had any idea what she was getting into – or trying to get into.

It was only a short time before the talk drifted to complaints about the boys.

While they picked delicately at their food with their chopsticks and the sky darkened over the twinkling lights of the harbour, Ellie braced herself for the usual litany of misery about the boys – tales of infidelity, unreliability with money, and secretiveness. After airing their grievances, the girls would tackle the murder.

Keiko had polished off a small seafood pizza and a pink cocktail, which was decorated with a tiny purple parasol on a toothpick stuck into a chunk of pineapple. She tossed back impeccably groomed, glossy, black hair and took a cigarette from her Louis Vuitton handbag. "It's his toys. That's what costs so much money." Keiko had an eight-year old son, Takao, and a six-year old, Yuji.

Ellie said, "You have to give Yuji or Takao expensive presents?" Keiko gave a bitter laugh. "Not my *sons*. Ben!"

"His toys…?"

"Computers, computer equipment, software, hardware, DVDs, iPods. Whatever he earns at his job, it's never enough."

"He doesn't give you his salary?"

"Bastard! He refuses to show me the pay slips."

Ellie could understand Keiko's fury. It was the custom in Japan for wives to manage the household finances. Although she knew little about her husband's work as a policeman, she was grateful he entrusted her with his monthly salary.

"I have the same problem," said Junko.

A hush fell over the table, chopsticks paused mid-air. Was Junko going to entertain them with her husband's antics? But there was sympathy in their expectant looks as well. Poor Junko had linked herself to crazy Karl. Not only that, Junko was plump and unattractive with a pockmarked face. She wasn't clever, couldn't match her friends in fashion sense, and her command of English was only adequate at best. The girls were in a constant state of competition. Who was the thinnest? The most attractive? The best at English? Who had the most successful *gaijin* husband? Junko wasn't even in the running.

She had a seven-year old son who was prone to attacks of rage and doing badly at school. That the little boy was a troubled soul was surely due to his scary father, but it meant poor Junko had yet one more problem on her hands.

Ellie's understood Junko's misfortune now but she hadn't when they first met. Keiko had introduced Ellie to Junko nine years earlier, when Ellie was still regarded as a newcomer. But for Ellie, the initial excitement of being in a strange new country had worn off: that thrill of being pointed at, stared at, a celebrity just because she looked different. In fact, a reaction had set in. She'd begun to fiercely guard her privacy. She was irritated when people made a fuss and hated all the personal questions directed at her.

At their first meeting, Junko seemed to regard Ellie as an unexpected treat. Ellie's hackles rose when the fawning questions started, and she replied in monosyllables. It was obvious Junko felt rebuffed, registering it as yet another failure in her life. Ellie then regretted her rudeness and tried hard to be especially friendly in subsequent encounters, carrying off the deception so well that Junko now regarded her as a close friend.

"I have same problem," Junko said, insisting on treating them to her broken English, despite Ellie's Japanese fluency.

"Karl give no money. He spend on girls. He find girls on Internet. He go Osaka and come back three, four days later, no money left."

Junko sighed. "Then he don't turn up for classes. We need that money! He hang around army base. What he do that for? No money there."

Ellie intervened to save Junko from making further embarrassing disclosures. She touched Junko sympathetically on the shoulder.

"Junko, that's terrible. And speaking of terrible things, I'm sure you've all heard about what happened at the university. "

"Yes, of course," said Misa. "We can think of nothing else. We wanted to ask you about it, Ellie, but you probably can't tell us anything with your husband involved."

"Ellie-*san*, it has been such a shock," said Keiko. "We're worried about our husbands' jobs at the university. You would be affected too, Ellie, because you work there part-time, don't you?"

"Yes, I do…the whole thing is horrific."

It didn't matter that Ellie didn't like Nomura. Had Professor Nomura looked down on her because she was a foreigner or because she was a woman? Either way, his disdainful look whenever their paths crossed had been unpleasant.

But she certainly hadn't disliked him enough to want him dead. His murder seemed a brutal act that stripped away the pleasant façade of Japanese society. She now saw that darkness and menace could lurk behind the conformity and routine of everyday life. If there could be murder here, at such an unlikely place as a university, it meant Japan might be, *au fond*, just like those misbegotten countries full of death and mayhem that featured in the evening news. It was a shock that here, even here, in peaceful and charming rural Japan, there could be danger and despair. She had felt so secure and happy here. And what troubled her was not just the murder but that her friend Andrew could be considered a suspect. She knew he couldn't have done anything like that.

"My husband is conducting interviews," she said. "I can divulge nothing because I know no details. My husband is professional that way, with work and home life kept strictly separate."

The girls exchanged disappointed looks. Ellie was about to mention Andrew but stopped herself in time.

Keiko suffered from no such compunction. She piped up, "My Ben says Andrew has been arrested."

Ellie was sorry she had brought up the subject. "I know nothing about it. But I can say with complete certainty that Andrew would never harm anyone."

The girls looked at each other speculatively until Misa remarked, "Well, I just pity poor Andrew finding the body. What a shock for the poor boy."

Keiko said, "And I don't imagine Alyson was much of a comfort. I've only met her a few times. She's beautiful of course, but like a store dummy: completely lifeless. I imagine you've heard the rumour that she was having an affair with President Nomura. And that Andrew has kicked her out. Well, he won't have much trouble getting a divorce, considering her behaviour."

"And I hear Akemi's having a hard time getting over seeing the dead body," Misa said. "I asked her to come out with us tonight, but she refused. She's scared! She won't get over it until somebody is arrested and put in prison. None of us can feel safe until the lunatic is caught. I'm relieved Billy doesn't work at the university."

"Andrew is like lamb," said Junko in her fractured English. "He always kind to me. So terrible he taken by police. He is not bad, not selfish like that Alyson."

Keiko looked thoughtful. "Ben told me there was some trouble with money at the university, that Professor Nomura was more worried and angrier than usual in the past few weeks."

Ellie said, "I wonder if it was anything to do about Professor Hunter's crusade for Koreans here to be given citizenship rights. I hear the army people are angry about it, seeing it as a slur on the government and its policies."

"And Professor Nomura's brother living at the army base makes it all the more awkward," Misa observed.

Junko broke in once more. "My Karl happy that man dead," she said. "He have some army friend here. He say Nomura-

sensei made trouble for army, trouble for Japan. Karl say he wish it double murder, Gerald Hunter killed too."

"Nomura-*sensei* had so many enemies. It will be difficult for your husband to find his killer," said Keiko.

Ellie resolved to tell the girls no more about the case and to avoid ever meeting them again for a meal or a drink.

Keiko had touched a sore spot. Ellie was worried about her detective husband. She knew he resented having that beady-eyed Takenaka taking charge of the case. He was being pressured on all sides to close the case quickly, even though the ultimate responsibility now lay with Takenaka. She was glad he'd been allowed to retain the

services of his two faithful lieutenants. She trusted that the three of them would find the murderer.

Luckily, the girls were tired of the topic. They moved onto the latest restaurants, bars, films, and hairdressing salons. They ordered another round of cocktails.

Oddly enough, as the girls parted that night, it was Junko who noted Ellie's concealed distress. She knew bad luck herself, so she could sense it in others.

"Take care, Eri-*chan*." She held Ellie's hand and gave her a big hug. That meant a great deal to Ellie. On such trying occasions, she needed physical touch, still anathema in Japan, where intimacy was often conveyed by nothing more than a glance or a bow.

Ellie's eyes filled with tears. "Thank you, Junko."

The Apprehended

Several police officers and a small man with bright black eyes and thick, black- framed glasses appeared at Andrew's house late Friday afternoon, two days after Nomura's murder. He had just got home from giving exams. He went with them to the police station.

Andrew made some discoveries about the Japanese legal system that day. Many of them were surprising. Nearly all of them were unpleasant.

He learned that he could be held in a police station for forty-eight hours with no questions asked. While he had a right to a lawyer, he would need to pay an enormous sum out to get one. Not enough money and he would need to wait two or three days before a lawyer would be appointed for him.

He expected an interpreter to make an appearance to read his rights. This didn't happen. Andrew was put in a cell for hours, and nobody explained what was happening. There was a tiny barred window and a small bed with a brown blanket. One bright spot: a gleaming new lavatory near his cell, and to use it he needed only to ask for an escort. He had imagined he might have a small, stained sink in one corner of the room and a bucket and a roll of toilet paper on a filthy floor.

Andrew knew he could count himself lucky on another point, too. Until a law had been passed several years earlier, specifically prohibiting the practice, Japanese police could use intimidation and even physical pressure to elicit a confession.

Andrew had never been in the Fujikawa police station before, a nondescript building in the town centre. Its prefabricated façade mimicking yellow brick could never pass for a properly constructed building. Or so Andrew used to think, as he drove past it. In the early days of his residence in Japan, he would marvel at the unsuitable architecture characterising nearly all Fujikawa's modern buildings. Whether they had been built for offices or for residential use, as flats or as factories, they looked like compact plastic boxes that must be suffocating in summer and freezing in winter, with synthetic walls absorbing the temperatures outside and compounding their intensity.

In those days of innocence, Andrew thought of the police station as a prosaic, unthreatening building. He confused it once with the post office nearby and had asked the duty officer at the entrance about buying a stamp.

Now that he was inside, held prisoner, Andrew saw the place in a new light. He was terrified. The smell was reminiscent of a hospital, a whiff of antiseptics and chemicals mingling with the aroma of over-cooked food. He had time, too much time, to think about the recent terrible events.

He sometimes reflected on what had happened the morning after he had found Nomura's body and learned of his wife's infidelity. Andrew had awoken on the uncomfortable living room sofa to the sounds of objects being thrown into boxes, bags, and suitcases. He'd walked into their bedroom where his wife was busily packing. "I'm only taking what's mine. I want nothing of yours. I want nothing of you or from you, ever again," she said.

Andrew was usually apologetic and mild, but the discovery of Alyson's affair had made him feel powerful, vindictive, and self-righteous. "I'll contact the Canadian embassy to begin divorce proceedings," Andrew had said, inwardly trembling but eloquent in rage. "And please drop the melodrama. I'd like to say it was you who destroyed what was between us. You were the one who betrayed our marriage!"

Alyson looked surprised but then uttered angrily, "Is that true, Andrew? I feel you've been looking for a way out for a long time now."

Andrew hid his shock. Had she indeed understood the real reason for Japan's initial attraction for him? It was a plan that had gone so badly wrong that, instead of escaping from her, he'd ended up marrying her.

"I've no idea what you're talking about," he said.

She looked at him pityingly. "My poor Andrew. So transparent. What a bore you are. Falling asleep like a log at nine every night, spending not the slightest effort on your appearance – that ponytail, your awful clothes. On these hot summer days you actually smell a bit: *eau de* salt-and-vinegar crisps. Can you wonder our love life fell apart? I stopped finding you attractive. Didn't you know any of this? And as for Masaki's murder, maybe any one of us is capable of atrocity if provoked enough."

Then she shook herself. "No! I can never, ever forgive who killed him. I would have won him back. We could have had a life together!"

After she'd gone, Andrew had felt guilty. I'm throwing her out on the streets, he thought, but then he was rescued by anger. *That's where she belongs anyway*, he told himself. *She's no better than a common streetwalker. Slut!*

He heard later from Ben that Alyson had simply turned up at Gerald Hunter's door, the taxi waiting outside loaded up with all her boxes, bags and suitcases, asking if she might stay with him.

If Andrew hadn't come to hate her so much, he might have marvelled at the way she had stood in the doorway on her way out, like a butterfly escaping a moth's pupa. She was a glamorous stranger. It seemed impossible she ever had shared their home, that she had holed up day after day in the smelly dark interior doing nothing. Hers was the role of the romantic heroine making some desperate gesture.

After she'd gone, Andrew wandered through their house, pacing back and forth like a prisoner. He took a shower. He thought of getting a haircut. He changed his clothes and washed what he had been wearing.

He got a call from Gerald in the afternoon. "*Moshi, moshi,* hello."

"*Moshi, moshi*. Andrew here."

"Oh, Andrew," Gerald said, "I feel I owe you an explanation, taking Alyson in." "Not necessary, Gerald. I feel grateful. I wasn't sure where she could go. She made

no friends during our time here. I felt guilty throwing her out, although I was very angry over her betraying me with that monster."

"It's all hard to take in. I would have said she was fantasising had I not heard a few rumours about Nomura."

"Rumours?" queried Andrew.

"That after Liza's death he liked the company of attractive female undergraduates and that recently he'd been seen late at night with some foreign woman." There was a long pause. "Please forgive my curiosity, Andrew, but had you no idea what was going on?"

Another long pause as Andrew clenched his fists. What a fool he had been. "None at all," he said. "I suppose I should be ashamed to admit that. But I want to say that while we may have seemed like some happy, devoted couple, there had been nothing between us for a long time, no real intimacy. I now see that we were like strangers."

"Interesting. I would have described you as a perfectly contented pair. In fact, I used to envy you. You two made me feel incomplete. I wondered why I had no such relationship myself. Listen, Andrew, I'm making this call while Alyson is out buying groceries."

"I'm sorry to cause you all this trouble."

"No trouble at all. I'll be glad of the company. I was a bit lonely. But I do hope it's a temporary arrangement. Although I've just mentioned I envied your apparent happiness with Alyson, I'm now used to living alone, preferring my own company. I hope Alyson doesn't plan to stay long. She hasn't said when she might be leaving."

"I'm wondering about that, too. There's nothing for her here. Not now, with Nomura dead and our relationship in pieces. She has no job, no friends."

"I hope she will count me a friend, just as I want to be yours…Oh, I hear her key in the lock. Better go, Andrew, I'll see you at the memorial service."

***

On Saturday, early in the morning after his arrest, having endured a dismal, sleepless night in his cell, Andrew was led down a maze of narrow corridors and escorted into an interview room. He was surprised to see Ellie seated at the table. She looked strained.

"Andrew, I'm so sorry," she said. "I've been asked to help with your interview as the police interpreter; Miss Shinohara, the woman who usually does it, is away."

Chief Inspector Inoue stepped in. Andrew was relieved he spoke English.

"Thomas-*sensei*. I am sorry. This is all…" he paused,

searching for the right word. Then he spoke quickly in Japanese to Ellie who translated, "Inspector Inoue wants me to tell you that he regrets having to ask me, his wife and your friend, to act as the interpreter at this interview. It is irregular. The Japanese woman the Fujikawa police station usually employs as interpreter has just left for a short trip to the States. She'll be back in a few days, but as they were unable to find anyone else, they've asked me to step in."

Inoue spoke again to Ellie, and she explained to Andrew.

"My husband says some new information has come to light, so you've been brought in for questioning. Superintendent Takenaka from the main police headquarters in Ishizaki will conduct the interview. Because I am to act as your interpreter, it wouldn't be appropriate if it was my husband who questions you."

The door opened. Inoue made a gesture indicating everyone should rise. Takenaka came in. Everyone bowed. The man looked sharply at Andrew and Ellie and then spoke abruptly to her. She responded. Ellie told Andrew, "He wanted to check on whether my Japanese was adequate. Also to tell you you have to pay if you want a lawyer present."

Takenaka looked at Inoue, who left the room.

"Perhaps I'm being naive," Andrew said, "but I don't feel I require a lawyer at this interview. I have nothing to hide. Apart from that, I can't afford one."

He waited as Ellie explained his answer.

Once the formalities had been observed, Takenaka began his questioning.

"Thomas-*sensei*, please be patient. I am new to this case. I have read the transcript of your first interview."

Takenaka consulted his notes. "Please clear up a few points. The first concerns your meeting with Professor Hayashi on the day of the president's death. You mentioned something about Mr Akamatsu that wasn't followed up in your interview."

Andrew loathed having to be a snitch, but he knew he would tell. I'm no better than Alyson, he thought – she was a faithless lover; he was a faithless friend.

"Professor Hayashi mentioned I should be on the lookout for rumours, *unsubstantiated ones*," he said, "about some financial impropriety committed by Akamatsu-*san*, who works in the accounting department."

"I see," said Takenaka, making a note. "That will have to be looked into. To move to the second point. Would it have been so bad for you to lose your job at the university?"

"I was worried mainly about my wife Alyson," Andrew admitted. "In fact, we've just separated, but I hadn't seen that coming."

Inspector Takenaka leaned closer. "Before I ask you about that, could you tell me why you were anxious about her?"

"Since coming to Japan, my wife has become like what you call a *hikikomori*. She rarely left our little house. She was quite dependent on my income. If I were to lose my job, I needed to know as soon as possible so we could make alternative arrangements."

Takenaka was still leaning forward, looking expectant. There was a long pause as the superintendent scrutinised Andrew's face.

"But it's because of your wife that we have brought you in today. Something quite unexpected has come to our attention. This morning we were contacted by a Mr Takeuchi. He is the owner of a small bar not far from your home. He told me that your wife and Professor Nomura had been regular customers, usually arriving late in the evening and staying several hours, and that this had been going on for about six months."

Andrew was silent.

"Thomas-*sensei*, does this come as news to you? Did you not know that your wife and the president were in the habit of seeing each other at night?"

Andrew felt humiliated and angry. "I only learned about it after I was escorted home by the police on the day of the president's murder. The news shocked Alyson into confessing that she and Professor Nomura had been friends...*lovers*."

Andrew was angry, his face was reddening. "I was stunned when she told me."

"As you say, they were not just friends. Mr Takeuchi tells me he observed them holding hands. He says they usually chose to sit in a booth at the back and once he saw them kissing."

Andrew bowed his head.

"You must see that this puts recent events in a whole new light. You were not only the first one to find the body, but we have now discovered that you had a strong motive for wishing Professor Nomura dead."

"I had nothing to do with his death! As I've told you, I only learned about him and my wife after Professor Nomura had been murdered. That's when Alyson told me the whole *sordid* tale."

"But we have only your word for that."

Andrew looked up. "I asked Alyson to leave, and she has gone. She has moved into Professor Hunter's house. I have no contact with her now. I never want to see her again. If you want to talk to her, you'll find her there."

"Oh, yes, you can be sure we will be contacting her," Takenaka said. "But I must say I find it hard to believe you were unaware of what had been going on."

The bald truth was painful, but Andrew decided it was best in the circumstances to reciprocate with frankness. "I think Alyson was attracted to Professor Nomura because he was powerful," he said. "And she wanted to engage in sexual experimentation. You may not believe me, but Alyson and I had been living together like strangers for some time now. Even so, I was surprised and very hurt when she told me what had been going on."

Takenaka looked at him doubtfully.

Takenaka's lieutenant knocked and entered. He bowed respectfully and asked to have a word outside. Takenaka was gone several minutes. When he returned he looked puzzled but also relieved.

He beckoned to Ellie, and they conferred several minutes in rapid Japanese. Takenaka bowed to Andrew and left the room. Ellie went to Andrew and said,

"Andrew, your interview is over for today. The police forbid you to leave Fujikawa. They say you may be summoned for questioning again soon, that you're still regarded as a suspect, but you may go home now."

She looked anxious and apologetic. "I'm sorry, Andrew, I don't know *what's* going on. I wish I could ask Kenji, but I can't. Apparently, he's now questioning another person involved in the case."

"Don't worry. At least I can leave. The thought that I couldn't, that I was being held here against my will has been unbearable."

Andrew wondered what had happened. Had someone else been arrested? It would be a relief but, on the other hand, Andrew felt in a state of limbo. While he was glad to be released from the ugly confines of the police station, he dreaded the thought of returning to the drab little home he had shared with Alyson. He wished he could escape himself. The saying *Wherever you go, there you are* kept running through his head like the line of an irritating song lodged in his consciousness.

At least Ellie hadn't abandoned him. They left the station together and stood huddled nervously by her car, as if expecting Andrew to be arrested again at any minute.

Ellie said, "Andrew, I was terrified when I heard you'd been arrested. I suppose you know Japan has a 99% conviction rate for suspects, people who've been arrested for a crime. It can't be true that *all* those people are guilty. That's why I was so scared for you, thinking they might make you confess to something. Even though my husband is a cop, I'm on your side. Please never forget that."

Andrew hugged her silently. He had a friend but nothing else it seemed. He had lost his wife and perhaps his reputation. He hoped he wouldn't also lose his job.

Worst of all, he felt he had lost a kind of innocence. He lived in a world where someone he knew could be murdered and the woman he had married could betray him.

New Developments

Since Nomura's murder, Inoue felt he had been subjected to one indignity after another. His authority had been superseded, just as he had foreseen. He had been treated as an underling in front of his own staff. When Takenaka interviewed Andrew at the station, Inoue had had to leave the room like a child dismissed from adult company.

Although Takenaka had trotted out the explanation that it was a conflict of interest with Ellie as interpreter, Inoue had felt the true reason was that he was regarded as superfluous.

"What happened?" Ellie asked her husband that night. "Why did Takenaka rush off and then have Andrew sent home?"

"Takenaka isn't exactly keeping me in the loop in this case," he admitted. "What I can tell you are only rumours, bits and pieces I've picked up."

Ellie sat down beside her husband and put an arm round his waist.

"The Fujikawa police force has been put under great pressure to solve this case," he said grimly. "I've never known anything like it. Even though Takenaka is officially in charge, representatives of Fujikawa's local board of trustees have been to visit me, and I've had any number of calls from Obuchi-*sensei*, now acting head of the university."

Inoue continued, "I wonder if that idiot Takenaka is just sending everyone with a question or a complaint to me. Maybe it's his little joke. I've become the Fujikawa police's PR man instead of its chief inspector. Everyone is desperate for a breakthrough, for an arrest."

Now Inoue looked around their tiny kitchen as if fearing he might be overheard. He said, "I place zero confidence in Takenaka's abilities as an investigator. Luckily, up until now, my encounters with him have been limited to the annual inspections. But now he's here, on my beat, in my office! It's almost unbearable."

Ellie looked at him sympathetically. "I'm so sorry. But why was Andrew suddenly released? Is he no longer a suspect?"

"Well, the case seems to be solved, but for the public and the press we're trotting out the line that 'someone is helping us with our inquiries'."

"You've actually arrested someone?"

"Yes, Takenaka has pulled someone else in for questioning, someone he says is a more plausible culprit. That's the good news."

"And the bad news?"

"I feel quite sure from the little I've gathered that we've arrested the wrong person. Again!"

Although these were the sentiments Inoue confided to his wife, he knew he was being unfair. Takenaka hadn't, in fact, behaved as reprehensibly as expected. He had looked apologetic after what Inoue thought of as the "Andrew incident". He had told Inoue that Mari Furomoto, the co-ed Nomura was reportedly having an affair with, had turned up at the station as requested. Takenaka had seemed sincere in saying he would be grateful if Inoue would interview her.

Still, Inoue thought Takenaka was following his own agenda and not confiding in him as much as he should have. It was a breach of professionalism, a flouting of the courtesy that Takenaka should have accorded him as the chief of police of this station.

Inoue was like a bystander, and that made him feel increasingly aggrieved and angry.

Because he couldn't rely on Takenaka to keep him abreast of developments, Inoue had been pursuing his own lines of inquiry. The president's home in Fujikawa had been searched and his office at the university gone over with a fine-toothed comb. Forensics had turned up nothing of value though. The post-mortem had served only to verify the obvious, that Nomura had been killed by a single swipe of a knife across his throat severing both branches of the carotid artery. Death had been instantaneous. The knife found outside Building Two had been established as the murder weapon, but it held no DNA or fingerprint evidence. Enquiries at local shops had turned up no likely purchasers. It was just a common kitchen knife of a kind sold in the kitchenware section of each of Fujikawa's three grocery stores.

It was important for Inoue to find the cleaner who had told Mr. Kawane of the trouble in Building Two. Curiously, enquiries had established there was no cleaner employed as maintenance staff who could be described as having a bulging belly. There was also the problem of Professor Nomura's computer and the folder of documents Miss Tanimoto had photocopied. Both seemed to have vanished. Another matter Takenaka hadn't even broached was the porcelain doll on the president's desk, with *ikenai* or 'forbidden' scrawled on its forehead.

Who were the suspects? Inoue had decided they should include the people he had interviewed on the afternoon after the discovery of the body but that the professor might also have been dispatched by someone unknown: a loner with a grievance perhaps.

The interview with Mari Furomoto meant that one suspect could be eliminated. She had been contacted after being singled out as the attractive student seen in the president's office in the weeks before. She had sounded incredulous and indignant when a policewoman rang to ask her to report to the police station for questioning.

Mari was angry when she flounced into the interview room three days after the murder. Inoue was still chafing at being unable to attend Andrew's interview. He had to content himself instead with interviewing a sulky lass with long black hair who was dressed in the latest summer fashion for trendy co-eds at Japanese universities in the second decade of the 21st century: a skimpy flowered tunic dress over short black leggings and platform sandals.

Mari had chosen to distance herself from what she obviously considered an ordeal that had nothing to do with her. She twirled long strands of hair around her fingers as she answered their questions in a dull voice, staring at the floor. She had a cast-iron alibi, having been on a shopping excursion with her mother in Ishizaki on that morning, with any number of shop assistants available to testify to the numerous purchases the pair had made. She admitted that Professor Nomura had made overtures but insisted she had rejected them. Inoue noted her simpering smile with some distaste.

He reluctantly concluded that, for the moment, only Thomas-*sensei* seemed a viable culprit. His gut instinct told him Andrew was no murderer, but there was motive and opportunity. Maybe finding out about Alyson had tipped Andrew over the edge. He had heard a little from Ellie about Andrew's partner. He thought she sounded a complete nutcase. But love was blind and maybe Andrew was crazy about her.

Still, this didn't ring true. He thought Nomura's murder was premeditated. Andrew seemed a bit clueless and helpless, with organising such a crime quite beyond his capabilities. Being a policeman meant being an expert in psychology. In his long years of service, Inoue had honed his skills at assessing character and, apart from the unpredictability of a spontaneous homicide, he felt he could spot a killer at a hundred metres.

After seeing Miss Furomoto off, Inoue was told by Kubo that Andrew had been suddenly released and allowed to return home and that Takenaka wanted to speak with him once he'd got off the phone to headquarters. More indignities. Takenaka hadn't conferred with him before releasing Andrew, and he kept Inoue cooling his heels in the corridor before he was finally summoned.

"We've let that foreigner go," Takenaka said smugly, "and made another arrest. This time I think we've got the right man."

"Another arrest?" Inoue said, shocked at the suddenness of it while resenting Takenaka's rudeness in not consulting him before taking such an important step.

"It's all clear, this tawdry but shocking event," Takenaka said, his beady eyes burning brightly. "Although, I must admit, we have a few loose ends to tie up."

"Please tell me more about it," Inoue asked, as calmly as he could.

Takenaka looked at him approvingly, but his words were tinged with mockery. "We have learned that a man, mentally defective – or, I should say, in these politically correct times, handicapped – has been employed at Fujikawa as a cleaner.

Of course, we're speaking off the record here."

"Yes, sir."

"You may remember that the university originated as a Christian institution and that its board of trustees actively pursues an ethical admissions policy, recruiting students who are in need or considered challenged in various ways. Well, I have now found out that they also hire staff, especially the cleaning staff and the grounds maintenance crew, using the same criteria. Or they used to, before President Nomura took charge."

"I'm not sure I understand," Inoue said.

"What I mean is this," said Takenaka confidently. "We have discovered that there is a man named Hiroki Suga with a very low IQ who has been working at the university for around ten years. He had been enrolled at special schools as a child. He can do only menial tasks."

"And his work at the university?"

"Emptying bins, washing windows, sweeping paths." "I see."

"But then President Nomura took charge. It came to his attention that Suga was frightening the students. He would sit on the benches and stare at attractive female co- eds. He was scolded by his co-workers, but he was incorrigible."

"And?" Inoue said, desperate for something substantial. He could imagine Takenaka later regaling his friends at the police prefectural HQ with descriptions of Inoue's bafflement: "His mouth was agape. He couldn't understand a word I was saying."

Damn that bastard, Inoue thought, as Takenaka continued his indictment of Suga. "A favourite chore, one he always volunteered for, was washing the windows of

the president's office even when the windows weren't *dirty*!" "Professor Nomura's."

"Precisely," said Takenaka approvingly. "Suga was *spying* on the president. And he had reason to hate him. The president had decided to fire him. His contract would have come to an end a few days after the president was murdered."

"But how did you discover all this? What happened just now, that you suddenly decided to release the foreigner?"

"There were several compelling reasons. First, Mr Kawane told us earlier that another cleaner had seen Suga cleaning the president's windows the morning of the murder, using a small stepladder."

"Aaach!" Inoue reacted with surprise.

"Yes, just what I thought," said Takenaka. "But it was another bit of information that made me release the foreigner. While I was interviewing Professor Thomas, my officers were busy processing the interviews of students and staff. One officer made an astonishing discovery and relayed it to my second-in-command. A student was sitting on a bench near the courtyard, drinking a can of cold coffee he'd got from a vending machine and studying for a test that was due to take place in the second period. He said he had seen a cleaner in the president's office at about the time forensics estimates the murder was committed. The student said he caught a glimpse of him through the window and that he also saw Professor Thomas hurrying out of Building Three, where his office was, and going into Building Two, apparently to see the president."

"And you think this implicates the cleaner Suga and clears Professor Thomas?"

Takenaka glared fiercely at Inoue. "But of course! Don't you? That's why I terminated the foreigner's interview and dispatched officers to arrest Suga."

But Takenaka had misunderstood Inoue, who saw how flimsy the evidence was against Suga.

"Congratulations, sir," Inoue managed. "But there are still a few aspects of the case that are unclear."

"Such as?" Takenaka looked impatient.

"The porcelain doll found on Professor Nomura's desk, for one thing. Why was it there? Whose was it? Who wrote the word 'forbidden' on its forehead? There's also the fact that Professor Nomura's laptop computer was taken, as well as the folder of copies and the original file that he intended giving to all the department heads."

Takenaka straightened in his chair. "As I've said, there are still a few loose ends. I expect you to begin working on those now." He dismissed him with a wave, turning back to the papers on his desk. Then he called him back. "I have issued a search

warrant for Suga's house, a dilapidated shack near the train tracks with his mother. He's a hoarder, living in the accumulated debris of decades: newspapers, magazines dating back thirty years. Apparently there are empty bottles, cans, and thousands of wrappers and bags, paper and plastic. It'll be tough finding anything in that chaotic mess, but I've got several officers working on it."

Then Takenaka delivered what he obviously considered his *coup de grace*. "I should also tell you this. Suga has a record."

"What has he done?"

"Two years ago he was arrested for aggravated assault with a broom." "A broom!"

"Suga has been a troubled individual all his life. When you speak to him, he sounds normal, but he was so delayed in language development as a child that his single mother – the father's unknown – thought she would need to enrol him in a special school for the mentally disabled. Turns out he could go through the normal school system after all, but he had no friends."

"And the assault?"

"I was getting to that," said Takenaka. "Suga lives in one of the meaner houses in the most rundown part of Fujikawa, one of those shacks bordering the train tracks. It's a bleak little place, but there was one spot of greenery in the vicinity, a big tree growing in a neighbour's front yard. Suga's mother, an old shrew who has worked all her life at a noodle shop near their home, was always complaining about the neighbour's not sweeping away the leaves and twigs from his tree. Human nature, full of contradictions – she lives in a pigsty but kicks up a fuss about those leaves. Anyway, one day, her son snapped, couldn't stand her going on about the leaves any longer. He ran out and attacked this neighbour when he was leaving home to go to work."

"With a broom," Inoue said.

Takenaka smiled. "In the right hands, it can be a lethal weapon. Left the chap with severe bruising around the head."

"And the result?"

"Suga was cautioned and given a suspended sentence. The neighbour cut down his tree and moved away shortly afterwards. The point is Suga is capable of violence. The case against that foreigner was never satisfactory. Once his partner's affair with the president had been discovered, I dispatched one of my best officers to interview her at

Professor Hunter's house. There's obviously no love lost between the foreigner and that woman. I got the impression she would have implicated him if she could, but she was vehement that Andrew Thomas knew nothing of her affair beforehand. Actually, she was quite pleased with herself for having deceived him so successfully."

"I agree, sir, Thomas-*sensei* was genuinely surprised to learn of her infidelity."

Takenaka shrugged and threw up his hands. "These foreigners with their messy love lives..." and then paused, recalling that Inoue was the wrong man to vent his prejudices to. "Anyway, with that motive gone, the case against Thomas-*sensei* seems to collapse. Nothing but circumstantial evidence, the foreigner guilty only of having found the body. Although I have the impression Miss Weller would like to have her estranged husband punished for something. Even though she was the guilty party."

"Ah woman, the mystery of thee…" "What's that?" Takenaka asked. "Nothing, nothing, sir."

Inoue left his former office in a black mood.

"It's our way," Inoue said to Ellie the next morning, as he tried to explain what had happened. "We try to erase or efface one mistake by making another that's even worse. We've arrested the wrong man. Now we're trying to make the crime fit this unlikely suspect."

"Oh god," she said. "What next?"

"What, indeed," he said. "How can we question a man who is legally classified as mentally deficient? What credence can we place on what he says? Takenaka places too much importance on the invisibility of the culprit. Suga was wearing the cleaner's usual outfit for summer: a broad-brimmed straw hat, a surgical mask, a loose shirt and trousers and, most crucially, white cotton gloves. This costume rendered him, to all intents and purposes, anonymous and even unseen. The gloves, of course, meant no fingerprints."

Inoue paused, lost in thought, and then continued. "From what I've heard of Suga, I can't imagine he would be able to carry out such a crime."

"Neither can I."

"He was cleaning the windows of Professor Nomura's office that morning, using a stepladder; it would have required considerable physical strength, not to mention cunning, for Suga to have got into the office through the window without Professor Nomura raising the alarm. Also, Professor Nomura had his throat slit while he was

seated at his desk. Assuming that Suga was able to enter the room through the window, how on earth could he have got up behind him to slit his throat? There is also the matter of the clothes. They would have been spattered with blood and would have been noticed by passers-by or fellow workers after Suga left the office. Takenaka has ordered a search of Suga's house. It will be interesting if clothing with blood on is discovered there."

"It does all seem wrong," Ellie said.

Inoue looked ironically at his wife. "At this point, I need all the help I can get. Please pray for me."

An Unlikely Suspect

Inoue attended the formal interview with Suga the next morning. Takenaka told Inoue to be an observer, sitting silently next to the policewoman working the voice recorder.

Suga was a gaunt, dull-eyed man in his late forties with scruffy hair and a wrinkled face. He wore a faded t-shirt and baggy jeans. He looked as if he hadn't had a proper meal in ages. Inoue imagined the officers searching Suga's house would find that he and his mother lived off Pot Noodles, rice balls and greasy snacks from the convenience store nearby.

Takenaka proudly took his place opposite the accused man, beaming at him as though he was new-found treasure.

"Please give your full name and occupation."

Suga looked up sullenly, warily, mumbling his answers. "Suga. Hiroki Suga. I'm a cleaner. Been there ten years."

"There, meaning...?" "The college."

"But I understand this employment was to come to an end imminently." "Sorry?"

Takenaka winked at Inoue as if to say, *Just as we thought, a halfwit*. "You were to stop work very soon, by next week, I believe."

The puzzlement on Suga's face was followed by relief at having understood. "Mr Kawane, the man who gave me orders, told me not to come anymore."

"Any idea why your employment was being terminated?" The puzzled look again.

"Why do you think you were losing your job?"

"Fujikawa has fewer students. Cuts had to be made. I'm not a teacher. I'm just old Suga, the man who takes out the garbage. Anybody can do that."

"Is that what Mr Kawane said when he explained your services would no longer be required?"

"Yes, but he also said something that made me mad."

Takenaka looked relieved. Finally the line of enquiry was producing satisfactory results. "And that was?"

"He said I had to return all my equipment, my mops and brooms. I keep some at home. I need them."

"I beg your pardon, Mr Suga. I think he had more to tell you than that. He complained about something, didn't he?"

Suga looked up slyly. "He said I shouldn't look." "Look?"

"At the pretty girls. But I laughed. That man didn't know the half of it. It was my job, wasn't it? Cleaning windows was part of my work. I saw things, didn't I? Things that maybe I wasn't supposed to see."

"Please be more explicit?"

"That old man Nomura, he liked young girls, too." Suga grinned. "So high and mighty. Lording it over everyone like he was god. He was the big professor, I'm just the cleaner, but we were the same. I like girls, too. He would have his blinds down, but I could see lots more than he thought. Girls! On the sofa with him. Not many times, mind you, but I saw him."

"Did you ever think of reporting President Nomura for misconduct?" "Sorry?"

"Did you ever think of telling anybody what you'd seen?"

"You're joking. He was the boss. I'm nobody. Who would believe me?" Suga smiled, lost in recollection. "Those girls, some real stunners."

"And did you ever try to enter the president's office, by the window?"

"That old man asked me to come in once. I was just outside on my ladder. He was having trouble opening one window and saw me was washing another. He asked me to step in and push up the window that was stuck. Then I left the way I had come."

"Where were you on the morning of Professor Nomura's murder?" "I just told you, didn't I? I was washing those blessed windows." "And did you see anything unusual?"

"I seen him walking up and down, up and down. Looked like he couldn't sit down. Got ants in your pants, old man, I thought."

"Do you know what time this was?"

"I could see the big clock on Building Four, about 8.30." Takenaka could hardly contain his enthusiasm. He leaned forward.

"And then?"

"I was laughing, wasn't I? I was thinking, hey old man, you

got stood up by one of your girls?" Suga's face darkened. "That's when the old man saw me. He pulled up the blinds. He was right mad. He told me to go away. 'You fool,' he said, 'get out of my sight. Go empty some bins and throw yourself in the garbage while you're at it.'"

Suga stared down at the desk, as if angrily recollecting the exchange. "He had no right talking to me like that."

Takenaka signalled to one of the officers standing by the interview room door. He went out and got a plastic bag holding the kitchen knife that had been found below one of Professor Nomura's office windows.

"Mr Suga, have you ever seen this knife before?"

Suga looked confused. "I got one at home in my kitchen. Everybody has one. They're sold cheap at the stores."

"I would now like to ask you your movements following your angry exchange with Professor Nomura. Did you climb in the window again?"

Suga looked at him as if he were crazy. "I told you, didn't I? He told me to go." "And so?"

"And so I did. Mind you, I was in such a rush, I forgot that ladder. I got yelled at when I got back to the garbage collection point."

"Did you go back to get the ladder later?"

"I did, maybe an hour or so later, but then I heard some commotion, somebody screaming from that old man's office, and I was too afraid to go near, so I just ran away. Lucky I found a broom near the car park. I just swept and swept until Mr Kawane finally stopped me and told me to go home."

Takenaka looked disappointed. "You know that's not the correct version of events," he said. "You were so angry with Professor Nomura after he scolded you that you pulled up one window and entered the office. When your employer turned away, seating himself at his desk, you took out that knife. You slit Professor Nomura's throat, making your escape through the same window. You wiped the blade and dropped the knife below the windows. You then hurried home and disposed of your blood-spattered clothing. Perhaps you even carried them to the university garbage site, to be incinerated with the rest of the burnable items."

"You what?" Suga looked incredulous, his mouth open, eyes bulging.

"I would like to formally charge you with the murder of Professor Nomura, the president of Fujikawa University. You need not say anything now, but it may harm your defence if, when questioned, you fail to mention something relevant to this case."

Inoue slumped in his chair as two uniformed officers came in to take Suga away.

Suga was stunned and put up no resistance; he just shook his head saying, "What in the world? What in the world?" as he shuffled off between the two officers.

"We've got forty-eight hours before we have to inform the

public prosecutor," Takenaka said. "But it doesn't matter. He's a good friend of mine. We can wangle ten more days of custody. Oh, and I heard from the search team. No blood-splattered clothing, but there was a large stash of pornographic material hidden under his bed. A classic peeping tom." He looked over at Inoue, standing silently by the door. "I know you disagree with me, you're fixated on the missing folder and Professor Nomura's laptop, but I think they were stolen in an opportunistic crime, someone who chanced upon the scene after the murder. We should question the people seen in Nomura's office after the murder once more." Takenaka shuffled papers on his desk and lit another cigarette. "What I'm proposing is two crimes here, committed by two separate individuals. Somebody killed the president. Somebody else stole the computer and the folder."

Takenaka folded his arms on the table and gave a small wintry smile. "Maybe what we're investigating is a miniature crime wave, centring on Miss Tanimoto's annex and Professor Nomura's office."

"I'm sorry, sir," Inoue said. "We secured the crime scene when we arrived. In addition to the missing computer and the missing folder, there's the mysterious porcelain doll on the president's desk. I expect you've heard that forensics confirmed the blood on the doll's forehead as Professor Nomura's."

"Yes, I did get that report from forensics. But this is a crime we must solve, one step at a time, and I consider Suga's arrest as one of the steps. We must concentrate on the missing items and the doll. There's also the disappearance of a pocket diary Kawane- *san* assures me was always in the president's possession. And now, if there's nothing else…"

"Yes, sir," said Inoue. He could think of nothing else to say.

Inoue Pursues Lines of Enquiry

Early on Monday, five mornings after that hot and bright July day when the president was murdered, Chief Inspector Inoue paced up and down for a good half hour. Five strides to the wall, then a tight swivel around and back to the opposite wall. Apart from the grim expression on his face, he could have been practising a dance manoeuvre.

His tiny new 'office' was like a storeroom, boxes stacked in a corner. It was at the end of the corridor, an afterthought. There were no windows, no large wooden desk, no comfortable chair with a view of the parking lot. Just a flimsy plastic table and a straight-backed chair.

He would have complained but that would be sour grapes. Never complain or explain. Ellie told him that was the way of the British monarchy. He admired stoicism. He tried to live like that.

Inoue was determined, his lips firmly pressed together. He had told Ando and Kubo to join him. He sat and clasped his hands on the desk, waiting for his juniors.

Inoue was furious to see that Ando looked more rumpled and frayed than usual. At least Kubo was neat and clean, even the brass buttons on his uniform twinkling.

His two protégés looked like models for the appropriate and the inappropriate- looking police officer in the cadets' training manual: Kubo with a big green check beside his picture; Ando, a big red 'X' scrawled across his.

"Sir?" said Kubo tentatively. "Just sit."

His officers looked anxious. They probably expected a dressing down. To their surprise, their boss was about to admit to a wrongdoing of his own.

Inoue took out a small volume, the sort of pocket diary used by most Japanese to record appointments and meetings.

"Do you recognise this?" he asked sternly.

Kubo said no, Ando hesitated, looking up with dread.

"Sir, it looks like the diary I saw you pick up on the morning of the murder. It was lying on the desk beside the corpse."

"Exactly," Inoue beamed. "And have you told anyone else?"

"No, sir. Of course not, sir," Ando said meekly. "Good. It's been a mine of information."

Inoue paused. For a moment he looked a tad embarrassed. "I had every right to take it from the crime scene, although I should have put on gloves before picking it up. I intended to study it and then have it officially docketed as evidence with everything else collected. That is what I *intended*." Inoue looked at his two officers listening to him. "But the next morning Superintendent Takenaka had been put in charge…"

He stopped again and then said, "I should have given this important material over to him."

Now the two junior officers looked at each other.

Inoue adopted a stern expression and spoke gruffly. "And if I find you two ever doing anything like that, I'll have you kicked out of the force so fast your feet won't touch the station floor on your way out."

"Yes, sir," Ando said. "Sorry, sir."

Inoue looked at him in exasperation as he seated himself again in his own uncomfortable chair. "You've nothing to apologise for! It's me who's apologising. What I did was wrong, and I want you to remember that."

"Yes, sir," Kubo and Ando chorused.

"This is your first murder enquiry," Inoue said. "A training opportunity for you."

Inoue leaned back in his chair, relieved at having made his confession. "Now, I'd like to hear your impressions of the case so far. You can begin, Officer Kubo."

"There are too many suspects, sir," Kubo said. "Almost nobody has an alibi for the time of the murder. Many of them seem not to have liked the victim at all."

"I agree, sir," said Ando. "It's baffling."

"But we have been able to eliminate several figures from our inquiry," said Inoue, consulting his notes. "Mari Furomoto, the student Professor Nomura is reported having an affair with has been cleared. She was shopping in Ishizaki that morning with her mother. We have CCTV footage showing she was at Ishizaki train station at

10.00. Also, Michiko Ota's colleagues say she never left her desk after the 8.30 staff meeting that morning."

Inoue picked up an official-looking document from the desk. "Good work, Ando, tracking down and interviewing those two men with a grudge against the president.

According to your report, the two men he had fired – the administrative officer Akiyama and the physics professor Horii – both have unassailable alibis."

Inoue squinted down at the report. Maybe he did need reading glasses, as Ellie had often suggested lately. "And those alibis were…Akiyama was visiting his aunt in Tokyo, and Horii was in a coffee shop in Ishizaki from 9.00 to 11.00 that morning."

"But, sir," said Kubo, "unfortunately, that's not the case with the others we questioned, individuals known to have been near the president's office when the murder was committed. Most have nobody who can vouch for their whereabouts."

Inoue smiled indulgently. "Yes, it *is* frustrating, but are there no other points about the case that stand out in your mind as requiring further investigation?"

It was a moment for Inoue to savour, a time he could feel superior. He needed it after having to suffer the indignity of his loss of position to Takenaka. He got up and stood before his officers as if to deliver a lecture.

"I would like to draw your attention to several salient

points. I want to do so because Superintendent Takenaka seems convinced that Suga is the killer and that all we need do now is clear up a few loose ends, including the presence of the porcelain doll on the president's desk and the disappearance of his computer and the folder of copies Miss Tanimoto had in her office."

Inoue continued, "First, why does Michiko Ota look so frightened? She has a firm alibi, so why should she appear so guilty?"

Kubo said, "Yes, I've noticed that. She seems terrified. Maybe she's just afraid because a murderer is walking loose."

Inoue approved. "I'm glad you took note of the state of mind of one of our suspects. We need to use intuition rather than just facts to conduct this kind of enquiry, but we should never take our assumptions at face value. And there are three more points to consider and investigate. The first concerns Professor Hunter. Why did he suddenly shave off his beard? Also, does he usually wear a hat?"

Now the juniors were afraid to look at each other. These were such odd questions they wondered if Inoue had taken leave of his senses.

His next words cast further doubt on his sanity. "The second point we must consider," he said, pacing back and forth, "is Professor Yamamoto's bag, the one she was seen carrying that morning. Why did it look heavier after her meeting Miss Ota in the mail room than it did while she was walking to the administration building to sign in? This fact was mentioned by Thomas-*sensei* with no idea of its significance.

And the third point. We need to identify the cleaner who heard Professor Thomas's cries for help and summoned Mr Kawane to the crime scene. We have Mr Kawane's description of the man: he was big bellied, suffering from a bad cold, wearing a surgical mask. We have reports from other witnesses of someone like that raking the courtyard about then."

Inoue paused. "You must have noticed that Suga is a very thin man, almost emaciated. He denies having been anywhere near the crime scene when the murder was committed. He said the president caught him peering through his office windows and yelled at him, that he ran back to the garbage collection area and was rebuked by other cleaners for forgetting his ladder. Kubo, after this meeting, I'd like you to go to the campus to interview all the grounds maintenance crew and the cleaners. We need to verify Suga's statement. We also need to find the person matching the description of the mysterious cleaner given by Mr Kawane. Ando, I know you've already questioned the cleaners about this, and they said there's no plump cleaner at the university, nobody who could be described as overweight. I'm sure you conducted the interviews thoroughly, but I think we need to broaden our search, asking if anyone noticed anything unusual on that day, like an imposter cleaner. I'm asking you to do this, Kubo, as

Ando has already talked to the cleaning staff. Enquiries by a different person can awaken memories."

Inoue stopped pacing back and forth. "Officers Ando and Kubo, as a sign of the trust I have in you, I want us to be like equal collaborators in solving this case. I'll give you some information from the diary which may open up other lines of enquiry or assist us in those we are pursuing already. Please take notes. I've looked specially at the entries in the days preceding the murder. Professor Nomura, like many academics, wrote in a tiny scrawl, but I managed to decipher most of what he recorded. There were also some interesting notes at the back of the diary."

Kubo and Ando both had pads and pencils at the read.

"Here are my conclusions," said Inoue, enjoying the moment. "Professor Nomura must have felt under attack from all sides. First, it appears, from calculations at the back of the diary, that he was being blackmailed."

Kubo raised his hand and said, "Any idea what about? Or for how long?"

"No, alas, the details are unclear. However, the foreigner Professor Thomas told us during his second interview that on the morning of the murder a Professor Hayashi visited him and mentioned some scandal surrounding a man named Akamatsu who works in the administration building. Some hint of financial impropriety. So, Kubo, this is the second job I'd like you to do, after you've interviewed the cleaners – find

Professor Hayashi and question him. Then find Akamatsu himself to see if he was involved in blackmailing the president or embezzling funds or whatever. There must be some substance to the rumour."

"Yes, sir."

"There's something else in the diary. President Nomura was the victim of threatening phone calls. He indicated the occasions with a tiny heart covered by a cross. This is a delicate matter. You may have heard the president was suspected of sexual harassment. There are also rumours that he was being targeted by people upset with his behaviour. I want to investigate this because I suspect the defaced hearts represent calls made by those individuals. A related line of enquiry concerns Professor Nomura's reported relations with Miss Weller. We arrested the foreigner, Professor Thomas, after we learned from a local bar owner that the president was having an affair with his wife. We released him because Takenaka believed the murder had been committed by the half-wit cleaner Suga. Then a student made a statement that he had been on a bench in the courtyard when Professor Thomas rushed from Building Three to Building Two, to meet the president, and that he had seen a cleaner standing by the window in the president's office just before then."

"I would say this conclusively establishes the foreigner's innocence. The murderer either had already killed the president and then made his escape, followed by the entry of a cleaner who has failed to come forward or, as Takenaka asserts, the cleaner the student saw in the president's window was the killer, presumably Suga."

"But what I want to tell you now is this. It seems Professor Nomura intended to break it off with the foreigner's wife the night before his death."

"From what I could decipher in the diary – some passages were not at all clear – Professor Nomura noted his assignations with Miss Weller with a tiny heart and an 'A' inside, drawn on the days when they'd be meeting."

"The nights, you mean, sir," Ando said.

"All right, nights, yes. We have only Miss Weller's word for it that she returned home that night after meeting Professor Nomura at a bar. She says he dropped her off near the house she shared with Professor Thomas. According to his statement and hers, Professor Thomas is a heavy sleeper, so he can't corroborate whether she was in that night or not. Was she driven to a murderous fury, a woman scorned?"

"As for you, Ando, while Kubo is interviewing the cleaners and then Professor Hayashi and Akamatsu, I'd like you to call at Professor Hunter's house, where Miss

Weller has been staying since Professor Thomas threw her out. See if you can get any more out of her."

"Yes, sir," Ando said, obviously pleased with the assignment.

"And polish your shoes before that interview and generally

tidy yourself up."

Ando nodded his head vigorously. "Yes, sir!"

As the two officers were leaving his room, Ando paused and looked back. "Please excuse my impertinence, sir, but may I ask what line of enquiry you will be pursuing?"

Inoue's face took on a grave expression. "No need for apologies, Ando. I need to inform you both that forensics told me this morning that Professor Yamamoto's fingerprints were found on the base of that porcelain doll."

Another Death

It was four o'clock on a sultry Monday afternoon, almost a week since the murder. Hideo Akamatsu, employed in the university's accounting department, was sitting, as usual, with his three colleagues in their crowded second-floor office in Building One. Keiko Araki was at the next desk. She glanced at him with pity tinged by contempt. Akamatsu had a huge stack of papers for processing and filing wedged between two improvised bookends on his desk: one was a statue of the Eiffel Tower and the other a plastic model of the Sacré-Cœur basilica.

Everyone knew Akamatsu dreamt of visiting France. He had even begun taking evening classes in French at a local community centre.

Keiko Araki gave a self-satisfied sniff. She was known for ruthless efficiency. Her desk was bare apart from the document she was working on. Akamatsu looked even paler and more frail than usual. She could hear his laboured breathing as he sat motionless.

"Akamatsu-*san*, *genki*?" Miss Araki asked. "Are you all right?"

He looked surprised at her unusual concern for his wellbeing. "Oh yes, perfectly fine. It's just this terrible business about Professor Nomura."

Everyone noticed Akamatsu had not been himself since the president's murder. He was irritable, did his work perfunctorily, and seemed heading for a breakdown. He looked about him furtively, often casting covert, suspicious glances at Miss Araki. He had a fearful expression.

They said it was nerves. Akamatsu was not the only one in any case. Many of the professors and administrative staff were dragging themselves through each day. Even Kawane, usually imperturbable, looked anxious, rubbing his big nose even more often than usual. But everyone knew they had to carry on – the final exams had to be administered, marks recorded and posted on the university's website. Still, they seemed demoralised, able only to muster strength sufficient to do the bare minimum in discharging their duties.

The students, on the other hand, were relishing it. There was a visible loosening of the bonds. In the two days of exams after the memorial service, the students were testing authority, seeing how far they could go. There was smoking in non-smoking

areas. Students cycled through the grounds, something expressly forbidden before the president's death. Litter was tossed in the courtyard, and one renegade soul had even scribbled graffiti on a wall by the main gate: *The president is dead. Long live the students.*

The general feeling was that the sooner the exam period was over, the better.

The office staff tried to pretend everything was normal, but with the flamboyant chain-smoking Professor Obuchi now in command, and looking more worried and dishevelled by the day, even the old troopers felt hard-pressed to keep to their routines.

"Well," said Miss Araki to Akamatsu, seeing him looking so poorly, "please take care of yourself. I hope one of your lucky charms will bring you some peace of mind."

Akamatsu reached up to fondle a rabbit's foot hanging from his angle-poise lamp.

That Akamatsu was superstitious had long been a source of amusement for his colleagues. The rabbit's foot was only one of Akamatsu's many charms to ward off ill fortune. The top left drawer of his desk was filled with tokens he had collected from local temples, assuring him of long life and happiness. His fellow office workers snorted about it among themselves, but said nothing seeing him bent over his desk.

Akamatsu's phone suddenly rang. Miss Araki was checking some figures first with her abacus and then with a calculator, but she overheard Akamatsu whisper into the phone, "I understand. At 9.00 then." When he hung up, Akamatsu looked pale and his hands shook slightly shuffling papers, as if he was making a great show of being busy.

Shortly after the mysterious call, Akamatsu was summoned downstairs to the annex next to the administration headquarters where twenty employees toiled with computers, papers and phones. Officer Kubo was standing at the annex door. Beside him was a strained-looking Professor Hayashi, wringing his hands. As Akamatsu and Hayashi passed each other, Hayashi stuttered, "I'm so sorry, I was only relaying a rumour I'd heard. I'm sure you are quite innocent."

Akamatsu spent the next hour strenuously denying any financial impropriety. Kubo wanted to question him further, but his physical condition was a concern. He was trembling so hard that that Kubo let him go, saying that he would contact him again.

At home Akamatsu watched television for an hour, eating a light meal of rice, miso soup, and a piece of broiled fish. His forehead felt hot and he wondered if it was a summer cold. At 8.30, he headed back to the university.

The muffled voice on the phone had demanded a meeting at 9.00 in the hallway of Building Two. The yellow tape had been taken down and the building unlocked for

the professors with offices on the second floor. The campus was deserted. Akamatsu felt feverish. The stars were strangely bright, and he felt as though he was the last person on earth. He thought about death. He longed for release, something to lighten the burden of guilt he had carried for six months, ever since Professor Nomura had requested his assistance with a delicate matter.

Akamatsu approached the building with foreboding. There was a light shining on the wall outside the door, but the corridor was dark. He checked his watch. It was exactly 9.00. When he tentatively opened the door and entered the hall, he could see, despite the gloom, a figure emerging from the men's toilet at the far end.

"*Konbanwa*," Akamatsu said in a quavering voice. "Good evening."

The figure approached in silence. There was no sound of footsteps. It was as if the man was moving through the air. As he got nearer, Akamatsu saw he was curiously dressed. He wore puttee trousers and a peaked hat with a neck skirting. Akamatsu realised with horror it was a man in the uniform of the Japanese Imperial Army. Was it the spirit rumoured to haunt Building Two, lamenting Japan's defeat in the war?

Was this delirium? Was he going to be accosted by a ghost? Anything was possible of late. Was seeing a ghost less likely than murder? He had always believed in ghosts actively populating the world. Akamatsu stumbled backwards back but the door was shut. He stood and stared, feeling more curious than fearful, but his heart was thudding and his legs were weak. When the figure was only a foot away, Akamatsu slumped to the floor and held up an arm for protection. The last thing he saw was a swarthy face and malevolent eyes. Then the figure bent forward, and white-gloved fists rained down punches on his head and chest in a relentless cascade of blows.

Visions of Paris floated, one by one, through Akamatsu's

mind even as he was being pummelled. He was strolling in Montmartre and having his portrait drawn by a street artist. He was cruising down the Seine on a *Bateau Mouche*. Promenading on the Champs Elysées, he wore a beret, a stylish green jacket, and light trousers. He was sitting at a café drinking a glass of Burgundy and eating Camembert. He had finally reached his goal: the City of Light.

Recovering consciousness, Akamatsu realised he hadn't taken a breath since the mysterious figure had launched its attack. He gulped and gasped. But breath no longer seemed necessary. He was freed from the most elementary fact of human existence. He was alone, in the darkness, under the night sky, the glittering stars coming closer and closer. They were a beneficent presence, beckoning him upwards to join their exalted company. Akamatsu's chest burst with a terrible pain. The stars were shining bright, coming ever closer. He felt himself swallowed up in their intense light.

A Fall From Grace

Ellie and Inoue were in bed in the early hours of Tuesday morning, six days after Professor Nomura's murder, when they got the call. According to Kubo, the office worker named Akamatsu had been found in the hallway of Building Two. He had been badly beaten, but the cause of death was a heart attack. Kubo promised to call Inoue when he got the coroner's report.

It was another hot day. When the phone rang, they had been clinging to each other so tightly it felt they were drowning in each other's embrace. But Ellie was wrapped around her husband in the throes of passion while Inoue clasped her to him not from lust, but to ward off despair.

He had been unable to find Professor Yamamoto the previous day even though officers had been dispatched to the campus and to her flat. He dreaded interviewing her about her fingerprints on the porcelain doll.

Damn, thought Inoue as he slammed down the receiver. *Building Two again.* Although he wasn't superstitious, he saw it as a benighted place, the site of two deaths now. Maybe it really was haunted, as he'd often been told when he was a student there.

"What is it?" said Ellie, sitting up and pulling the sheet around herself. "That office worker, Akamatsu, has been found dead."

"Akamatsu?"

"He worked in the accounts department."

"My god! I'm supposed to meet the girls for lunch. I won't go."

"You won't do yourself or me any favours by staying at home moping. Who knows, you might even hear something of interest relevant to this case."

"I did pray for you yesterday," Ellie replied.

"And now you can do one more thing for me," Inoue said, rolling over to give her a hug before explaining his request.

Over breakfast, a phrase kept repeating in his mind: *a damnable job*, *a damnable job*, an annoying jingle he couldn't get rid of. Then he got a second phone call telling him Professor Yamamoto had voluntarily presented herself at the station and was waiting to be interviewed.

Takenaka insisted on being present. But Inoue felt grateful. This time he would be allowed to conduct the interview and the superintendent would sit in a corner as the observer. When Ando escorted Yamamoto-*sensei* to the interview room, Inoue was surprised to see she looked completely relaxed, her lips softly curled in a grin. She bowed towards Takenaka and sat opposite Inoue.

After he had offered her the services of a lawyer, which she declined, he asked her why she was smiling.

She was clad as usual in her faded yellow Indian tunic and

baggy orange trousers, a purple scarf around her neck and the perpetual beaded bag on the floor beside her chair. Inoue thought she looked like a dried-up raisin with her tiny head, her lined, sallow face, her hair back in a long braid, but she showed how attractive she had been when her mouth parted in an even broader smile.

"I'm so sorry, Chief Officer Inoue. I hope you can forgive me," she said, resting her head dreamily on her hand. "I understand you tried to find me yesterday. I needed to get away, just briefly. I went to a hot spring resort near the coast, only half an hour's drive from here. The scalding hot water was a great relief. Then I had a few beers, a nice meal and a good night's sleep. It was a very comfortable hotel. I'm sure it has affected you, too, all the stress of the president's murder. I was smiling just now because I was reflecting on my misdeeds catching up with me and how I'd never thought they would. My prints are on file, and I imagine you want to question me about the prints on the porcelain doll. I've been waiting for you to arrest me."

"I'm sorry, Professor Yamamoto, but I must tell you again to remember that this is a murder enquiry, and you are implicated. As you surmise, your fingerprints have been found at the base of the porcelain doll found at the scene of crime. There was also blood on the doll – Nomura's blood type – meaning it must have been near Nomura and got spattered when his throat got slit."

Professor Yamamoto suddenly looked older, Inoue's words seeming to have added ten years to her age in less than a minute. She was now seriously frightened. Inoue hated having alarmed her. *What a damnable, damnable job.*

"Do you know where the doll was from? Did you bring it into Professor Nomura's office?"

"I will tell you all about it. But first I need to briefly explain the background of what I did, why I did it. Some years ago, I founded an informal group of like-minded souls. My protégées and some of the female employees at Fujikawa banded into a kind of sisterhood. We wanted to celebrate women's achievements and protect women from

the predations of Japanese men who consider us second-class citizens, who adopt the so-called *droit du seigneur* in their relations with the fair sex."

"You mean ..."

"Yes, that's why I instituted a campaign to lecture staff and students, male and female, about the hazards and injustices of sexual harassment. I've leafleted the campus, held seminars on the topic, and we run a help line for any victims of assault, including rape."

"How has this worked in practice?"

"Male professors who are known to 'hit' on female students or employees at the university have been targeted by our group. We bombard them with phone calls. We tell them we know who they are and that we consider their activities despicable."

"Was Professor Nomura one of these targeted professors?"

"Yes." Professor Yamamoto paused and looked at them thoughtfully. "It was obvious he had dearly loved his wife. After her death two years ago, he tried to alleviate his misery and loneliness by seeking out the company of vulnerable female undergraduates. We found out he was preying on one of my students, Mari Furomoto." She struck the desk, and Inoue admired her show of spirit. "This was contemptible, a blatant abuse of privilege."

"How did you combat this?"

"The sisterhood rang Professor Nomura, muffling our voices. We put notes under his office door. We made it known we denounced his exploitation of women."

"And yet, all the while, he was having an affair with Thomas-sensei's partner, Alyson Weller."

Yamamoto-*sensei* looked thoughtful. "Of course, she is a foreigner, a Canadian, I believe. My sisters and I contacted her, but she disdained our services. She apparently had a relationship with Nomura of her own free will."

Yamamoto-*sensei* flushed. "I'll admit it. The whole set-up made me angry. From what I understand, Andrew didn't know she'd betrayed him. In my opinion, betrayal is unforgivable whether it's the man or the woman."

"And the porcelain doll?"

"It was a symbol that *we* were watching him."

"Can you tell us where you got the doll and how you put it on Professor Nomura's desk?"

"I may as well tell you everything. You'll find out anyway. One of my best friends here is an officer worker named Michiko Ota. She had invited me once to the old farmhouse she shares with her grandmother just outside town, and I noticed a porcelain doll in a glass case on the shoebox in the entranceway. Ota-*san*'s grandmother is in the early stages of dementia. Also, age and injury mean she is nearly immobile. She relies on a cane or a stroller to get about. And she has slowly been going blind."

"I take it you thought this old woman wouldn't notice if the doll went missing."

"Yes. Or she'd forget it was there altogether. Even if she managed to get to the hallway, her failing sight would mean she might not notice it was gone. We only intended to use it for a day or two. The plan was that I would put the doll on the president's desk with that word *ikenai* pencilled on its forehead – which he would be able to interpret perfectly, I thought – and then, when I had my chance, I'd take the doll away again, clean its face and return it to Miss Ota, to take home."

Yamamoto-*sensei* placed her head on her arms, folded on the table. "It was such bad timing," she moaned, "putting that doll on Nomura-sensei's desk when I did."

"I'm not sure there could have been any good timing for

doing that," said Inoue.

"Mari Furomoto rang me up the night before the murder, a bit hysterical, saying she felt desperate. She was in her fourth year at the college and had already secured a job, but it was conditional on her graduating in March. She knew she was failing one required class. She'd gone to Professor Nomura to ask him to contact the professor involved, but he suggested rather unpleasant compensation for efforts on her behalf."

"I see."

"That's when I got the idea of borrowing that doll from Ota-*san* and scrawling 'forbidden' on it. That type of doll is typically given to female children on Girls' Day on March third. The president would make the connection: innocent girlhood should be off limits."

"And how did you carry out this plan?"

"I rang Ota-*san* after I got off the phone with Mari Furomoto. Ota-*san* was reluctant, even frightened, but she eventually agreed to bring the doll to the university the following morning, hidden in a bag. We met in the area for professors' mailboxes, a room on the first floor of Building One. As you know, professors rush in, sign their names in the attendance register, collect their mail, and leave. At the time of meeting Ota-*san*, it was unlikely anyone would be there."

"And did that prove the case?"

"Yes, Ota-*san* appeared at about 8.25 with the doll in a pink bag. I transferred it to my shoulder bag. But it was a close call. First Professor Hunter and then Miss Tanimoto turned up just after I'd put the doll into my bag. I hadn't expected either of them at that time. I grabbed a paper from my mailbox and pretended to read it."

"You hadn't expected anyone to be in the mailroom?"

"Well, we knew it was a risk, but I hadn't counted on meeting those two. Professor Hunter usually arrives after 9.00 and Miss Tanimoto was early for the staff meeting. Anyway, Ota-*san* collected a broom from the adjoining utility room and went out to help her workmates sweep in front of Building One. Then I rushed to my office in Building Eight. I deliberately hadn't signed the register book in the administration building so that gave me an excuse to go back. I took my bag, of course, with the doll in it, and signed in. Then I loitered in the mailroom, reading the official reports on the bulletin board. After a few minutes, I went to the vending machines near Building Two and bought a can of cold coffee. By this time, I thought the coast must be clear. I went into Building Two, entering Miss Tanimoto's annex. I knew she was at her staff meeting, and I was fairly sure I'd been unobserved. My initial intention was to leave the doll on the table in Miss Tanimoto's room. But my plans went awry."

"What happened?"

"Imagine my horror when, on entering Miss Tanimoto's office, I heard a chair creaking in the president's room. Nomura was there and had just stood up."

"Why were you so horrified at that?"

"It seemed likely he would appear in Akemi's annex. It would have meant I couldn't have gone ahead with my plan. Not a catastrophe, I admit," Professor Yamamoto said. "And, of course, given what has happened, it would have been better if Professor Nomura *had* come in."

"But he didn't enter Miss Tanimoto's annex?"

"No, I heard his corridor door open, and I realised he must be going to the toilet down the hall. It was well known that he drank great quantities of coffee, so he had to go to the toilet often."

"You saw that as your chance?"

"Yes, I put the doll on the president's desk rather than on that table in the annex. Of course, I first knocked on the door connecting the two offices and, when I heard no response, checked he wasn't there, put the doll on his table in a prominent place, and

then left. I waited briefly in the annex until I heard his footsteps coming back down the hall to his office. After that I rushed out, back to the mailbox area in Building One."

"I have a few more questions for you, Miss Yamamoto," said Inoue. "First, when did you scribble that word forbidden on the doll's forehead?"

"When I briefly went back to my office. I picked up a pencil and scrawled the word quickly before going back out."

"When you put it on Professor Nomura's desk, did you see

his laptop computer there?" Inoue asked.

"Yes, it was there as usual. I placed the doll beside it." "Can you be more exact?"

She frowned. "I placed it to the left of the computer, between the laptop and a big stack of papers. I wanted Professor Nomura to see it as soon as he sat down to work. May I ask why? Is the president's murder related to his computer?"

"I can't comment on that."

"I can't forgive myself for getting poor Michiko Ota involved in this. She's been in a terrible state ever since the murder. She somehow blames herself."

"But why didn't you come forward when the president's body was discovered to tell us about the doll? Didn't you realise it would be important?"

"I'm sorry for my cowardice, I'm so ashamed. I think I was affected by Ota-*san*'s terror. I didn't imagine the doll could be traced back to us, so I said nothing. I wasn't sure how my little revenge tale would be received, no idea she and I might end up being considered suspects."

"I'm afraid that's just what has happened. While you didn't kill him, you will be charged with obstruction of justice or as accessories."

"Wait one minute!" said a loud, stern voice. Inoue and Professor Yamamoto both jumped at Takenaka's command.

"Chief Inspector," he said impatiently. "I don't think we can so readily dismiss Professor Yamamoto as a suspect. We have only her word for it that she placed the doll on the president's desk and then left his office before he had returned from the toilet."

Takenaka looked at the elderly woman suspiciously. "Wasn't there a decorative screen just behind the president's desk? You could have hidden behind it and waited for your chance to strike after the president had returned to his office. Then you made your escape just before Professor Thomas ran into Building Two. As I recall, there's a

woman's toilet just opposite the president' office. You could have rushed in there and hidden in a stall."

Takenaka consulted his notes. "I see that the president's door to the corridor was unlocked. Professor Nomura would have locked it on returning to his office. It's possible you unlocked it when you were rushing out."

"No, no," Professor Yamamoto said in great distress. "I detested him, but I couldn't kill anyone."

"Perhaps that's true, perhaps not. May I see your hands, please?"

She held them out in front of her. They were wrinkled, but they looked strong enough to run a knife across someone's throat.

Takenaka said: "Forgive me, but for a woman your age, you look very fit."

"I don't want to end up like poor Miss Ota's

grandmother. I train twice a week at a gym, run on the treadmill, lift weights. I don't want to become a burden on anyone."

Takenaka said, "I am going to charge you as a possible suspect, in addition to the other charges concerning your little trick to upset Professor Nomura. We haven't got enough yet to arrest you, but I must ask you not to leave Fujikawa for the foreseeable

future."

Professor Yamamoto hung her head in despair. An officer was at the door, waiting to take her away, but first Inoue had a question.

"Do you know someone named Suga, Hiroki Suga, who has been working as a cleaner at the university?"

"No," she said, and again Inoue would swear her surprise was not feigned. "I always greet all the cleaners on the campus, but I can't say I'm personally acquainted with any of them. On the morning of the murder, on leaving the president's office, I did notice a cleaner raking the courtyard beside Building Two. Was that Suga?"

Inoue didn't answer.

Professor Yamamoto continued, "Later there was all the commotion when the president's body was found, and I saw the cleaner again, still raking the courtyard."

She rubbed her forehead. "Wait, I think that's wrong. By the time I'd realised Nomura had been killed, I was in such a state, but I think it was another cleaner I saw then, somebody who was a bit overweight. Well, his shirt was bulging out over his trousers. I remember thinking that we Japanese need to be avoid getting fat like westerners do."

Inoue thought of Ellie.

"What happens now?" Professor Yamamoto said. "It was just unlucky timing, an unfortunate coincidence."

"As Superintendent Takenaka has said, we have to charge you as a suspect. We will also need to summon Miss Ota to the station for questioning."

Professor Yamamoto said fervently, "I am glad my parents aren't still alive to see their treasured daughter, their only child, named as a suspect in a murder enquiry."

Girls and Boys Go Out to Play

Ellie Inoue was used to obeying her husband. Despite feeling reluctant, she rang Keiko saying she'd like to join the girls for lunch at Café de Fleur, an up-market restaurant.

Housed in a yellow building with a red tiled roof and bay windows framed by neatly trimmed shrubbery, it had chintz sofas and chairs, and freshly cut flowers to attract Japanese women of leisure and means. The prices displayed on the menu outside told Ellie it wasn't for the likes of her, working women on a budget. The cafe specialised in exquisite and healthy delicacies, colourful masterpieces of culinary art on huge platters.

Misa and Junko would be there but the real attraction for Ellie was that Akemi Tanimoto had promised to pop in during her lunch hour. They had not met since the murder and Ellie wondered how she was.

Keiko was there early to nab the best table by the window. She had arranged the lunch meeting and was impeccably dressed in a powder-blue two-piece suit, her thick hair dyed a fashionable light brown and secured in a ponytail with a pink ribbon.

"Sorry we're late," Misa said. "The traffic was terrible."

"No problem. We're still waiting for Akemi."

A waitress brought glasses of ice water, *oshibori* for them to wipe their hands before eating, and menus. "Our special today is ginger-flavoured beef slices with salad. Please let me know when you're ready to order."

"Just waiting for one more friend," said Keiko.

Ellie felt dowdy and fat with Japanese women. She wished another westerner were there to share her lonely contrast with these women's perfect stylishness. Keiko was the pampered darling daughter of a wealthy businessman. Misa was in student chic – a loose but expensive-looking blouse over fashionable blue jean shorts and black leggings, hobbling about in sandals with absurdly high heels. Junko was more human, Ellie thought, someone who made mistakes. Her hair was a little greasy and her clothes not as stylish as those the others wore. She sat awkwardly, tapping the table with her fingers, as if preoccupied.

Keiko said to Ellie, "The stir-fried vegetables are amazing. The tofu is marinated in a special sauce."

"The beef for me," said Junko. "I'm a confirmed carnivore." She translated for Ellie in her fractured English, "Me, meat. Like meat." Ellie wondered why Junko did that. Maybe it was her appearance. Ellie knew some Japanese couldn't believe a big pink western woman could become fluent in their language.

"Did you have to become a big meat eater for Karl? He must eat great hunks of it at every meal," said Keiko. Then she exchanged looks with Misa and laughed. "Maybe he eats it raw so no there's no need for you to cook it first."

Junko didn't register the insult. "That's right. Meat for breakfast, lunch, and dinner. He wishes he could kill the animals himself. He wants to hunt the wild boars in the mountains with bow and arrow."

Keiko looked at her watch. "Akemi's late. Let's go ahead and order."

When Ellie was dining with slim women, she felt self-conscious. She tended to order the least fattening item on the menu, usually a salad.

From the menu items they turned to talk of summer bargains and where to buy the cheapest western clothes, Gouda cheese and flax seeds. Ellie's eyes glazed over. She liked her Japanese friends and enjoyed speaking freely with them. She knew they liked her, too often inviting her on their outings. But she didn't have much in common with them, with no children and no interest in fashion or shopping.

Akemi finally arrived. They all jumped up to greet her as if she were a celebrity. None of them had seen her since the murder, only spoken to her on the phone. They scrutinized her, wondered if she'd been changed by the tragedy.

But she looked the same as ever, her thick black hair falling long and lustrous past her shoulders. Ellie wondered if Akemi hid behind it. When a lock fell across her face, she didn't brush it back. Although she seemed relaxed, her eyes were sad.

Ellie asked sympathetically, "Are you okay?"

"As well as can be expected. The acting head, Professor Obuchi, has asked me to stay on as his secretary. I was surprised and glad. And also relieved. He's moved the president's office back to the admin office so I don't have to *remember*."

She heaves a great sigh. "It's like a new start but until the president's killer has been found, I'm worried, even a bit scared. It's like a black shadow over my life."

"I have troubles, too," said Junko, unexpectedly. They stared at her.

"My husband acting strangely lately. I worried about him."

"What's been happening?" asked Misa.

Junko paused, rice dish in one hand, chopsticks poised in the other."I'm not sure, just feeling I have. He won't tell me anything. He gone a lot and won't tell me where he go. Came home late last night with hands bruised. I see him put clothing in a bag in the hallway cupboard. I think he hang around the army camp next to the college. What he do that for? He talk a lot about when he was a soldier, how happy he was then."

They wanted to hear more, even if her account was delivered in fractured English.

Ellie said, "Everything's so strained now with this unsolved murder on our doorstep. I'm sure we all feel it."

Keiko said, "But the case has been solved. I heard on the

news there was an arrest."

Ellie suddenly lost her appetite. She smiled wanly at Keiko. "You must understand, I can say nothing about any case my husband is working on."

"Of course, of course," Keiko and Misa echoed together, but Ellie could see the disappointment in their eyes.

"In fact," Ellie continued, "you probably know more than *I* do. I never watch television or listen to the radio, so I'm usually in the dark about what's happening. And Kenji is very tight-lipped about his work."

"I'd prefer not talking about it anyway," said Akemi, "it's still painful. Anyway, I must be going. Obuchi-*sensei* is particular about the one-hour lunch limit. But he's not so bad once you get to know him."

"And have you?"

"Well, in a way. His cigarette smoke wafts under the door from his office to mine. If I get lung cancer, I'll demand generous worker's compensation."

Keiko ordered a *cappuccino*; Junko had a *café au lait*, the others had black coffee. "Isn't it amazing?" Misa exclaimed. "Ten years ago, nobody here had heard of *cappuccino* or *café au lait*; now they're everywhere."

Ellie turned pale with the smell of her coffee. Junko placed her hand over Ellie's. "Are you all right, Eri-*chan*?" Ellie leapt up and ran to the toilet.

A few minutes later, standing unobserved by the door, she

overheard her friends talking. Junko said to Keiko, "I was just the same in the early months before I had my boy. Nothing made me more nauseous than the aroma of coffee."

Keiko recalled, "For me it was the smell of frying bacon. I couldn't stand it when Ben was making one of his English breakfasts." She shuddered. "Or fry ups" as he called them."

***

It was with reluctance that Andrew Thomas agreed when Ben rang up asking him to join in a night out at a bar with the boys.

"You haven't been out for ages, Andy," Ben said. "We miss you! Please come." "Don't call me Andy. You know I don't like it. Can't you manage Andrew? I

thought you Brits liked formality."

"I wish you Yanks could remember, I'm Irish, not a frigging Brit. Listen, I'll call you anything you like, old sausage, just come out with us tonight," said Ben.

"And I'm not a Yank, I'm Canadian. I'm from a *different* country! Who is us?" "Just the usual suspects: Billy, Karl, Stephen, the Carrel boys. Tell me, Andrew,

what's a derogatory term for somebody from Canada?"

"There isn't one. We're too perfect. Nobody has a bad word to say about us."

"Too boring you mean."

The boys would meet at the usual place, the bar called *Izakaya*.

For all his shortcomings, Stephen was punctual. He could be counted on to get to any meeting place early enough to get good seats. At *Izakaya* he had secured them the usual booth near the toilets. He was wiping beer foam from his moustache when Ben turned up, followed by Billy. The Carrels arrived, chatting about some Japanese girls they'd met, comparing numbers on their mobile phones. "You got the high school girl's? I got the office lady's. Let's call them later," Pete said.

"Good location beside the toilets for Billy," Ben said, laughing.

Billy scowled, took a long draught of his beer and muttered, "Next time you have computer trouble, Benji-*chan*, you can whistle in the wind. No help from me."

The door of *Izakaya* slammed. "Oh, charming," said Ben. "Here's our little half- breed, the poster child of good manners."

"What did you say?" Karl asked throwing himself heavily into a seat, forcing Billy to move over.

"I said we need to order some food to go with these drinks," Ben said.

They ordered boiled octopus, a Salad Niçoise, deep-fried tofu, slices of raw fish on grated radish, vegetable *tempura*, miniature hamburgers and a plate of sausages smeared with vivid yellow German mustard. Billy insisted on more drinks.

"This is just starters, of course," said Karl, greedily eying the food. Ben held out a large brown mug full of chopsticks. Stephen gave a small white dish to each of them. Karl filled his dish, gobbled the lot, and took a second helping.

"Good to see a man with an appetite," said Ben. Karl was too busy eating to reply.

Stephen was sitting unusually quiet. "Sorry, thinking about what's happened here. Been nearly a week now."

"Well, your wish was granted. Our Andrew got arrested for it."

"It was a joke, okay? I said I hoped he was a suspect, but I didn't mean it. Thank God he's been released. Any of you seen him since then?"

"At the university, of course," said Ben, a trifle pompously. Stephen groaned at his patronising air, his sentiments shared by everyone present. They all gave Ben a hard time because he was the only one who'd snagged a full-time position at a university. Granted, he had a doctorate in linguistics but that didn't make it any more palatable.

"You deign to turn up there once in while?" said Stephen.

Ben's red face went redder. "I have to be there every working day, go to lots of meetings and write papers. I can't just turn up for a class like some of you."

Ben and Stephen stood up as Andrew approached. It was fine gossiping about someone, but Andrew had seen tragedy. He'd even been on the national news.

Karl was on his third plate. Without looking up he

bellowed, "And here's our murder suspect. How are you, Andy-boy? Feeling guilty?"

"It's Andrew, I'm fine. And innocent for your information."

Somehow Andrew's words set Karl off. He began guffawing uncontrollably, spitting out food fragments. "Innocent…innocent…tell it to the Marines!"

More food: smoked salmon, potato salad, Korean pancakes, Japanese savoury omelettes, egg mayonnaise, more raw fish and *kushiyaki*, barbecued chicken on skewers. Billy ordered more drinks.

Karl's hunger was temporarily sated. He put down his chopsticks and placed his big brown hands meditatively on the scuffed table surface.

"Looks like you've been in the wars," said Ben. Everyone looked at Karl's bruised and scratched hands.

"None of your bloody business. But if you have to know, I like to go hunting. I been tracking some big prey lately."

"Did the officials grant you a license to hunt wild boar with a bow and arrow?"

"No, not wild boar, just a bore," Karl said, throwing back his head in laughter. They all looked away – Karl in a jovial mood was not a pretty sight.

Stephen distracted everyone's attention with a strange moan. "What is it, something you ate?"

"MDBB alert," Stephen muttered.

Only Ben understood. "It means 'momentarily distracted by

beauty.'"

"A tasty morsel," Stephen said. Not more food for Karl, not a gorgeous chick for the Carrel boys; only the waiter, a stocky young lad, come to take orders.

The Carrels consulted their mobile phones. They glanced at each other and nodded. "Well, boys," they said, "hot dates await."

"Don't forget to pay on your way out. I recall you two skipping off early the last time without setting your bill," said Ben.

Karl also decided he'd had enough. Nobody dared ask him where he was going or reminded him to pay. They just said goodbye, glad, if truth be told, to see the back of him.

By now, Billy was nearly comatose, at passing out stage.

"I can't think why I keep inviting Karl to our gatherings," said Ben.

"Don't make me laugh," said Stephen. "Of course you know why. Karl would slap us if he heard we'd got together without him."

"Well, it looks like he's been up to something. See the state of his hands?" "Now we're rid of the riffraff," said Ben, "tell us how you really are, Andrew."

"I'm still in a state of shock, to be honest. Lord knows I didn't like that old bastard, but I wouldn't wish him dead. And then there's Akamatsu. His body was found in Building Two yesterday morning. He'd been attacked, but they say the cause of death was a heart attack."

Andrew sighed. "I thought him the one decent bloke on the staff. In the accounts department. The only one who ever tried to help me," he said. "I couldn't sleep last night, thinking of what had happened to him."

"Me, too," said Ben. "He was one of the few office workers who had any time for us foreigners. Shame he never made it to France."

"It's the nightmares, worse than the insomnia," said Andrew. "Nightmares?"

"Oh, bodies, blood, death. Weird stuff. Who will be next? I hope I can get over it."

"Bring on the day."

Billy by now was slumped forward over their table, his forehead lying on its beer- stained surface, as if in silent communion with it. He always passed out, but they never had any difficulty rousing him.

Stephen said, "Alyson was never my cup of tea. Can't think what you saw in her." "I thought she was drop-dead gorgeous," said Ben.

"As my dear departed mum used to say, 'pretty is as pretty does'."

"I talked to your mother on the phone recently. She's not dead!" Ben snorted. "Is she still sponging off poor old Gerald?" Stephen wondered.

"The man's a saint," Andrew said.

Ben was a Catholic and felt the need to say, "Well, he is a missionary."

"Okay," Stephen conceded. "My mum isn't dead, still alive and kicking in a semi in Birmingham, making my father's life a misery, but she always used to say, probably still does, 'Beware a man of principle'."

"What's that supposed to mean?" Ben demanded. "Don't know. I have a creepy feeling about Gerald." "You have an allergy to organised religion."

"That too."

"Alyson's a puzzle, not one I'd like to try to solve," said Stephen. "Still waters run deep," said Ben.

"I still can't believe it. The betrayal, her little fling with Nomura right under my nose. The humiliation! It's odd. But somehow, I feel I deserved it. I wanted to leave her before coming to Japan. She must have sensed that." Andrew shook his head in puzzlement. "But I ended up marrying her! What does that say about me?"

"I'd put my bet on self loathing," said Stephen.

"I'm glad she's out of your life. Out of our lives soon if what I've heard is right," said Ben.

"Oh?" said Andrew. "What's that?"

"She's booked on a flight to Canada leaving from Fukuoka next week."

Blackmail and Brotherly Love

"That's one loose end tied up," said Takenaka the day after Professor Yamamoto and Michiko Ota had been formally charged and detained. "But I'm disappointed in you, Inoue. It was unprofessional to be so hasty in dismissing Professor Yamamoto as a suspect. Best keep an open mind, even if we each draw our own conclusions. As you know, I still think it was Suga. I'm checking on what he said about rushing back to the cleaners' compound after being shouted at by the president."

"I'm sorry, sir. You're right. I was relying on feelings rather than facts. I felt there was contempt but no real hatred in Professor Yamamoto placing the doll on his desk. Thinking her innocent was intuition, not detection."

Takenaka's pasty forehead was creased with worry lines. "Well, never mind. We all make mistakes. Maybe I've made one myself. What if the other cleaners can provide an alibi for Suga? That would be terrible. We can place him outside Building Two that morning and a student has testified to seeing a cleaner in Professor Nomura's office."

Inoue was seated in his own office but sitting opposite his old desk. Takenaka was in the comfortable leather chair swivelling back and forth in it, his glasses glinting under the fluorescent light.

"Let's think this through again," he said to Inoue. "The murder was committed exactly a week ago. How far has our investigation progressed?"

Inoue assumed his role was to act as a sounding board.

Takenaka sank back and stared straight ahead, the wrinkles in his forehead deepening. "We've arrested the suspect *I* think most viable. We have Suga, a man with a history of violence, who had a grievance, who was seen near the crime scene at approximately the time of the murder. He had a ladder propped against the president's office window and has even admitted he entered Professor Nomura's room that way on a previous occasion."

Now Takenaka looked up at Inoue with a slight hint of malice and said pointedly, "My man Suga had motive and opportunity. I know you've been fixated on the mysterious appearance of the porcelain doll but that's been cleared up."

"Yes, sir," said Inoue in a subdued voice. "However, there's also the matter of the two missing items that remain unaccounted for: the president's laptop, that vanished from his desk, and the folder containing files to be distributed to the department heads from Miss Tanimoto's."

"Yes, yes, yes," Takenaka said impatiently. "And, alas, our search of Suga's filthy cluttered home failed to turn up either of those."

He stopped swinging in his chair, planted his elbows on the desk, propped his face on his hands, and said, "There's also the attack on Akamatsu. What has that got to do with things? According to his co-worker, Miss Keiko Araki, he was suspected of the theft of considerable sums. If it hadn't been for her vigilance, he just might have got away with it. He had switched funds to different accounts and almost succeeded in the deception."

"Sir," said Inoue. "I need to talk to you about this. I have information implicating Professor Nomura's younger brother in Akamatsu's death. I'd like to bring him in for more questioning."

Takenaka's gloom vanished. He looked up, bright-eyed. "Really? Tell me more."

Inoue continued, "Sorry, sir. If you don't mind, I'd like to have my suspicions confirmed before going into the details. Sir, I hope you won't think it improper, but I've pursued my own lines of enquiry already. I need to tell you, sir, that I've even taken the liberty of sending Officer Kubo off this morning to question one of the foreigners resident in Fujikawa, someone I suspect."

"Another *foreigner*?" asked Takenaka. "And some people say Japan should admit more immigrants."

Inoue said, "I think this man, Karl Matthews, an American, actually carried out the attack on Akamatsu, acting on the president's brother's instructions. If you can issue me a warrant, I'll arrest him now."

Takenaka nodded and said, "I'd have preferred to be kept

up to speed but I commend your initiative. Get the president's little brother. I'll sit in on the interview."

Teruo Nomura didn't come willingly. He protested that he had too much to do at the base, that he was under no obligation to attend, and acceded only when Officer Ando produced an official warrant for his arrest.

Nomura was escorted to the interview room. Inoue took the leading role in the questioning, but Takenaka pointedly joined him beside the recorder.

"Nomura-*san*," said Inoue. "Thank you for granting us this interview."

"It's not as though I had any choice," Nomura said sulkily. He wore his Self- Defence Forces uniform and sat, muscular and impatient, looking as if he might spring up at any moment and leave. "And if you're going to ask, I don't need a damned lawyer. It's my brother who was killed! I'm a victim, nearly as much as him. I had nothing to do with Masaki's death. I'm up to my eyes in work and I'd like to make a formal protest to the authorities at being questioned again. This is a serious disruption of my schedule. We're busy training a new batch of recruits."

"Sorry to inconvenience you. Before we begin our formal questioning, I would like to express my commiserations again on your brother's tragic death."

"More useful than your sympathy would be your agreeing to release his body. It's been a whole week. I want to hold his funeral service and cremation in Kyoto. Our parents are dead, so I have to arrange for the Buddhist priest from the temple closest to our family home to conduct the ceremony. I also need to issue invitations."

"I thought Professor Nomura was a Christian, that all the full-time staff at Fujikawa University were required on being hired to show proof of baptism."

Nomura's lips curled in a contemptuous smile. "For Fujikawa's top police officer, you are ill-informed about the town's leading institution and employer. That requirement was dropped five years ago."

"I didn't know. You say five years ago? Presumably, that change was introduced by your brother. Do you know the reason for it?"

"My brother felt he had to. With Japan's economy in the doldrums for decades now coupled with the low birth rate, drastic measures were required. Kindergartens, schools, universities, all have fewer students these days. You must have noticed that the junior college near Fujikawa train station closed three years ago. Well, that's exactly the fate my brother dreaded for his precious university. But how could he save it? He couldn't exactly force couples to have more children. He couldn't do anything about the economic menace posed by China. He had to make the university as attractive as possible to applicants."

"And the connection of all this to the university's Christian requirement was…" Nomura began to speak in the clear slow voice of an adult speaking to a child.

"The rule that the university could hire only baptised Christians meant that the pool of qualified candidates to teach was small to begin with, there being few Christians in Japan. My brother wanted to be able to employ the people he thought the best, irrespective of their religion. He opened up a few more departments – theatre

studies and cultural management – to attract students, hiring some famous names from as far afield as Tokyo. It was too much to expect that all these experts would be Christian."

"Thank you for your explanation. Do you know if there was much opposition to your brother changing the rule about hiring baptised Christians?"

"Of course there was!" he blurted out. "From those mealy-mouthed Bible-thumpers who couldn't see what side their bread was buttered on. They put on their pious faces, spoke with their pulpit voices. They said the whole purpose of the university was to bring the light of Christianity to our town so darkened by nationalism and militancy during the war years."

Nomura sat glowering at them for a full minute before continuing.

"My brother came to his senses when he became president. I admit we had our differences. I hated him for many years for all the pain he caused our parents. He was a rebel as a high school student and then he got even more messed up. I think he was corrupted by becoming a Christian, by staying in America and consorting with all sorts. Then marrying that black woman! It's a mercy they had no children."

Inoue winced involuntarily. Married to an American Christian wife whose own childlessness was a source of pain, he felt these comments cut too close to the bone.

"Do you think he renounced his own faith?"

"He didn't bother doing anything like that, not publicly, at least. He knew there was no point in further antagonising the Fujikawa staff. I am glad to say that, shortly before his death, my brother visited me in my quarters at the camp and brought an offering for the family altar in my room. He prayed, burned incense, and lit a candle in front of the photographs of our parents. Does that mean he was no longer a Christian? I don't know. But it was proof enough for me that he wasn't denying his Buddhism anymore, that he was paying the proper respect to our ancestors."

"And that pleased you?"

"Naturally! I just wish our parents hadn't gone through the pain of witnessing their son's abandonment of our traditions. He was the eldest, the one they counted on to maintain the family altar."

"You are contradicting yourself," Inoue said forcefully. Nomura was taken aback.

"Your comments today about your brother are at variance with the statement you made three days ago, when you told us the two of you were implacable enemies. Now you are implying that there was a truce before his death."

"I was feeling angry that day," Nomura hastily sputtered. "Angry my brother had been murdered, angry at his behaviour that had caused our parents so much unhappiness, angry he had been killed so ignominiously. I feel calmer now and I can draw the picture for you more clearly. You should know that shortly before his murder Masaki had a change of heart. And I had, too. I could see us as friends again. I'm grieving that that won't be possible now."

Takenaka looked puzzled. He was obviously wondering where this line of questioning was leading.

Inoue said, "Mr Nomura, it has come to our attention that you may know something about the attack on a long-serving clerk at the university named Akamatsu. An attack two nights ago that resulted in his death."

There was an immediate change in Nomura's demeanour. He had been from relaxed. Now he looked tense and grim. "I think I've heard the name Akamatsu. I seem to recall my brother mentioning him. Maybe he was in the accounts office."

"Did you ever meet Akamatsu? I'd like remind you this is an official interview.

You are expected to tell the truth."

Nomura said casually, "I may have bumped into him once or twice when I was visiting my brother at the university."

"I would like to put it to you that you knew Akamatsu well. It was true you and your brother had reached an uneasy truce, but it suited you both to pretend the old enmity continued."

"What possible reason could I have had for pretending I hated Masaki longer than was actually the case? You're wasting time spinning improbable scenarios. You would be more profitably occupied in making a watertight case against the suspect I hear you've arrested for Masaki's murder."

"Don't worry. We are vigorously pursuing various leads. But this is a related issue, one for you to clarify. Akamatsu had been suspected of embezzling money from Fujikawa University."

"Oh, yes. Now I remember," Nomura said. "My brother was quite worried about it, upset because he'd always trusted this man. Akamatsu, eh?"

"I suggest that Akamatsu was embezzling funds on orders given by your brother at your request."

"Ridiculous! Why on earth would my brother secretly authorise his employee to steal money from his university?!"

"Your brother trusted Akamatsu more than was good for that poor sickly clerk with his heart condition. Akamatsu was instructed somehow to get money to you. Let's call it a bribe. It was to persuade your right-wing fanatic friends to stop harassing the university, to stop circling the campus in their blaring trucks, to abandon their protest at Professor Hunter's mission to help second-generation Koreans born in Japan."

"A fairy tale!" Nomura sneered. "For one thing, I wouldn't have wanted anyone to stop attacking that stupid *gaijin* do-gooder. Also, my brother was doing everything in his power to save the college from bankruptcy and closure. It's like I said. He instituted new programmes. He hired famous professors. He dropped the Christianity requirement in his hope to attract quality staff. He was responsible for improving the infrastructure of the college. He got a beautiful new library built, older buildings painted and renovated, and had the grounds professionally landscaped. Masaki made a demoralised institution a much better place."

"But there was still one worry," Inoue said. "He must have worried that Professor Hunter's crusade to help the Koreans was attracting unwanted notoriety to his university, especially as it had provoked a right-wing backlash."

There was a brief silence and then Inoue continued. "And that is where you come in. Your brother must have approached you, offered you something in an attempt to appease you, to use your contacts with right-wingers to get them to back off."

Nomura sighed impatiently. "Theories, suppositions…."

"Brotherly goodwill alone was not enough. You required cash to silence your sympathisers. Your brother didn't have enough money to pay you himself. He entrusted Akamatsu with the task of siphoning off funds from the university budget. And the plan might have worked, you might all have got away with it, but for a sharp-eyed woman in the accountancy department who noticed discrepancies in the books."

Inoue consulted his notes. "A Miss Araki, I believe," he said. "No proof," Nomura muttered.

"Speaking of 'no proof,' again, we only have your word as to Professor Nomura's sudden burst of fraternal feeling for you. I think your first witness statement revealed the true state of affairs: that you were sworn enemies and have been since boyhood. But let's return to the matter at hand. We are investigating the financial matters lately handled by Akamatsu. Officers will soon bring an American resident in Fujikawa, a

Karl Matthews, to the station. We have reason to suspect he is implicated in Akamatsu's death. We know that Mr Matthews, who teaches at one of the local language schools, has been an occasional visitor to your army camp. Yesterday evening, he was seen in a Fujikawa bar with badly bruised and scratched hands."

Nomura looked at his watch, indicating he had other things to do.

Inoue doggedly continued. "We are going to question Mr Matthews about the attack on Akamatsu last night. We think this assault was intended to warn Akamatsu not to mention anything about stealing money from the college to pay you off."

Nomura looked down at the table in silence.

"Akamatsu had a cruel trick played on him. Many people believe Building Two to be haunted by a ghost. I believe you persuaded Mr Matthews to put on the uniform of a Japanese soldier from the Pacific war taken from the office of your commanding officer. Maybe it was only a warning to Akamatsu. But he was terrified, especially when the "ghost" began hitting him. Tragically the beating triggered a heart attack. It also may well be that you thought the uniform could be returned that night, no questions asked, but it got spattered with blood in the assault. We also know that Matthews has trouble controlling his temper and keeping his mouth shut when he's in a rage. We expect interesting revelations from our interview with him. We are going to search his home and we expect to find the uniform."

"We have also sent officers to search your quarters. Others are going to the local bank to find out if large sums have been deposited in your account recently."

Nomura said nothing.

"And now, if you would like to add to or alter your original statement, we can revise it. Although you have dispensed with a lawyer for this interview, you should contact one now as you will be formally charged with blackmail, extortion, and conspiracy to commit assault. You and Matthews will also be charged with involuntary manslaughter."

Nomura suddenly came to life and spat out, "That damned

do-gooder Hunter! And that damned other foreigner. I told him just to frighten Akamatsu. The *fool!* He couldn't control himself. He wasn't supposed to hit him."

"I'm sure your lawyer will make the most of such touching protestations when he pleads your defence." Inoue looked at Kubo angrily. "Book him."

Takenaka Eats Humble Pie

Inoue was peremptorily summoned to Takenaka's office eight days after the murder. He didn't want to go. Ever since Takenaka had appropriated Inoue's territory at the police station, Inoue had found it painful to be in his old office. He hated seeing his desk, his chair, his phone, even his computer being used by the petty tyrant. And now the room stank like an old ashtray and everything was untidy. Inoue wondered how long it would take to get the place back to the spick-and-span order he liked.

Takenaka wore an aggrieved expression. After Inoue had sat down, he exploded. "It beggars belief," he said, looking accusingly at Inoue. "Suga has dredged up a plausible alibi. We've had to let him go."

"Yes, sir," said Inoue, struggling not to smirk. "Sorry, sir. I heard the news. As you say, it appears to be a watertight alibi. Suga's claim to have left the vicinity after being told off by Professor Nomura is confirmed by witnesses near Building Two who heard the president yelling at somebody and saw a cleaner rushing away. It's also verified by the cleaners who were sorting through the rubbish when Suga turned up."

Inoue paused, not wanting to rub salt into the wound. "And those cleaners have confirmed it was a little after 9.00 when Suga returned. That's before the time forensics has pinpointed for the murder: that is between 9.30 and 10.00."

"Well, I see you've heard the full story," Takenaka said almost angrily. "I wonder if you also know the cleaning crew gave Suga a real roasting for having come back without the ladder."

Takenaka sighed, looking deflated, his glasses gleaming vividly black against the pallor of his doughy face. "I'd like to give him a roasting myself, but what good does that do us? Now we seem to be back at square one."

"Not quite, sir," said Inoue, feeling relieved Takenaka had accepted Suga's innocence. Inoue had never thought Suga a viable suspect – it must have been hard enough for him just to manage to get dressed for work on time and to perform his menial chores at the university. Suga signally lacked the audacity and cunning to commit murder. "I do have a few theories…"

"I would be grateful to hear them now, Chief Inoue, and I want to apologise if I've seemed less than receptive to your ideas in the past," conceded Takenaka. "You and your two juniors have done exemplary work in clearing up some of the mysteries surrounding this case. There's the matter of the porcelain doll and also the rumours about Akamatsu being involved in some sort of financial impropriety. I was particularly pleased that you managed to identify the culprits behind the fatal attack on that poor man."

"I want to give credit where credit's due, sir," Inoue said.

"It was my wife who put me on to Matthews. She'd gone out for lunch two days ago with *his* wife, who complained he'd been acting strangely lately and making lots of visits to the army camp. Matthews' wife also told my wife that he seemed to have been in a fight, returning home late one night with his hands damaged and concealing some clothing in a cupboard. It was all a matter of chance, even of coincidence."

"And why did you suspect Nomura's involvement?"

"There was the fact of Matthews' frequent visits to the army camp. Also, something had been troubling me lately, niggling away at me. It was that the right-wingers' harassment of the university suddenly came to a stop a few months ago. Those vans had stopped circling the campus. I thought there must be some reason and that money was involved."

Takenaka grinned and said, "A valuable ally, your wife. I wonder if she'd care to give us her thoughts on who killed the president. We need a breakthrough."

He must have seen Inoue glare because he changed the subject, saying, "We've released Professor Yamamoto and Miss Ota under caution. We've got the president's brother and Matthews under lock and key. Pity about Akamatsu, I suppose his death could be considered collateral damage, a result of his having been dragged into the whole business by Professor Nomura. He must have been a *very* trusted employee to be given that task."

"Yes, sir," said Inoue. "From what I gather, it was the

president who was primarily culpable in the affair. He abused his position of power by asking an employee to do his dirty work – as you say, a trusted employee who felt compelled to comply. According to witnesses, Akamatsu had been under a lot of strain the past six months. Miss Araki, a fellow clerk, had her suspicions, but she thought that Akamatsu was just trying to fiddle the books to line his own pockets. She had no idea, of course, that it was Professor Nomura who had asked Akamatsu to make funds secretly available to bribe his brother. Nomura would have done anything to save the university. We're now actively pursuing the money trail, checking Akamatsu's accounts

for the funds. We'll be making a few more arrests soon – right-wing fanatics and a few army officers complicit in the whole affair."

Takenaka frowned. "Even with the release of Professor Yamamoto and her accomplice, you seem to be filling up the cells of this police station. Do we have room for any more lawbreakers? Speaking of which, are you convinced the feminist and her friend had nothing to do with the murder?"

"Yes, I'm quite sure," said Inoue decisively. "It was just bad luck, just unfortunate timing, that the little trick they played on Professor Nomura backfired so spectacularly."

"Bad taste, I'd call it," said Takenaka. "What can they have been thinking of, placing that silly doll on the president's desk?"

"Just trying to make a point," said Inoue.

"So we can rule out the president's younger brother and those two harpies. Suga is in the clear, and Professor Thomas has managed to get an alibi, thanks to the student who was sitting in the courtyard and saw him rushing to Building Two after, it seems, the murder had been committed. But how about his wife? I think you mentioned the president had been on the point of dumping her. That's a motive I should say."

"She has no license. She would have needed to get to the campus from her home, half an hour's drive away. We've interviewed bus and train staff and no foreign woman was seen that morning."

"Damn!"

"Nor was she seen on campus that day. She would have been easy to spot. But sir, there is some good news. You may recall that that student who testified to seeing Professor Thomas rushing to Building Two also said that he caught a glimpse of a cleaner standing by the window in the president's office. Presumably it was that individual who murdered Professor Nomura."

"Of course, I remember! That's why I thought we had a good case against Suga."

"The point I'm trying to make," said Inoue calmly, "is that if that cleaner wasn't Suga, who was it? Another cleaner? Or somebody dressed as a cleaner?"

"Good lord, I hadn't thought of that. We'd better get

someone over to the university as soon as possible to interview the cleaning staff."

"I've already done that, sir. As you'll also remember, Mr Kawane was alerted to the attack on the president by a cleaner who suddenly turned up, looked a bit stout, was wearing a hat and a surgical mask and had a blocked nose and muffled voice. Well,

Officer Kubo has ascertained that there are no cleaners at Fujikawa University who could be described as in any way fat and no cleaners who have had colds in the last week or so."

"But doesn't that put us right back at the starting point?"

"Not quite, sir," said Inoue. "But before I go on, I need to confess to something else that has been bothering me. When I sent Officer Kubo to the university to interview the cleaning staff, I asked him also to question Akamatsu about his alleged fiddling of the university accounts. I'm now worried that I might, in doing so, inadvertently have caused the man's death. The campus is next to the base. Nomura may have seen the police car pull into the university or heard Akamatsu had been questioned again. It was that very night the American dressed up as a ghost and attacked Akamatsu as a warning he had to keep his mouth shut. What it boils down to is that I feel personally responsible for the poor man's death."

"We have to carry on with our duties," said Takenaka severely. "If certain unpleasant consequences occur, best not take them too much to heart. Again, it's collateral damage.

You were just doing your job. You weren't to know this office worker had a heart condition, that Nomura would arrange an attack on the clerk and succeed in literally frightening the poor man to death."

"Thank you, sir," said Inoue.

Takenaka wriggled in his chair as if this conversation made him uneasy. He changed the subject, saying, "I'm sorry to have to drop Suga as a suspect, I don't mind telling you. An unsavoury character if ever I met one. The way he and his mother live in that tumbledown shack! As I told you, hoarders the pair of them. Unwashed dishes, plastic wrappers, empty cartons and bottles, piles of unwashed clothing everywhere. My officers nearly keeled over from the stink."

Inoue tried to say something and paused.

"What is it, man?" Takenaka asked impatiently. "More qualms about the fate of that office worker?"

"Sir, it's interesting that you've mentioned the topic of collateral damage. I think murder in particular is an event that leaves a great deal of collateral damage in its wake. While it was the president and Akamatsu who actually died, there are many other casualties in this case. We've disturbed a wretched old woman and her half-wit son and ransacked their home. Professor Yamamoto may lose her job when Obuchi-*sensei* learns of the extreme measures she adopted in her crusade against male sexual predators at the university, and poor Miss Ota, who is probably her grandmother's only source of financial support, is also at risk of being fired."

"But Yamamoto-*sensei* is a bit long in the tooth, must be nearing retirement age."

Inoue had to suppress a snort. That was Takenaka all over, he thought, casually betraying the traditional Japanese male's contempt for women. Inoue felt a sneaking sympathy for Professor Yamamoto and her band of feminists. Their lot could never be easy with men like Takenaka holding the lion's share of power in Japanese institutions and businesses and in government. No matter what qualifications or honours these women held, they would still be regarded as second-class citizens.

"But being fired would be an ignominious end to what has been a long and distinguished career," Inoue said.

"Well, we can only hope she still qualifies for a full pension," said Takenaka dismissively. "Speaking of casualties, once everything comes out, I imagine the president's younger brother will lose his commission in the army. And then there's the foreigner. He'll get a few years for attacking the office worker and then be deported after he's served his sentence. I agree: there are many repercussions. But murder's not a garden party."

Inoue said, "It's like having a big stone thrown into a murky pond. Unpleasant things rise to the surface."

"I had no idea you were so poetic, Inoue," said Takenaka with a grimace, looking as though it was a regrettable tendency that should be suppressed.

"I wonder about that Miss Weller. Is she leaving Japan soon?" he went on.

"Apparently so. That's why I asked Ando to talk to Miss Weller again. I wanted to get any more information from her before her departure."

"And the result?"

"Not what I expected, but Ando's report of that interview has set me on the right track. To be honest, I've been suspicious of this individual for some time."

"*Dammit*, man, tell me!"

"When Ando returned to the station after the interview, he said that Miss Weller had talked a bit about the porcelain doll on the president's desk that had been spattered with blood. That was the clue I needed. First, though, I need to send Ando and Kubo to see Miss Tanimoto, Miss Ota, Professor Yamamoto, Mr Kawane, and the foreigner Mr Thomas and ask each of them a specific question. In an hour or so, I'll be able to report back to you."

"Fine, do whatever you need to do, but let's wrap this up. Professor Obuchi's been on the phone again today, shrieking at me to nab the culprit and get everything back to normal."

"I'll do my best, sir," said Inoue. "If my suspicions are confirmed, there'll be another arrest."

The Wages of Sin

Eight days after Professor Nomura was murdered, Chief Officer Inoue set off on a bright, hot, late July afternoon to arrest a person 'of interest'.

Ando was driving and had been instructed not to use the siren. They entered the side entrance of the university as discreetly as possible. The tests were over, so the campus was deserted apart from clerical staff, cleaners, and a few professors.

Going through an ornamental iron gate, Inoue squinted, noticing the outlines of the buildings they passed – the boys' dormitory, the cafeteria, and the bookshop – were blurred by the shimmering heat. A hydrangea bush that had been frothing with purple blossoms a few days before was now browned and withered, its leaves drooping down like the wings of sleeping bats. It was so hot that everyone was sheltering in some air-conditioned spot.

The narrow road curved left. Professor Hunter's house was opposite the tennis courts, next to an archery range. It was a big blue clapboard house. Most modern Japanese homes were made of synthetic materials that glittered in the sun, but Professor Hunter's house was wooden, dully reflecting the light, and it had white- framed windows. There was a grassy lawn, a veranda, and a porch swing. Two palm trees planted at the back looked incongruous, like a semi-tropical garden tacked on to a residence that looked like it belonged in the American Midwest.

Then Inoue glimpsed a face pressed against a downstairs window. "Looks like the foreigner, Miss Weller, sir," Kubo said.

"Yes, I knew she was still here. Apparently she'll be returning to Canada at the end of this month."

The doorbell made a hollow echoing sound. Nobody came. Then Kubo rapped the brass lion's head knocker on the white wooden door. Again, there was silence. They tried the knob. The door was unlocked. They entered a dark hall.

"Hello, anyone there?" Inoue called out. An attractive young blonde woman materialised from the shadows.

"I don't think I've had the pleasure, Miss Weller," Inoue said.

"And you're the cops...pigs, as we say at home. I have nothing more to say to any of you, hoped if I didn't answer the door you'd just go away."

"We haven't come to see you. We'd like a word with Professor Hunter."

"I don't think he's in."

Inoue didn't bother asking permission. He nodded at his officers. Kubo and Ando kicked off their shoes in the entranceway and set off to do a search. Ando went upstairs, and Kubo explored the rooms on the ground floor. Kubo reported back first, saying, "He's at the back, in a study."

Alyson Weller resignedly shrugged her shoulders. "Be my guest. Come on in if you have to see him so desperately. Can't think why you have to bother innocent people going about their daily business."

"That's the point, miss. Some of the people we're talking to aren't so innocent," said Inoue, kicking off his own shoes and following Kubo to the study.

Professor Gerald Hunter, missionary and Christianity professor, was sitting motionless at his desk in a high-ceilinged room lined with bookshelves. He was completely clad in black, the outlines of his figure hard to distinguish in the gloom. He supported his head with his hands steepled under his chin as if in prayer, his face a pale oval.

"I'm sorry to disturb you, professor," said Inoue. "Can I turn on the light?"

When he flipped the switch, Inoue saw that the room was comfortable, even cosy with black leather sofas, chintz-covered armchairs and small tables cluttered with magazines. There was a long crucifix on one wall and the head of Jesus in his final agony, wearing a crown of thorns, tears of blood streaming down his anguished face, on another. The professor's face looked no less troubled.

"Yes, do whatever you like. But please call me Gerald, everyone does, even my students, even Fujikawa's cleaning and maintenance staff."

"Very well, Gerald then."

"You can have tea or coffee, but I don't imagine this is a social occasion."

"No, it isn't. We would like to talk to you in private, please," said Inoue, looking at Alyson. She flounced out, slamming the door.

"But I can offer you a seat," Gerald said, indicating the armchair near him.

Inoue shook his head, approached the desk and said, "I plan to arrest you for the murder of Professor Nomura. You are entitled to the services of a lawyer, but you will need to pay. If you can't pay, you'll have to wait a few days for the court to appoint one for you."

Gerald looked at him impatiently and defiantly. "It's so tedious being involved in all this," he said. "I know the absurd system here. As an American, I find it outrageous not to be offered the services of a lawyer free of charge. Equally disturbing is the fact that you can hold me for forty-eight hours for questioning before making a formal charge. And that there are heavy-handed officers allowed to try to extort confessions."

Inoue was offended. "Laws have been passed banning such interrogations. That method to get a near perfect conviction rate is no longer permitted."

"Well, thank God for that. May I ask your grounds for arresting me?"

Inoue sat down after all, with Kubo and Ando at the back of the room, standing guard by the door. Inoue held up a hand, counting off the charges finger by finger. "First, you have no alibi for the time of the murder. Second, you had a motive. Third, you had the opportunity. Fourth, you told us you had seen Professor Nomura the night before his murder and that you had argued. Fifth, Miss Weller mentioned that when she saw the professor shortly afterwards, he told her he was upset about that argument and that you'd threatened him over the changes he'd planned for the university."

"Yes, what the president told me that night about his proposals was very unpleasant, but hardly grounds for murder."

"Please tell me about those changes."

"The president explained that he had already drafted a new university constitution acceptable to the board of trustees – who are all, by the way, his buddies and allies to a man. And I use that term advisedly. The old-boy system still rules in Japan. There's not a single woman on the board."

Inoue said nothing. Gerald continued, "This new constitution included the provision that the office of president was to change from an elected position to a tenured one. Nomura was a wily old devil. He wanted to hold the reins of power until his retirement, wanted time enough in power to ensure his new policies were implemented permanently. That would have meant at least five more years of Nomura in charge."

"What other changes were proposed?"

"Too many to enumerate. To add insult to injury, he gloated as he outlined them all. Particularly rankling was his claim he'd ditch the college's Christian orientation and even planned to break the historic link with my Presbyterian missionary board – for financial reasons, apparently. There was to be a wholesale firing of foreign staff on contracts. Several departments, including English, would be dissolved or merged with others. He was going to allow the lowering of academic standards to attract more applicants. He was tired of problems caused by our Korean exchange students and would scrap that programme, hoping, incidentally, to scupper my campaign to help Koreans born in Japan to get Japanese nationality. And on and on."

Gerald Hunter suddenly clutched at his head with his hands, the fingers scrabbling through his hair, leaving it standing up in little pale tufts. He sighed and glared at Inoue. "Anyway, what proof do you have that I had anything to do with that bastard's death? Yes, we quarrelled but murder's another matter altogether."

"Miss Tanimoto, Professor Thomas and Professor Yamamoto have all testified that you turned up unusually early on the day of the president's death, that you met and greeted them in the mail room in Building One. It occurred to me that you might have wished to be seen, to be conspicuous."

"I was preparing for end-of-term exams. I had to get to my office earlier than usual."

Inoue said severely, "Miss Tanimoto also remarked on your having shaved off your beard and, when I questioned you, I noticed your hair was flattened and you had a red mark on your forehead, the type of mark left by wearing a hat. Everyone has said you never wear a hat."

Gerald smiled. "It was a bright, hot day. Surely it's no crime to turn up for work early, to shave, or to wear a hat."

"I think the hat was a large straw one, the type preferred by the university's cleaners. I believe that, at some point, you also dressed yourself in their uniform of a loose white shirt, baggy trousers, and white cotton gloves. That the reason you shaved off your beard was not because of the heat but because you didn't want it to show beneath the surgical mask you also put on. That all of this was done so you could hide your real identity, to look like a cleaner who happened to be raking the courtyard shortly before Professor Nomura met his end."

Gerald had been shuffling papers on his desk, but now he looked up with a derisive expression. "An intriguing, attractive fantasy. Do you have any hard evidence? Isn't it all just supposition? Aren't you just clutching at straws, coming up with any old theory in your desperation to find a culprit?"

"I have obtained a search warrant for your house," Inoue said. He turned in his chair, nodded at his officers, and Kubo and Ando left the room.

Inoue continued, "I've been looking over your statement. You were seen at 8.25 and after 10.00 when we arrived to investigate the president's death. But nobody saw you between those two times."

The professor looked exasperated. "I was in my *office!* Of course, nobody saw me. It's like I said. I'd got to the campus early to sign in, get mail, and check on my exams. I stayed my office until I heard the commotion outside. I made my way downstairs and could see policemen standing in the courtyard. It was only then that I realised something was amiss."

Inoue plodded on, ignoring the professor's words. "You argued with Professor Nomura and were so enraged by the plans he'd made for the university that you decided to murder him. I have officers searching not only your house and office at this moment, but I've dispatched others to visit local shops to make enquiries about anyone matching your description buying certain items on the night of July 20th, the evening before the murder. They are asking if a short, thin, bearded foreigner purchased a straw hat, white cotton gloves, white baggy shirt and trousers."

"This house is surrounded by a sizeable bit of land. Perhaps I did buy such items within the last week or so. I've been thinking of growing vegetables."

"A student chanced to see a cleaner in the president's office at the time of the murder. It was a coincidence, good fortune for you. It led to the arrest of Suga. But he had a firm alibi."

Gerald said in a dull, tired voice, "I haven't felt lucky for a long time now."

"Then there's the porcelain doll," said Inoue. Yesterday afternoon Officer Ando interviewed Miss Weller. She let it slip that she knew such a doll had been found on the president's desk. We know that Professor Yamamoto placed it on Professor Nomura's desk about 9.30, when Miss Tanimoto was in the photocopying room down the hallway. She has told us she wanted to leave the doll on Miss Tanimoto's desk in the annex, but hearing the president leave his office, she rushed in and put it beside his computer."

"A piece of childish nonsense," Gerald murmured.

"Whether or not you agree with Professor Yamamoto's feminist views, the important point here is you knew of the doll and passed that news on to Miss Weller. Only six other people knew about the doll and where it was placed that morning. They are Miss Ota, who took it from her grandmother's house; Professor Yamamoto, who misguidedly placed it on the president's desk as a warning about sexual harassment; Professor Thomas, who saw the doll when he found the president's body; Miss Tanimoto, when she appeared in the office after hearing calls for help, and Mr Kawane and Mr Akamatsu, who had been summoned by a cleaner to the crime scene. The doll was shielded from view from the windows by a large decorative screen. As I've said, only those six people could have known of its existence. Before coming here today to interview you, my officers and I met the five *surviving* individuals and asked them if they had mentioned it to you. They all said no. Poor Akamatsu would have taken that information to his grave. Only the murderer could have known of that figurine. And the murderer could only have been that cleaner, glimpsed by a student sitting in the courtyard. You masqueraded as a cleaner to kill the president."

It happened in an instant. There was a sudden flurry of movement. Inoue saw Gerald open a drawer, withdraw something from it, and in a fluid motion plant against his own throat a kitchen knife that looked like the one used to kill Professor Nomura. He stared in motionless horror as Gerald calmly prodded his neck with the tip of the blade, saying "I bought two. Got an extra in case I got found out."

Inoue made as if to rise, but Gerald shook his head. He prodded his neck again and then displayed a knife that now had a few red bright spots glistening on its blade.

"I was raised on a farm. I slaughtered pigs from an early age. My father was a harsh man who allowed no squeamishness. It was an attitude that came in handy a few days ago. Simple to slit that bastard's throat. Now I can try it on myself."

Again, it was the work of a moment. Inoue heard the door thrown open. Alyson must have been listening at the door.

She ran in and sprang at Gerald, screaming as she aimed blows at his chest with her small white hands. Gerald dropped the knife onto the desk, using both hands to shove Alyson back so hard she fell and lay sprawled on the floor. Inoue rose but Gerald was surprisingly strong and quick. He pushed Inoue away next, and again so hard that the chief also found himself on the floor. In an instant Gerald managed to pick up the knife and draw it swiftly, deeply across his left wrist. A thick spray of blood shot over the desk. Gerald slumped back in his chair as he transferred the knife to his left hand and held it over his right wrist.

It was a blur of action: the struggle, the knife, the slashing. As Inoue was struggling to stand, Ando ran into the room. Rushing to the professor, he wrested the knife away and threw it on the floor. Then he whipped out a handkerchief and wrapped it tight around the gushing wound, pinning Gerald into the chair with one hand while holding the makeshift tourniquet in place with the other.

Inoue reached for his mobile phone, called for emergency backup, and allowed himself a moment to marvel at his junior's presence of mind. And to feel irritated by his predilection for apologies.

"Sorry, sir," said Ando. "I was upstairs and happened to look down the stairwell and saw Miss Weller listening at the door. Then I heard a commotion down here."

"You did well, Ando, lucky you were in the right place at

the right time."

Inoue took a plastic bag from a shirt pocket and, using another bag over his hand, placed the knife in it. He drew a handkerchief from a tunic pocket and gave it to Ando to reinforce the tourniquet

Alyson was standing now, too. She seemed dazed, confused. But then she glared at Gerald, reduced to a huddled, trembling heap in his chair.

"Nomura wasn't the bastard. It was you, it was you, it was you!" she shrieked. She rushed over and renewed her attack, hitting Gerald in the torso while Ando tried to protect him, holding the tourniquet with one hand and using the other to deflect the blows. Luckily Kubo reappeared just as Inoue grabbed Alyson. Together they pulled her back and forced her into an armchair.

An ambulance arrived, and then two squad cars. Medics treated Gerald by untying the two sodden handkerchiefs and binding his wound expertly before putting him in the ambulance. He looked ghostly pale.

Inoue and Kubo followed the ambulance to the local hospital, the sirens ensuring they arrived within minutes. Thanks to Ando's quick-witted action, Inoue was confident he wouldn't lose his prime murder suspect.

Inoue stood for a moment looking at the red smear glistening across Gerald's desktop. A long blood spatter stretched across the carpet as far as the armchair. Gerald must have severed an artery, he thought.

Confessions

Inoue commandeered one of the squad cars to take him to the hospital. The ambulance had arrived just minutes before, with Professor Hunter already rushed into the emergency room. As Inoue stood beside the open door of the back of the ambulance, staring at its floor, splattered with blood, Ando appeared.

"Don't worry, sir," he said. "A medic told me the wound isn't as serious as it looked. Blood began spurting out halfway here, but they put another tourniquet on. I think we got him here in time."

Inoue said, "Thank you, Ando. Professor Hunter needs be closely watched. He may well try to kill himself again."

Kubo was dispatched to wait outside the emergency room where Gerald was being worked on.

Ando ventured an opinion. "I think sometimes it can be dangerous to hold beliefs too strongly."

"What are you talking about?"

"Professor Hunter reminds me of one of those Jesuits."

Jesuits?! Inoue held himself in check, waiting for Ando to elaborate.

"I watched a television programme about them once, sir. They were men who had complete certainty in their convictions. They were religious. They did much good. But because of their beliefs they were willing to do evil, too. They tortured people who didn't share their way of thinking."

Inoue was surprised at Ando's perceptiveness. Yes, he could see Gerald as a Jesuit, too, with his austere face and black clothing, his uncompromising outlook on life.

A young, exhausted-looking doctor appeared and assured them that Gerald's condition was not life threatening. He had lost a lot of blood and had required an infusion. They had stitched up the wound in his wrist. He could probably be transferred to the prison hospital in as early as two or three days.

Inoue instructed Ando to contact police headquarters to arrange for a guard for Gerald's hospital room and that a watch be kept on him as a possible suicide risk.

Back at the station over drinks, Kubo admitted he couldn't understand Gerald's motives.

"It's inconceivable to me, sir, that a professor would kill another professor. And for what? Just because the president wanted to make a few changes at the college? It just doesn't make sense."

Inoue made no reply. From long experience, he knew that anything was possible with people, no matter how intelligent or prestigious they were.

The next morning, on hearing that Gerald had passed a good night and could be questioned, Inoue and Ando made their way to the hospital, Ando taking along a voice recorder.

There was a guard outside Gerald's private room, and Inoue found Gerald had been handcuffed to his bed. He got the guard to take off the cuff, at least for the duration of the interview.

While Gerald struggled to sit up in his bed, rubbing his right wrist, Inoue wondered whether Gerald was, in fact, well enough for an interview. He seemed a hollow shell of his former self, whiter and thinner than ever, almost wraithlike, and he was on a drip. Inoue thought Gerald looked as if he had been sedated. His lifeless, glazed eyes were fixed on the floor; he spoke in a low, dull voice.

"I want to tell you the latest developments in the case," Inoue told Gerald, "so that you can make a full confession if that is your intention. My officers discovered some interesting items in their search of your home and garden. Professor Nomura's laptop computer was found under the mattress of your bed. We inspected a small bonfire beside your house and retrieved scraps of paper that indicate that you tried to destroy Miss Tanimoto's photocopies of the president's report for the five department heads. My officers also found bits of clothing corresponding to a cleaner's uniform in one of the incinerators at the rubbish collection site."

Gerald nodded at Ando, and he turned on the voice recorder.

"Tidying up. That's what I was doing two nights ago, anticipating you might turn up wanting to arrest me, hoping

I'd have the courage to kill myself before you could." He groaned suddenly. "The pain in my wrist is nothing like my aching ribs. I had no idea Alyson could pack such force in her punches!"

"I suppose she felt she had her reasons," said Inoue. "What I want to know is how you gained entrance to the president's office. He wouldn't have welcomed a cleaner, especially after he'd spent a sleepless night worrying about the reception of that controversial report on changes he wanted to make to the college."

Gerald gave a faint smile. "I knocked on the corridor door and muttered through my surgical mask that I'd been sent to look at that noisy air conditioner. It worked like a charm. The fool opened the door, barely gave me a glance."

"A good disguise."

"Yes, and a good reason to get in the room. That machine made the most infernal racket."

Gerald looked at Inoue with a piteous expression, like a bid for his understanding and sympathy. "You see, Nomura had waved that damned file in my face the night before taunting me with it, saying I was powerless to prevent copies being made and delivered to all the department heads. In the last few years, he had consolidated his grip on power to such an extent that nobody would object to the report, that nobody *could*. It was a foregone conclusion everyone would meekly agree to it and then he could make the changes official. I saw red. I felt I had to do *something*."

He's lying, Inoue thought, while maintaining his calm, impassive expression. Does he really think he can persuade us the crime wasn't premeditated?

Gerald was going on: "I had no concrete plan apart from turning up as a cleaner and carrying a knife. I never meant to hurt Nomura. I just wanted to frighten him. Seeing his secretary with the report that morning gave me hope that I could stop him before it got distributed."

"Are you saying you only meant to threaten Professor Nomura?" Inoue asked.

"Yes! I don't expect you to believe me, but I had no plan to *kill* the wretched man. My sole hope was my dramatic ploy might inspire him to delay the release of the report, to hold further discussions on it. Of course, I knew I would lose my job in any case and probably be deported from Japan and that the mission board would dismiss me. Still, it seemed worth staging this protest. Many of my Japanese colleagues felt the same disgust at the changes as me, but none of them had the guts to do anything."

"A martyr to the cause," Inoue interjected.

"Exactly. Someone had to make a stand."

"Let's backtrack a little. Tell us your movements after you ran into Miss Tanimoto."

"As I approached Building One, I saw Professor Yamamoto and Miss Ota through the window of the mailroom. Miss Ota had her arms out, holding some heavy object. I delayed a few seconds then went in, pretending I hadn't seen anything. I signed in and got my mail. I saw Miss Tanimoto pass through carrying the file to her meeting. I exchanged a few words with Professor Yamamoto before going up to my office. That's when I changed into the cleaner's clothing I had brought in my briefcase."

"And put a knife in one pocket?"

"As I've told you, it was only to threaten Nomura, not to kill him."

"And then?"

"I left my office in my disguise without seeing anyone or being seen, getting to the courtyard at about 9.30. I'd found a rake in a utility cupboard in Building Five. I

collected it and started raking the courtyard. Then I saw Professor Yamamoto again. This time she was rushing away from Building Two in the direction of her office. Of course, once I was in the president's office and saw the porcelain doll, I knew why she was in such a hurry and what Miss Ota had given her in the mailroom. It seems reprehensible to admit it now, but I was amused. The word 'forbidden' scrawled on the forehead was perfect for our lecherous old friend. He thought he'd been so discreet, but he'd been found out. I propped the rake up against Building One and went over to Building Two, wanting to check whether Miss Tanimoto was in the photocopier room. She was there on her own. I wanted to get the original and the copies from her, but I wasn't sure how to do it, so I decided to carry through with my original plan of knocking on the president's corridor door, in my disguise. He looked so distracted that he didn't question my being there even though it was highly unlikely a cleaner would have been sent to repair office equipment."

"The president sat down again at his desk after opening the corridor door to you?"   "Yes, he had a heap of papers on the desk, something about next year's budget. He

was tapping away on his laptop as I stood behind him, pretending to examine the air conditioner. Then I shouted out 'You bastard!' and pulled off my mask. Nomura stopped working on his computer and looked back at me with a stunned expression. Then he laughed. He thought it was a joke."

Gerald paused, reflecting. Remembering. He gave a small shudder. "He didn't think it quite so funny when I got my knife out of my pocket. He stopped smiling and asked me what the hell I thought I was doing. I grabbed him and put the blade to his throat. It all happened in seconds!"

Gerald shook his head, as if wanting to shake off the memory. "Can't you see?" he pleaded. "I just wanted to stop that laughter. I didn't mean to kill him. But the blade was sharp, and suddenly there was so much blood... It was everywhere: on the pile of papers on the desk, on that damned doll, on his suit."

"You say you slit his throat unintentionally. So why not call for help?"

"There was so much blood it was obvious he was dead. He was slumped over, perfectly still. It was convenient he collapsed over those papers he'd been looking at rather than over his computer. It was a matter of seconds: closing the laptop and putting it down the front of my shirt. I glanced out the window. I was shocked to see a student sitting on a bench in the courtyard but, even worse, there was that fool Andrew coming to see the president. I just had time to hide myself behind the screen before Andrew rapped at the door and came in."

"And what was your plan at this point?"

"I had no plan, dammit! Nomura was dead. I had suddenly become a murderer. It took ages for Andrew to realise Nomura was dead. He started shouting his head off. Miss Tanimoto heard and came in. She began giggling hysterically and fainted. I knew I had to get out of there! I put my mask back on pushing my hat down well over my eyes. I wiped the blade of the knife and put it in my pocket. Because Nomura had been facing forward when I slit his throat, I had only a few small bloodstains on my clothes. When I stepped out from behind the screen, Andrew took no notice. He was in shock, sitting in a heap on the floor, completely out of it."

Gerald groaned again and softly patted his ribs before continuing. "It all went better than I could have planned. I walked out through the annex and saw a thick folder on Miss Tanimoto's desk. I put it in my shirt, next to the laptop, and went on to Building One. I went in by the back door. Mr Kawane was seated near the rear of the staff office, facing forward, so no danger of seeing me. Anyway, I was still disguised. I stood near Kawane and I whispered that something was amiss in Building Two. After that I went back to the courtyard and kept on raking. When I saw Kawane run across the courtyard, followed by Akamatsu, I sauntered over to the grassy verge by Building Two and dropped the knife there, under one of Nomura's office windows."

"But why did you try to tell Kawane anything? Why didn't you just go off to your office and change your clothes?" asked Inoue.

At least the mystery of the plump cleaner was solved. It was Gerald with a laptop and a thick folder stuffed under his shirt.

"I thought it would look too suspicious if I scampered off," Gerald said. "And I was sure Andrew would, at some point, remember having seen a cleaner in Nomura's office. If that cleaner made no subsequent appearance, suspicion would have fallen on that mysterious figure. I was able to make my getaway when you lot arrived. I went back to my office, changed clothes, stuffing all the cleaner's gear and the laptop and the folder in my briefcase. I had the presence of mind to seat myself at my desk and start marking some exams. I simply went back to being myself again as if nothing awful had happened."

Inoue said, "Are you really expecting us to believe you took a knife to your interview with the president but didn't mean to kill him?"

"As God is my witness, yes! And I also meant to kill myself when you found out."

"As I've said before, a martyr to a cause." "One I believe in completely. Even now."

Ellie Has Some News

A week after Professor Gerald Hunter's arrest, Inoue sat at the table in his small kitchen. It was a pleasant room with frilly white curtains, yellow walls, and gaily painted cupboards filled with neatly stacked dishes. He watched Ellie open the fridge and take out a bottle of beer beaded with condensation. She flipped off the cap and poured him a large glass. He took a drink. He was still celebrating having solved the case.

But his happiness and relief was tinged with a sense of disappointment, even sadness.

By identifying the killer and arresting him, Inoue knew he had vindicated himself while redeeming his standing as a career police officer promoted at a young age. But he felt he had also been defiled by the whole experience, and that left a bad taste in the mouth. The chain-smoking Inspector Takenaka had invaded his life and not only left his office stinking, but also humiliated him in front of his men.

Inoue didn't want to become one of those individuals – mostly men, he thought – who harbour grievances. Women could drain off emotional poison by gossiping about troubles with their friends. Japanese men were reluctant to do that. They inhabited a culture that promoted uncomplaining endurance of pain. Takenaka had praised Inoue when Gerald was identified. He was grateful the case had been solved. But then he had remembered he was the superior officer and recovered his usual air of haughty dignity. An hour or so after Inoue and his officers had submitted their report, Takenaka had summoned Inoue to his old office.

"I'll admit it," Takenaka had said, "I had doubts. I should have had more faith in you. I thought it impossible that an arrest could have been made so soon, let alone followed by a full confession. Well done! You've really got me off the hook. As you know, since the murder, Obuchi-*sensei* was constantly on the phone asking about our progress and demanding results. And I don't mind telling you, I was also being closely supervised by Tokyo HQ. It was a terrible strain, like being under attack from two sides."

Inoue was glad he had not been the only one to feel the pressure.

"A press conference will be held today," Takenaka added. "Local and even national news teams are expected. We'll feature on television tonight and have a full spread in the Fujikawa and Ishizaki papers tomorrow."

Inoue nodded, anticipating Takenaka intended to hog the limelight himself and take all the credit.

"I will mention the important role you played," Takenaka said, sitting up straight and stubbing out his cigarette. "But you must understand that, as the chief investigating officer, I'll be expected to take centre stage at these public events."

Back to condescension, Takenaka continued, "You had a few lucky breaks, Inoue. However, we would have got there in the end, with or without your help. I think a few words I let drop early on put you on the right scent. You'll recall, I'm sure, that I said the culprit was most likely a foreigner. These foreigners! Either too fat or too thin. Professor Hunter looked almost skeletal. After reading your report, I formed the impression of a disagreeable character. Hellbent on a mission, the type to avoid."

Then to Inoue's great relief, he said, "My men and I will be returning to headquarters later today, so you can get everything back to normal." He looked at Inoue and grimaced: "Job well done!"

What followed was even more surprising. Takenaka concluded by saying, "I'll be giving you a very glowing report. You may even be in line for a promotion."

Anything so long as I'm not transferred to Ishizaki and never need have anything to do with you ever again was Inoue's thought. He merely bowed deeply.

He waved goodbye to Takenaka later that morning, standing sombrely by the front door of headquarters. Inoue felt reborn returning to his old office and opening all the windows. He set Kubo and Ando the task of scrubbing surfaces and sweeping the floor, try trying to rid his office of not only dirt but also the stink of cigarette smoke.

What Inoue couldn't dispose of so easily was the way he'd

been treated by Takenaka. Also, fingering Gerald as Professor Nomura's murderer had shaken his self confidence. In his long career, Inoue had often had occasion to rely on his intuition. But it had let him down badly this time. It still seemed incredible that Gerald had killed Nomura, especially as Inoue sensed a fundamental goodness in the man.

And it was unfortunate he was American, with the media adopting the angle he had feared would attract them, reporting that the law-abiding Japanese populace was in danger from foreigners in their midst.

It was a bittersweet victory.

But one good result of it all was a new appraisal of one of his junior officers, his protégé Ando. An unpromising officer had been Inoue's initial appraisal, but he'd certainly exceeded expectations in rising to the challenges presented by this case.

That night Ellie awoke to hear her husband groaning as if he was having a nightmare. She turned on the lamp beside their bed and gently shook him awake.

"How is it possible?" he said. "How could a distinguished man like Professor Hunter do something so far from my judgement of him, something so purely evil?"

"But he said he killed the president on the spur of the moment," Ellie said.

"I don't believe that. There was premeditation in every step. But perhaps he'll be able to get some hotshot lawyer who can convince a jury otherwise."

Inoue turned over on his side to face his wife. "You know, he said he got the idea for dressing up as a cleaner from seeing Suga playing the fool, looking through the president's office windows, leering at the young girls from there."

"What I can't understand is *why*," Ellie said. "Did he really think that murdering Nomura would put a stop to all those plans he'd made?"

"He *says* he thought threatening the president might give him breathing space, make Nomura reconsider, hold off for a bit. But I think he intended murder from the start. When Gerald managed to carry through on his plan, he stole the laptop and the reports the president was going to distribute. Maybe he thought that would make the whole problem disappear."

"I always found Gerald slightly intimidating," said Ellie, "but I certainly never thought him capable of anything like that."

Inoue said, "To me, the worst of it isn't that he killed Professor Nomura. It's that I can't understand how, as a devout Christian, he could allow first Andrew, then Suga, then Professor Yamamoto to be accused of the murder. How could he square *that* with his conscience?"

Ellie had told Inoue of her loss of faith before they met. He had only known her as a nominal Christian. He couldn't imagine her being any better as a person if she regained her belief.

As she caressed her husband's face, she said. "It's odd. Gerald's despair has lifted me out of mine. It's somehow energised me. I want to find my own way back to my faith."

"In my eyes, you are perfect now," Inoue said. "It's all very well for you. You have something to fall back on. I don't. My faith in human nature has been shaken. I wonder if I'll ever feel able to believe in anyone again…except you, of course."

Ellie felt this was her moment. They were lying opposite each other, limbs intertwined. "I have something special to tell you…" she murmured.

He gazed at her expectantly.

"We've had enough bad news, now for some good news, something nice," she said.

It was the two of them in their bedroom in the small town of Fujikawa in western Kyushu, a naked couple in bed cooled by an air conditioner on a warm humid night. All ordinary and mundane. Still, their lives were about to be changed forever. Ellie leaned over to her husband and whispered in his ear, hearing his gasp of delighted surprise, watching his face brighten. Then he threw his arms around her and embraced her as if he would never let her go again. After a bout of lovemaking, Ellie told him such activity would be possible for another five months at least, according to her doctor.

Ellie awoke to find her husband mumbling in his sleep: "Ando, not Kubo. Ando, not Kubo."

She shook him gently. "Ando understands…understands people," he said before falling back into a heavy sleep. They slept until the disgracefully late hour of eight o'clock the following morning.

As Inoue was hastily dressing, Ellie mentioned his words to him.

Inoue put on a mock display of displeasure. "I hadn't expected my own *wife* to be acting the detective," he had said.

"But you want our baby to be like Ando. I think that's what you meant."

He grimaced and said, "I'm not at all sure I want our son to be a police officer."

"Our son or our *daughter*!" she pronounced triumphantly, jumping out of bed,

wrapping herself in a light summer kimono and fleeing to the kitchen to make coffee for her husband.

Epilogue

"Why are we all so obsessed by death?" Stephen asked. "Why are we so interested in it? Ben, you're our resident intellectual. You tell us."

The boys were at Fujikawa's Irish pub on a rainy evening in early August. A typhoon was approaching, offering a welcome respite to the merciless heat. Big fat drops lashed the windows, and the room was comfortably cool. The landlord, obsessed with all things Irish, who had dyed his hair green and always wore clothes festooned with shamrocks and harps, beamed at them with a rosy drinker's face, grateful for their regular Saturday night custom.

Stephen, Ben, the Carrel boys and Billy were preoccupied with tipping their glasses slowly from side to side. The trick was to get the shamrock imprint in the inch of head on their glasses of Guinness to go round the rim in a perfect circle without breaking up.

Ben gave up and took a long gulp as though to seek inspiration. With a cream moustache on his upper lip, he solemnly said, "Crime fiction is a huge seller and there are countless police dramas on television."

Stephen said, "We all know that, fool, but why?"

"It's because we've excluded the physical fact of death from our daily lives but know it's the fate that awaits us all."

The Carrel boys' eyes glazed over. They were rescued in the nick of time. Two attractive young Japanese girls walked in wearing thigh-high boots. They deposited furled umbrellas by the door. They were heavily made-up and patted raindrops off their fancy hair dos. The Carrels acted of one accord, rushing over to ask if they could buy them drinks.

Stephen remained on his uncomfortable stool by the window as Ben pontificated.

"In the past, we *saw* the dead. They were a part of daily life. Families bathed and dressed their dead and then personally arranged everything for their burial."

"Oh, yes?" said Stephen, looking out the window at the bright reflection of a neon sign on the wet pavement below. He knew somebody he wished were dead, although he probably wouldn't want to wash the corpse.

"Yes," said Ben, pleased that Stephen was listening for a change. "And that intimacy with death is still present in Japan but not in our own countries."

"And?" Stephen asked, trying to sound interested.

Ben continued, "And there was religion. The church offered us answers to why death occurs and consolation to deal with loss. That's all gone now. In many countries elderly people are shipped off to so-called care facilities or they die, miserable and alone, in crowded hospital wards. The funeral homes take over, and we get sanitised, prettified corpses in a coffin before they're whisked away for burial or cremation.

But Japan is an exception. Close relatives bathe the body and dress it in a white death kimono. Then it is burned, and the relatives pick out some bone fragments with chopsticks to bury in the family grave. That's getting up close and personal with death. But in the west, death is the new taboo. It used to be sex, of course."

"Sex," Stephen repeated. He decided to order fish and chips.

Ben looked pleased at having been asked to impart fragments of enlightenment. "In fact, I think it all goes much deeper even than that," he went on, but he soon realised he was addressing the empty air. Stephen had jumped up to order his food at the bar, and Billy wasn't listening at all.

"Sorry, Ben, do carry on," said Stephen when he returned.

"No, don't laugh. It's something that interests me," said Ben. "We all suffer a great deal in ordinary life, what Shakespeare called 'the slings and arrows of outrageous fortune'. Somebody cuts us off on the road; somebody gets a raise or promotion before us; somebody says something cruel or unkind. As Sartre said, hell is other people," he concluded.

"These blows in life…like *you* getting tenure and not me?"

"A crime novel, with a clear victim and villain, satisfies our thirst for justice. Retribution is dealt out to the unjust. Good people are rewarded and the evil punished."

"But it doesn't always work like that, does it?" Stephen

said. "Nomura was a nasty piece of work. It's right he paid the ultimate price for acting the tin-pot dictator."

"Yes, the corrupting nature of power."

Billy grunted and went off to get another drink.

Ben said, "What I can't understand is how Obuchi-*san*, so officious and controlling, never stopped Nomura from hitting on young girls on campus."

"Frightened of the old man or didn't dare. More than his job was worth."

"Okay, but why did none of us twig Gerald was on the brink? We were supposed to be his friends," Ben queried.

"He may be facing only manslaughter rather than a murder rap," said Stephen.

"He'll still need a good lawyer," said Ben.

"He's been dismissed by the Presbyterian mission people he used to work for."

"No wonder."

"And they may be severing their link with the university."

"God, I shudder to think how long poor Gerald will languish in a Japanese jail," said Ben. "His trial is next month. He's been put on suicide watch."

"Keiko told me that Ellie is going there every day to pray with him."

Billy, now nursing another Guinness, sang out, "*Ellie*! What a sweetie! Does anyone have news of scary old Karl?

I'm glad they've locked *him* up. They should throw away the key."

"Oh, Billy, you've condescended to talk to us?" said Stephen.

Billy stood beside Stephen's stool, lurching from side to side. "Karl's been involved in all kinds of shit. I hear he even experimented with cat vivisection, performing makeshift surgery on the poor creatures he found in his neighbourhood. Just as well he's been put away before he did something even worse."

Ben said: "He's still acting true to form. He was sentenced to only two years for involuntary manslaughter for that attack on Akamatsu, but he's been so unruly in prison they've upped his sentence by a year. Still, it's hard luck on Junko."

"She's well rid of him, I reckon," said Stephen. "Ellie told me Junko's filed for divorce."

The door opened, and a young man walked in. Thin, wearing smart khaki trousers and a fashionable linen shirt, his hair slicked back, he looked like a forties film star.

It was late and they had given up on him, so his appearance was as joyfully greeted as if they'd not seen him in years rather than just over a week.

"Andrew-*chan*!"

"How are you, old boy?"

"Glad you've decided to rub shoulders with us plebs."

When questioned about his appearance, Andrew wouldn't

be drawn. *Just something Alyson said* was all he would offer. Then he added, "I need a fresh start! I'm tired of being so useless here, unable even to manage simple conversations. I'm going to take

Japanese language classes and enrol in a distance-learning programme for a master's in teaching English as a foreign language. I've even asked the university for an apartment nearer campus. Anything would be better than the awful place I shared with Alyson for two years."

They all gazed at Andrew in astonishment. "And I'm divorcing Alyson," he added. "I need a change!"

"Good for you, Andrew," said Ben, finally. "But I wonder, can people change?"

"I think they can, if they really want to," said Andrew. "I feel I've been sleepwalking through life up till now. I want to make the most of my opportunities. I like it here. It's like I've been given a new chance. I can make something of my life. I'm *alive!* Not like poor Akamatsu. Did you know he had a dream of visiting Paris?"

"Akamatsu?" asked Stephen.

"The office worker Karl beat up, the man who had a heart attack and died. He was delivering bribes for Nomura to his brother at the army camp, the weird militaristic guy."

"What's happening with that brother?"

"His case is pending. He's been charged with bribery and involvement in Akamatsu's death. I hear he'll get a dishonourable discharge. He's scampered back to the family holdings in Kyoto."

"Hey, Billy," said Stephen. "What's your take on death?"

For a drunk, he was surprisingly lucid. "There's death and then there's death," Billy opined. "A violent death isn't the same as gaga granny slipping away in her sleep."

He looked at them with a sage expression. "I think that when we do violence to others, we do violence to ourselves. A murder, a crime of passion, that's like, like … the heart of darkness. I know you all think I'm just a computer geek, but I like reading."

"Well, poor Gerald sure screwed up his own life."

"And making it all even worse is that Nomura's reforms are going through. In killing Nomura, he accomplished nothing."

"Those reforms included getting rid of the English department. I'm okay, I'll be teaching English to students in other departments, but does that mean you contract teachers will be fired?" Ben asked.

"No, you should be so lucky. We've been told we have at least a year's reprieve."

Ben said: "It's the vicious old law of unexpected consequences. Gerald took drastic action to prevent the university changing in ways he hated, but he's ended up making things even worse. And life won't be a bowl of roses for us foreigners. Pity it was an American who killed the president."

"Life is a vale of tears."

They looked out the window at the rain now falling heavily. "Even the sky is weeping for us," snorted Stephen.

The Carrel boys briefly returned to make their farewells, Pete saying to Andrew, "One of our birds wanted to be introduced to you, said you look distinguished."

Andrew grinned and felt his spirits lift. *Back in the game*, he thought.

"I imagine some of you've heard that Alyson's gone back to Canada and managed to get a job at an art gallery in Winnipeg," he said. "No doubt she'll wax eloquent on Hokusai's views of Mount Fuji even though I was never able to drag her to the art museum in Ishizaki."

"Good riddance," said Ben.

"Who's buying the next round?" Stephen asked. He thrummed the table impatiently as he stared at his empty glass but brightened when a large plate of fish and chips was placed in front of him.

"Do we all drink so much because we're afraid of death?" asked Ben.

"I drink...because I drink," said Billy.

"Billy boy, you're on top form tonight, you closet existentialist."

"Stop!" declared Stephen dramatically, placing a hand over his heart. "It's a DBB moment."

"Distracted by beauty," Ben explained.

A young, handsome Japanese boy with long black hair had just walked into the bar. They all gazed at him. But a pretty girl soon joined him, and they stood at the counter holding hands.

"Life is full of disappointments as well as tears," said Stephen, looking at the pair with sad eyes.

"Never mind, Stephen," said Andrew. "I have a bit of news I think you'll like. I've heard that Ellie and her Japanese cop husband are having a baby."

"Hooray!"

As soon as he'd made this disclosure, Andrew regretted it. *That was indiscreet*, he thought. Ellie probably would prefer not to have that fact bandied about by the boys in a bar.

"I bet it'll be adorable," said Stephen.

Billy unexpectedly piped up: "Misa told me Ellie couldn't have babies."

"The Lord works in mysterious ways," said Stephen.

"I know something else that's amazing. Ellie's going to move into the Inoue family home," Andrew went on. "It's one of those old farmhouses with an annex and a big courtyard. Ellie's mother-in-law is desperate to have the new baby live there. She'll move into the annex, giving up the main house to Ellie and her husband and the kid."

"Ellie's such a private person. I never thought she'd go native, moving in with the in-laws," said Ben.

"It just shows we're all capable of surprising each other,"

Stephen said.

"Maybe it's a blessing. If we knew each other too well, we probably couldn't keep up the pretence of friendship," Andrew said.

"I'm ready for another drink," mumbled Billy.

"Let's all have one," said Andrew, "And toast Ellie's baby. Death is too long and life's too short!"

"It's your round," Ben said.

Glossary of Japanese Terms

Azuki bean paste: Dessert paste made from sweet red beans.

Bento: Japanese lunch boxes, usually containing rice, vegetables pickled or cooked, fish or meat.

Burakumin: Traditionally an outcast group at the bottom of the Japanese social order who worked in 'unclean' trades (for example, butchers or tanners). *Burakumin* face discrimination even in modern-day Japan.

Chan: An honorific, '-chan' is often substituted for '-san' when speaking to a close friend or family member.

Doozo: A phrase meaning 'here you are' or 'go ahead'.

Futon: Mattress-like bedding that is folded up and stored during the day in a large special cupboard with sliding doors.

Gaijin: A term that literally means 'outside person' referring to anyone in Japan who is not Japanese.

Genkan: The small enclosed entrance to a Japanese home, just inside the front door, where people slip off their shoes before stepping up into the interior of the house.

'*Genki?*': 'Are you well?' 'Are you in good health?'

Girls' Day: *Hinamatsuri* on the 3rd of March, also called 'Dolls' Day,' when families with girls display a set of ornamental dolls, special food is eaten, and girls' health and happiness are prayed for.

Hikikomori: A term that literally means 'pulling inward,

being confined' referring to reclusive adolescents and adults choosing to isolate themselves from society, a phenomenon occurring in Japan since the 1990s.

Izakaya: A drinking place where typical Japanese dishes are also served. '*Konbanwa*': 'Good evening.'

Kushiyaki: Charcoal-grilled skewered poultry or other meats or vegetables.

Manga: Japanese comics.

Meishi: Name/business cards that have a great significance in Japan where the individual is identified by the group he belongs to; they are routinely exchanged on a first meeting, with a strict etiquette of exchange observed.

Minshuku: A family-operated Japanese-style bed-and-breakfast.

Miso: Fermented bean paste widely used in Japanese cookery.

'*Moshi moshi*': Phrase used to say 'hello' when starting to talk on the telephone.

Obaachan: An old woman or 'grandmother'.

Office lady: A female office worker in Japan, often single and living with parents, given menial tasks such as photocopying and serving tea and expected to resign on marrying.

'*Ohayo gozaimasu*': 'Good morning.'

'*Okaerinasai*': A greeting said by person at home when someone returns (translating loosely into 'Welcome home').

O-mochi: Rice cakes made by pounding the rice into a paste.

Oolong-cha: Traditional Chinese tea.

Oshibori: A wet hand towel given to customers in restaurants.

Rakugo: An ancient tradition of comic story-telling in Japan.

San: An honorific; the Japanese automatically attach '-san' to the name of anyone other than close family members as a sign of respect.

Sensei: An honorific attached to the name of anyone who works in any capacity as a teacher.

Shoji: Sliding latticed doors with panels made of paper.

Tempura: Battered, deep-fried vegetables or seafood.

'Tadaima': A phrase uttered by someone on returning home ('I'm home!').

Tatami: Traditional floor matting made with rice straw and rushes.

Yakuza: Japanese criminal gangs.

Yappari: A common term meaning 'It was only to be expected'.

Printed in Great Britain
by Amazon